D0718823

Tania Kindersley

Tania Kindersley was born in 1967. She read history at Oxford and currently lives in London, where she is working on her fifth novel.

SCEPTRE

Goodbye, Johnny Thunders

TANIA KINDERSLEY

SCEPTRE

First published in 1996 by Hodder and Stoughton
A division of Hodder Headline PLC
A Sceptre Book

10 9 8 7 6 5 4 3 2 1

British Library Cataloguing in Publication Data

Kindersley, Tania
    Goodbye, Johnny Thunders
    1. English fiction – 20th century
    I. Title
    823. 9'14 [F]

    ISBN 0 340 66024 4

Typeset by Palimpsest Book Production Limited,
Polmont, Stirlingshire
Printed and bound in Great Britain by
Mackays of Chatham PLC, Chatham, Kent

Hodder and Stoughton
A division of Hodder Headline PLC
338 Euston Road
London NW1 3BH

To Valentine, Lulu, and Georgia.

Acknowledgements ∫

For all their advice and help with this book, I should like to thank Louisa Kulukundis, Lucy Goldman, Matthew Miller and William Ogden. Special thanks also to Richenda Todd, David Herbert, and Dinah Wiener.

∫

I met Jack at the start of my first summer in London. It was May, it was hot, I remember it. I was young and free and the whole world was just an oyster to me. It seems a long time ago now. I suppose it was a long time ago, in a way.

I wish I could have said that Johnny Thunders brought us together, that I met him by chance in one of those second-hand record stalls that cluster together under the Westway, sorting through the boxes with that look of frowning concentration that marks the vinyl buff from the casual browser, hunting for a bootleg album by the New York Dolls, or a remix from the Heartbreakers. But I can't. I hadn't heard of Thunders, in those days. I wasn't even a record buff.

I had a collection, quite respectable in its way, all the usual names – the Doors (dreaming of Jim before he got fat), Lou Reed, Bob Marley, Iggy Pop, the Velvet Underground, Ray Charles and Otis for nostalgia. I had the *White Album* and *Exile on Main Street* and *Highway 61 Revisited*; I had ska and soca and reggae and everything Leonard Cohen ever recorded.

It would have been fitting, in a way, if we had met like that, a curious piece of symmetry, but life doesn't imitate art quite so much as we like to think, which is why, I suppose, we fall back so gratefully on fiction – never let the truth get in the way of a good story, or so the man says. I know I never did, not then, I was too young.

But we didn't. Nowhere near the Westway, or Portobello, which wasn't my neighbourhood. I was just another Chelsea girl, battling through life in the genteel confines of SW3. Not that that was my neighbourhood, either. I didn't exactly have anywhere I came from. I liked London because it was all new to me, and it was a long way away from my parents. They had left England years before, before I was even thought of – although I was never really thought of, a nice little accident, that was me. Children wasn't one of the things my parents had ever considered, but my mother got careless one night, and nine months later I was born, late December in Washington, DC. It was raining. I knew this because my father told me how hard it was to get a taxi. He didn't say much else about it.

My father was a writer, a famous writer, the kind that people sit up and take notice of. I remember that still minute hush that followed the mention of his name, from when I was very small, a child, and I didn't know why, or what it was.

Respect, that's what it was. People silently taking their hats off. He deserved it. He was remote and otherworldly and not like a human being at all, but he wrote clear untrammelled prose, truthful and sure. He didn't care to enter into the human condition, but he knew all about it, and he observed it ruthlessly and set it down in all its strange confusion, and everyone said they didn't know how he did it.

I certainly didn't. We didn't really talk, my father and I. He wasn't one of those men who are a Dad. He was just there, every day, behind a study door, and occasionally he would come out and make pots of strong thick coffee and remark on something altogether bland and unimportant, like the weather or an avocado plant he was growing from seed. He liked growing things, clipping and pruning and watering, with care and precision. He was good with inanimate objects.

Often he looked at me with a curious speculative glint in his eye, as if wondering who I was, or how I came to be there. He always seemed a little amazed by me, as if I were some kind of obscure scientific phenomenon; not so much when I was a child, but as I grew up, passed puberty, grew girlish things like breasts and cheekbones and painted lips. He had a mistress, so he must have known about sex, which always surprised me, but he didn't seem to understand that one day I might be able to do it too.

I never forgot the first time I brought a boy home. I was eighteen and we were living in one of those nice old houses on Russian Hill and I asked if I could bring someone for dinner. Danny, that was his name, second generation Irish, and no doubt what he was built for. He had that smart physical knowing look about him which went best with having no clothes on.

Perhaps that was why I chose him. There are people who say there is a reason for everything. I didn't resent my father, but I wanted to jolt him, to shock him out of his dream world. Short skirts and late nights and my own latch key were a start, the usual adolescent badges of independence, the flags of doing it my way. I scattered Marlboro packets behind me wherever I went and dyed my hair dark pink. I even wore black nail varnish for a while, hoping my father might notice. He didn't.

But Danny really delivered, in spades. He arrived at eight wearing torn jeans and that disreputable just crawled out of the wrong bed look that was his stock in trade, and my father didn't say anything to him, not one word. He just stared at him in mute horror all night as I chattered in delight and my mother made those vague urban observations that went for conversation with her.

*   *   *

It wasn't so very bad, having these strange distant creatures for parents. I went through a stage of being jealous of people who had close cosy families, mothers who made them chicken soup when they were ill, fathers who helped with the homework, real Brady Bunch families, who sat down to eat with each other, who teased and bickered and gave each other nicknames, who shared private jokes and holiday reunions. I thought for a long time that I wanted that, that I had been deprived, that I had nowhere I belonged. But as I grew older, I realised the advantages. I could do what I wanted after all, and that's worth something. There were no expectations put upon me. We didn't ask anything of each other. It was quite restful, in a way.

It's not so terrible, being someone's daughter. That's what I said, when I was asked. People complain about it, cry that they want to be taken on their own merit, by their own lights. I said I didn't mind so much. I learnt not to mind. There wasn't anything I could do about it. Besides, it opened doors, my name, it was useful. I used it. I wasn't ambitious, that was what I learnt.

I can't remember if it came to me suddenly, in a flash of revelation, a blinding insight. I don't think so. I think it just came gradually, crystallised one day, like one of those things you've always known, in the back of your mind. Oh yes, you say, that's it, I knew it all along. It's a responsibility, ambition. You can't just have it, there, for granted. You have to work at it, justify it; dignify it, I suppose. You have to deserve it.

I didn't want to shoot for the moon, not even the stars. I'd seen it for too long, those peaks and troughs. I'd watched my father, the days when he lost the muse, when he battled to find his way out of the darkness. I watched the strain in his eyes, and learnt not to ask him questions, because he didn't hear them. He rarely told me anything, but I remember once, he said that he had no brief for half measures. It was all or nothing, with my father. He didn't want to be good, he needed to be great.

There's no respite from that, no room for weakness. If you want success and recognition it's a life choice, growing stronger with every passing day. I think that's why my father had no time for living. He couldn't afford to. I didn't know him, but I could see what he was like, and I knew that I didn't want what he had. I wanted it easy, I suppose. I wanted a clear run, a smooth ride. That's what I said. No sound and fury for me, no sir, no tempest tossed. I could see it, but I didn't want it. I wasn't built for it. I was a rowing boat to my father's clipper; or a punt, maybe.

People said it was a reaction, that I was afraid of competing, of being held up against my famous father, and found wanting. I knew this because my mother told me. She wasn't very sensitive, my mother, she was too busy giving parties.

Furious, I told myself I didn't care. It wasn't true, after all. It was so far off the mark, it made me laugh. I didn't care when everyone commiserated with my brilliant father on his directionless daughter, that they held up their hands at a girl with so much expensive education under her belt, with so many exams to her name, and all for nothing. And what are you going to do with it, everyone asked, of my privileged education. I thought it an asinine question. I wasn't going to do anything with it. It was just book learning, after all. Life, I said, a little haughty, as if it had never been said before, you have to teach yourself.

So that's what I was doing, that first summer in London. I wasn't looking for Jack. I wasn't looking for anyone. I was on my own in a new city and I thought that would do for the time being. I thought I could learn a few of those things that were still a mystery to me, which was practically everything.

I had just hit the age when it becomes clear that everything you thought you knew was wrong. Or not so much wrong, as misplaced – something to do with arrogance and youth. I thought it was time to put all that behind me. I had been in the city for three months, and I was just getting used it, the newness and strangeness were wearing off. I was starting to find my way around without a map. I wasn't looking for a man. I didn't think I was looking for anyone. So Jack was a surprise, in a way. It was all a surprise.

It was a party, a Friday night, in someone's garden. It was one of those upmarket affairs, carefully orchestrated, where everyone looks pretty and sounds witty, even if they aren't, particularly. There was good champagne and men in white coats to pour it out, and no reason to be invited. I didn't know why I was there, but I went anyway. No-one seemed to know the host – there was a touch of the Gatsby's about him, he had come out of some obscure jungle in Brazil the year before with money to burn and an impressive guest list, and he entertained with a feverish intensity all that summer before disappearing as abruptly as he came.

I didn't mind about not knowing anyone. I was used to it. I had been moving on since I could remember. Wherever I lay my hat, I used to tell people, that's my home.

So I dressed up a bit, and tripped about the garden, from arm to arm, picking people up as I found them.

Eventually, inevitably, I got round to Jack. He was standing by himself, apart from the rest, and that was challenge enough. It had all been easy pickings so far, and I was starting to get restless. So I walked up to him and looked him very straight in the eye and held up a cigarette and asked if he had a light.

He looked back at me for a while, not much expression in his face, and then he said,

'No.'

That was all. That was all it took. Before he said that I was just playing, but now I was in earnest.

I laughed, as if he had said something amusing. It was a laugh that couldn't care less, that skated over the surface of the night and broke up into a hundred pieces when I was done with it.

'Dear me,' I said. 'That didn't work, did it?'

I took out a fold of matches and lit my cigarette myself, taking my time over it. Then I looked at him again, just to show I was mistress of my own composure.

'No,' he said again.

I wish I could say that there was some hidden note of amusement in his voice, some buried flash of interest, but there wasn't. It was just a voice, low and a little broken and flat with disinterest. It was a clarion call to me, that voice.

'Well,' I said, bold with illusions. 'We had better start again.'

I paused, and looked away from him, out into the party, where people were walking and talking and having a nice time. Then I turned back, and gave him a sudden smile, one of the best in my repertoire.

'Hello,' I said, as if I meant it.

'Hello, Society Girl,' he said.

I remember thinking that he sounded like something out of a novel. I thought he must have been reading Colin MacInnes. Later, I discovered that he didn't read, it was one of the things he didn't do.

Hello, society girl. What was that about? People didn't talk like that, not any more. But if that was the way he wanted it, I was willing to suspend disbelief. He was the kind of man it was worth suspending disbelief for.

He had one of those hollow wasted faces that spoke of secrets and sorrows and night-time living, and strange transparent washed-out eyes, not quite blue, not quite green, and black hair to his shoulders. He wore a white

T-shirt, ancient with washing, that draped over his thin shoulders, formless, and black jeans, and narrow boots in dark green leather, and a heavy silver earring in his right ear.

I wondered if he were gay – I never could remember whether it was the left ear or the right ear that signalled sexual bias, or even whether that rule applied any more, now that we were all supposed to be bisexual at heart. I hoped he wasn't.

I waited, wearing half a smile, smoking at my cigarette. I hoped I looked enigmatic. I had always wanted to be an enigma, like the Czechs and Greta Garbo, but I was never sure how to go about it. I thought if I let him, he might start a conversation. People usually did. It was a party, after all.

Nothing happened for a while. We stood in developing silence. I'm not good at silence; it bothers me, I feel responsible for it. It didn't seem to affect Jack.

'So,' I said, cracking under pressure and trying not to show it, 'do you come here often?'

I hoped I sounded ironic. Irony, saviour of the bland remark.

He was surprised into a smile. Well, not quite a smile, but something moved in his face, although it could have been the light.

'What?' he said. 'Does this party happen every night?'

I took this for encouragement.

'I don't know,' I said. 'I just got here myself.'

He looked weary.

'Do you want some blow?' he said.

I hesitated, unsure. I didn't know the jargon, in those days.

'No, thank you,' I said. 'Not just now,' I added, to make it sound better. I didn't like to betray ignorance.

'OK,' he said.

I looked away. It seemed the interview was over. Across

the garden I saw a session musician I had met before. I was tired of casting seeds on rocky ground, so I smiled at Jack again, a small tired it could have been great but where did we go wrong smile, and I didn't wait to see what effect it had. I just walked away.

'So,' I said, to the session musician, who at least looked pleased to see me. 'What about this gig, then?'

2 ∫

'What's blow?' I asked Louey, the next day.

Louey was my boss. He was one of the reasons I thought maybe I would stay in London. He was the twenty-third number I'd tried, when I first arrived, looking for a job, and he was the first to offer me an interview. So I went in to see him, and he looked at my CV and asked me if my father was who he thought he was, and said, 'So you worked in the Village?' and wouldn't you never guess, it turned out he had worked on exactly the same publication, years before, in his salad days. So now tell me the world isn't the size of a boiled egg. And he asked me about it and I told him, because he had one of those faces, the kind you tell things to.

I told him that after a lifetime on the move, my parents had got to New York, and stopped.

I remember the first time I drove over Brooklyn Bridge, and took a look at that skyline, with the shock it always gives because it's so familiar from all the films and pictures and postcards, but absolutely new and strange all at the same time, and for a moment it seemed as if it had just been invented for me, sitting there, waiting for me to find it – a whole party of a city, mine for the taking.

I discovered nightclubs and late bars and drinking tequila

out of shot glasses, straight up, and boys, straight up too, and the Village and Soho and Little Italy, and bagels at noon on Sundays in lofts full of dim sunshine and reruns of *Charade* at the Bleecker Street cinema, and that I didn't want to be famous, like my father.

I learned to do all the New York things, just like I was supposed to. I watched performance art and off-Broadway shows and obscure Japanese films. I knew where to find the best espresso, the best thrift shop, the best blues bar, the best place for Singapore noodle at four in the morning. I knew all the words to *Annie Hall*, and I developed a deep passion for Woody Allen, but in a cerebral sense of course, none of us could ever bring ourselves to think of him without those baggy corduroy trousers.

I got work on one of those underground publications that come out of Greenwich Village. I'm still not sure how I got hired – I met someone who knew someone, in one of those New York bars where everyone knows everyone, and I hadn't yet discovered my self-doubt, so I said I knew all about magazines, and before I knew it, I had a job. That was how things happened in those days, it was strangely easy. And there was my name, of course. It looked good on the masthead.

It suited me, for the time being. It made me independent. I liked that. I felt it meant something. I lived in a walk-up on West Fourth Street and paid my own rent. I listened to Bessie Smith and had people round for pot roast. (Only once, to tell the truth. I burnt it, and we had to send out for pizza. After that I went back to eating out.) But most important, I had somewhere to *go*. Each day, as I walked the four blocks to 8th Street, I wanted to stop the passers-by and tell them. Directionless, I wanted to say, you can keep it. I have somewhere to go.

So I worked for not much money in my stuffy little office, and worried about the ozone layer and AIDS and there not being enough venues for experimental jazz and bitched about the Republicans and wore all black, all the time.

'Come on,' as my friend Jeanie said. 'Please. *Of course.*'

I turned twenty-four, and on my birthday the office clubbed together and bought me a bottle of tequila, the real kind, with the worm, and a giant pack of rubbers, ribbed for extra sensation, and much later, the arts editor, who had pale sorrowful eyes behind thick spectacles and politics to the left of Lenin, helped me use them.

I told Louey that the next year it was my turn to get restless.

My parents seemed to have settled, perversely, high up in one of those venerable apartment blocks that mass the Upper West Side. My father even gave lectures at Columbia, that was how much part of the scenery he was becoming, and his wanderlust was bequeathed to me. So I went on a road trip.

They didn't ask why. Why wasn't one of the things they ever wanted to know, not about me. That, of course, was the other advantage of having these strange parental pods. Everyone minded for them, but they didn't care what I did. I could have married a crack dealer and gone to live in the South Bronx and all my mother would have worried about was what flowers to have at the wedding and whether to wear a hat, or not. I didn't bother them, they didn't bother me. It was tacit. (From the Latin *tacitus*, past participle of *tacere*, to be silent. Perfect.)

So at least I didn't have to answer any awkward questions. I wasn't sure I knew the answers anyway. I just said I felt like a change. I didn't tell them that my heart was broken. I didn't tell them that the arts editor had told me he loved me. I didn't tell them that he had lied.

It was a shock, at the time. It's always a shock, however long you see it coming. Not knowing what to do with it,

I pretended I was fine, young enough to take the knocks and get up again. It was just timing, I told myself, that's all. The wrong time and the wrong place, not my fault, it could have happened to anyone.

Of course, deep down, there was a part of me that believed it was very much my fault, that I had done something fatally wrong, or not even that, not even done something, just not been good enough, that perennial fear, our universal demon, not being good enough. But it was easier not to admit that part, although I didn't think of it that way. I was devoted to fooling myself in those days, something I was exceptionally good at, a professional in self-deception, and I told myself that it couldn't have been anything to do with me, that it was his loss, that he was too young and foolish to know what he did.

But all the same, I didn't want to stay around the scene of my failure. I made a whole load of excuses. I told myself that maybe it was time to get away from my father. I said I was tired of being asked if I had any literary pretensions. I thought I was getting boxed in in New York, that I wanted open spaces and green things. I said to myself that the Village wasn't really the same since the Beats had all got old or dead.

Whatever it was, I packed my bags and cashed my savings and said that I needed a change. That was what I told my parents. They nodded without interest, gave me a nice fat cheque and some letters of introduction and didn't ask when I would be back, and I went to look at America.

I saw it. It was big, and dirtier than I expected.

'What did I tell you?' said my friend Jeanie, down a late-night connection to New Mexico. 'I've *seen* Albuquerque.'

There were long stretches of flat desert and sudden dramatic bursts of scenery and strange small towns with dark bars and dilapidated general stores. I liked Chicago, Chicago, it's my kind of town, and I hated Florida, and I nearly died of suffocation in Vegas, but Sinatra was there, his eyes still blue, and he sang *The Lady is A Tramp* just as sweet as he ever did, so it was worth it.

I worked for a while on a Grunge magazine in Seattle, but it wouldn't stop raining, so I went into Kansas and hung out with some cowboys who thought Johnny Cash was God, and after that I drove down to New Orleans, and took a job in a book store, and got a taste for cajun food and blues guitar.

I finally arrived on the West Coast, hitching up on Venice Beach just as the sun was going down. I looked for the ghost of Jim Morrison, but he wasn't there, so I cruised up to Santa Monica and gazed out over the ocean, which was big and blue and shiny with the setting sun, and everything it was supposed to be. I had a beer in a bar with a long mahogany top and football pennants hanging on the walls and every drink known to man arranged on long glass shelves, and then I took Wilshire and drove the long curving drive up to Hollywood.

I lasted a week in Los Angeles. It might have been the City of Angels, but it wasn't celestial enough for me. Or perhaps it was too celestial, it was hard to tell.

I blew the last of my father's guilt money and sat in the Chateau Marmont, which I did like, because it had seedy brown carpets and fifties' tiled bathrooms and a swimming pool with leaves in and room service that didn't mind if you called it at two in the morning and asked for thirty-seven bottles of Budweiser and it was the only thing I saw in that entire city where I felt that I didn't have to apologise for not being Elizabeth Taylor.

I went to a few parties and I clubbed in a few clubs, and I met a few people, and I watched the interest in their eyes fade the moment they heard I wasn't in the business, and I saw enough Barbie Doll would-be starlet girls in tiny bra tops and eternally sprung hope to last me for the duration.

Tired of the film crowd, I fell into a renegade gang of English boys, all one-way tickets and attitude, who hung out in blasted pool halls the wrong end of Hollywood Boulevard and drank too much sour mash bourbon and played in undiscovered rock bands. That's who the thirty-seven Budweisers were for.

When the bars closed we would go back to my room and sit up until late, but they knew all the words to Beast of Burden, and that was worth anything. They had a startling beauty, and they all looked the same, bright staring eyes looking out from chiselled faces, and long black hair, and Harley boots. They used to fight a lot, proud of their temperament. There was always someone jumping out of the window in a fit of rage, because no-one understood what it was like to be an Artist. Lucky my room was on the ground floor.

In the day, while they slept off the night before, I sat by the pool and ate club sandwiches and listened to Lou Reed singing about what it was like being high in the city and wondered what I was going to do next. I didn't know. I wished someone would tell me. I felt it was time for my life to begin, but I didn't know how, or where.

So I went to London. I'm not sure why, exactly. Maybe it was all those pretty boys talking about the King's Road and Soho Square and gigs at the Marquee. Maybe it was just that I was English, after all, I even had the nice blue passport to prove it. I had some confused notion of nightingales singing in Berkeley Square and big red buses and wide garden squares. I thought maybe I'd like all those English things like irony and understatement and soccer matches.

So I packed up again and paid my bill and sold my car to the only one of the renegade boys who actually had any money (a cash deal, that was life on the Strip for you), got a cab to LAX and took an aeroplane and when it arrived, I was in London.

When I went to see Louey and told him some of this, he laughed quite a lot, although not at the bits I would have expected, and gave me a job, which was even less expected, and we became friends, which was the best part of all.

'Blow?' he said now, giving me a sidelong look. He had a thing he could do with his eyebrows which made me mad with jealousy. He could do everything from cryptic to quizzical through faintly disbelieving with those eyebrows.

'Yes, yes, yes,' I said. 'Come on, sheriff, give me a break. I just hit town,' I said. 'I don't know nothing.'

Louey knew everything, it was part of his charm. I wanted him to become a shrink, so I could go to him, but he wasn't interested. He said that if he did have a philosophy, it was intimately connected with the songs of Bob Dylan.

He looked wise and worldly and indulgent. He indulged me most days, it was one of his favourite games.

'Cocaine,' he said, not having to add the of course. 'Snow, charlie, toot, blow.'

'Oh,' I said, trying to sound blasé. 'That old chestnut.'

Louey leant back into my sofa and drank the beer I'd given him. He liked my place. He said it had a nice empty impermanent feeling to it. What he really meant was why didn't I have any furniture. I said I thought it was romantic, property being theft and all. I had bought a bed and a sofa and a table and a chair and a pot to put flowers in, and left it at that. I had some books and some records and a stereo that stacked up three feet high. I didn't have any of those tired middle-aged things like carpets and curtains and fitted units. I didn't have occasional tables or conversation pieces. I liked it empty. I liked sitting on the floor. I liked my two rented rooms, and my one gas ring, although I couldn't work out how to light it.

The French windows were open to let in the sun. It was one of those brave bright late spring days that promise summer. It was a Saturday, and we were just sitting. We did that most weekends. Louey wasn't big on action. He didn't go in for all those male bonding things, like playing football in the park or racing go-karts. He just liked to sit and talk and drink some beer. I said it was his female side, but he said it was idleness.

'Why?' he said.

Why was always what he wanted to know. With Louey, there really was a reason for everything.

'Oh,' I said, 'you know. Someone asked me if I wanted some. I didn't know if it was sex or drugs, so I said no.'

'Someone,' said Louey, getting it at once. '*Someone.*'

He smiled, just left of centre. Girls had been known to do foolish things over that smile. Louey had an effect on women. He was tall and wide in his shoulders and well-made, assembled with care, and he was funny and clever and comfortable in the world, as if he understood it, and he could do a perfect impression of Tony Curtis impersonating Cary Grant.

'Someone,' he said again. 'Where have you been hanging?'

He squinted at me. He did that when he wanted information. It made him look innocent and goofy, the kind of person a girl could tell all her secrets.

'A party,' I said. 'That party you wouldn't come to.'

I gave him a reproachful look. Louey didn't do parties. He said they gave him a rash.

'Ah,' he said. 'The gun-running gig.'

'It's not necessarily guns,' I said. 'How do you know it's guns?'

'Stands to reason,' said Louey, as if teaching a child its

ABC. 'Mystery cash, isn't it? No pedigree. Flash suits, big cigars, shiny new motors, hired mansions, rent-a-crowd parties. It's got Kalashnikov written all over it.'

'Yeah, yeah,' I said. 'I suppose you'll tell me that he fixed the world series. I suppose you'll tell me that he killed a man once.'

'That,' said Louey, 'is small potatoes. Packet of fags for people like that. Trip to the corner shop.'

I didn't bother to ask how he knew about people like that. He knew about people like everything. I had once asked him where all this knowledge came from and he just said that he'd read the Encyclopedia Britannica as a child.

I didn't buy that for a minute. Louey had never been a child. He'd come into the world fully formed, twenty-one with a hundred-year soul and not a fly in sight.

'So who's this geezer, then?' he said. 'This *someone* cat.'

Louey sometimes liked to talk like Keith Richards after a hard night, I never knew why.

'I don't know,' I said. I didn't. I hadn't asked. 'I don't know at all.'

'A dish, was he?' Louey said, squinting more than ever. 'Handsome? Tall and dark, all the right stuff?'

'Yes, yes,' I said, impatient. 'But it didn't work.'

'What didn't?' He was laughing at me now, but that wasn't anything new.

'Nothing,' I said, turning up my palms to show him. 'None of it. Me.'

Louey laughed some more. He often found me amusing, as if I had been invented especially for his entertainment.

'Shucks,' he said. 'And ain't it just a bitch, being you?'

'Ain't it just?' I said.

I didn't mean it. It wasn't, not then.

Summer came early that year. There were no late un-seasonal snows, no unheralded frosts to kill the roses. It just got hot. The city was warm and dusty and *en fête*, a shifting carnival, theatre in the streets. I liked it, summer in the city, the unexpected London sun forcing life up to the boil, out from behind closed doors, throwing up windows and opening shutters, putting an end to privacy and whispers and secrets and small talk. It was a celebration, a big communal all-day party, with everyone invited, the melting pot of races and colours and creeds cooking up in the sun, the thick air cut with jazz and reggae and rhythm and blues, with babel jabber and pidgin exclamation. That was the way I saw it, anyway. I was good at looking at the parts I wanted to believe.

I walked through my two white empty rooms, watching the sun fall into pools of light and shade, and drove into work with the roof down. Watch me, won't you please? I have somewhere to go.

Louey ran his magazine from a long bright office down by the river. It used to be a wharf where grain was shipped and stored, in the days when the Thames was a working waterway. Now it housed chi-chi restaurants and snob wine merchants and society photographers' studios – very gentrified, very uptown, very up-river.

The magazine was one of those part cult part fashion off centre off beat off Broadway productions that no-one can categorise and everyone expects to fold after six months of hysterical success. But Louey was cannier than that. Defying pessimistic odds and cynical prediction he was still in business after three years, filling a carefully carved niche, and doing very nicely.

It was good work; I liked it. I had been quickly promoted, I had a section all to myself, my very own six pages, to do with what I liked. It had to be about London, was all. I was the man on the Clapham omnibus. It was typical of Louey that he gave the London pages to me, that I was the one on the bus, when I didn't even know the routes yet. I still thought the underground meant people sitting in dark rooms plotting the downfall of the government.

He said that they had been getting predictable, and he might as well try a fresh pair of eyes. I liked being a fresh pair of eyes. I sat looking over the river and thought up quirky articles and new angles and savvy interviews. It wasn't subverting the English language, or redefining the use of prose. It was just a job. But it was mine, and it suited me, and I did it well, and it had nothing to do with my father.

3 ∫

I didn't think much about the man at the party, after that. I had other things to think about. I had my work and Louey and people to see. I had the city to discover.

I liked it in London. I liked it better than New York. I liked the changing rhythms of the city, I liked the spaced-out sprawl of it, the different neighbourhoods. I liked Hampstead Heath and Hyde Park and Richmond with all those deer. I liked Soho with its peep shows and old-fashioned shops and drinking holes. I liked the Bar Italia and the Colony Room and the French House. I liked Piccadilly Circus and Speaker's Corner and the fountains in Trafalgar Square. I liked it that there really were wide garden squares, and big red buses, and cab drivers who talked about the weather. I thought there was something more forgiving about it than New York, something older, more resigned, allowing everyone their own pace, like an elderly lady who's taken off her corsets for the last time and settled into her dotage, shaking out a long sigh of relief.

So I wasn't thinking about the man at the party, but I found him again even so, just when I wasn't expecting it.

It was one Saturday in May, and I went up to see my friend Lil in her new apartment. I had met her at a club opening, one of those things I got asked to as part of my job. All the new places wanted their three inches of copy in the magazine, just so everyone knew they existed. Lil and I met in the lavatory, and spent half an hour redoing our lipstick and discussing how second-rate it all was and where did they get crowds like this one and how the combined IQ of the entire room would not even hit double figures.

'Probably means the whole thing will be the biggest success of the year,' said Lil. 'Queues round the block by next week, you'll see.'

I told her that I had just arrived and I didn't really know anyone yet, and she said we should go for lunch, and the next week we did, and we discovered a mutual admiration for the novels of Scott Fitzgerald and the songs of Edith Piaf, and we became friends. She was older than me, and she had been living with a man, one of those rich Italians with a nice line in suiting and a broken accent and a big stucco house looking over Chelsea Hospital.

She had been living the high life: fast cars and society parties and dinners in Mayfair and all those other things that the Europeans like. He even gave her a dress allowance. I think he expected her to spend it in Bond Street, but Lil had a strange quirk about clothes, a kind of fancy dress sense, so she shopped in the markets, Saturdays in Portobello, Sundays in Petticoat Lane, and haunted Oxfam and those dark dusty shops in the back streets of Victoria. There was a streak of the theatrical in her family, her great grandfather had been in the music hall, so perhaps that was it.

She had moved out when she discovered that the Italian was cheating on her with four other women. She cried quite a lot and made a scene, and then she packed her bags and left. She rented a room at the end of Kensington Park Road and said that she had never loved him anyway, and I pretended to believe her.

* * *

So that Saturday, I took her a bottle of Chilean wine and a bunch of flowers and went for lunch.

'New World,' she said, looking at the bottle. 'What do you know?'

'Pre-philoxera,' I said. 'That's what the man in the shop said. I don't like to think what he meant.'

Lil laughed, a little ragged round the edges.

'It sounds like a sexually transmitted disease,' she said. 'I'm thinking of calling Paulo and telling him I've developed herpes. Herpes Simplex,' she said. 'It sounds like a character in Star Trek. I'd like to tell him he's going to break out in scabs and sores and then his dick will drop off.'

I wondered if it was too early to tell her that she was better off without him, and decided it was.

'I should,' I said. 'Really. It's all he deserves.'

'Four women,' she said bitterly. 'Four. It would have been better if it was only one. Or another man. But *four*.'

'The Latins,' I said, as if I knew all about them. 'They always revert.'

I had heard someone say that once. I wasn't sure exactly what they were supposed to revert to, but it sounded good.

'I know, I know,' she said, with that awful resigned look that women wear when they have been made to look like a fool. 'Don't tell me. I should have gone out and found a nice cosy Hampstead brain surgeon, just like my mother always wanted.'

'It could have been worse,' I said, without much conviction. 'At least you have an extensive wardrobe and a sure grasp of the Italian idiom.'

'There is that,' said Lil, with even less conviction.

The Italian had been something I hadn't understood about Lil. He had seemed such an unlikely choice for a girl like her. I hadn't liked to ask her about it at the time, and now it seemed even more indelicate, so I left it. But I think she knew, all the same.

She smiled at me, only a little forced. Lil didn't believe in dwelling on the past, even if it was only yesterday. She thought a great deal about the shortness of life and how many buses there were out there with her number on them.

'Let's drink this wine and have a nice time,' she said bravely. 'Living well is the best revenge.'

We drank the wine, and talked about safe neutral subjects, and put up some pictures. Lil looked right in her one room, more in place than she ever had in the grandeur of her Italian's mansion. He had made her store all her things in his basement. She had a great hoarding instinct, and he hadn't liked all her junk (his word) sitting among his carefully orchestrated interior designed rooms.

Now the junk was back, surrounding her, suiting her, lying where it fell. There were chipped busts of heroes so out of date no-one knew their names, a deck chair from Brighton pier, a tuba and two guitars that she couldn't play, a ship in a bottle. There were Indian wall hangings and statues of Ganesh and incense burners from her hippy stage, Russian icons and Eastern prayer mats from her spiritual stage, Lalique glass and Tiffany lamps from her deco stage, and one scaled down matt black minimalist stereo system from her eighties designer stage, which hadn't lasted.

And books, that was the other thing, books everywhere and by everyone, from Enid Blyton to Marguerite Duras and back again, although she drew the line at Joyce, who she said was too silly. It was one way of putting it. I had never managed Ulysses myself.

'I love it here,' I said. 'I love your things.'

Lil looked about her. She was dressed as a sailor today, right down to the bell bottoms, a jolly jack tar ready to do any hornpipe she chose. Because she was tall and narrow, and because she didn't care less, she got away with it. She made me think of some errant seaman, on shore leave, looking for a brothel, who had strayed into a junk shop by mistake, and was not quite sure what to do about it.

'I had forgotten,' she said, looking around with a steady kind of deliberation. 'I had forgotten how naked I felt, without my books.'

We finished the bottle. It seemed like the right thing to do, fitting, I don't know. You have to do something with pain, and I wasn't yet sure what it was. I wasn't experienced enough to give her advice or direction, I had just a bare slice of the world at my disposal, and I felt a little helpless, because she was older and she knew some of the answers to some of the questions I hadn't even started to ask. But I knew that she needed something, something to help her through, something to smother the sharp sting of rejection. I knew about that anyway. I might tell myself that I had forgotten, but there were times when it seemed like it was just yesterday.

I watched her hurt, and I watched her deny it, and I let her, and we talked of other things. I wanted to make everything better, but they don't hand out magic wands with the price of admission, so I made bad jokes instead.

That was all right, in a way. We grew into the irresponsible garrulous mood that daytime drinking can induce. We were girls together, and we laughed and got dirty and told each other how absurd men are. It was one of our favourite conversations, even on a good day.

'You see,' said Lil, 'the point is . . .'

For a moment, she forgot the point, and looked about her jumbled room for a while, to retrieve it.

'The point,' I said, helpfully.

'Exactly,' she said, with authority. 'The point is, that when a man gets an erection, all the blood from his brain goes into his penis. Which is why men can't think and fuck at the same time.'

'Poor sad things,' I said. 'I feel for them, really I do.'

'Whereas,' said Lil, not to be put off her stroke, 'a woman can lie there and plan her spring wardrobe, consider her next career move, wonder whether to paint the bathroom green, compose a letter to the bank manager, and take responsibility for her own orgasm, *all at the same time.*'

She paused for a moment, for dramatic emphasis. I watched in admiration. It was dramatic. It was front row of the stalls and no mistake.

'That,' she said, with the air of one finishing a controversial debate on molecular biology which, in an oblique way, she probably was, 'is the difference between men and women.'

'It is,' I said.

There was a kind of madness in Lil that day. I watched it grow as the afternoon wore on, escaping in sudden incongruous bursts of laughter and mysterious *non sequiturs.*

I hadn't seen her like this before, but then I had only known her since she had been with the Italian, and for all her idiosyncratic dress sense and her determined way with her hair, she had been his creature. He didn't like his women wild. He said that the English were effete, fast and decadent. I said just look at the Roman Empire, not so staid last time I looked.

But he was right, in a way. The modern Italians don't seem to have that drive to excess that the English do. They have cast off the soft indulgence of togas and orgies and dancing girls and evolved a kind of stately grandeur, a civilised latin deference to social mores and cultured politesse. They don't have the same hanged if we do hanged if we don't up the hill backwards breakneck fever that drives English men to foolhardy drinking and staying up all night and dressing in women's clothing.

This Italian didn't, anyway. There had been a curious old-fashioned routine to Lil's time with him, a great many dinners at eight and weekend house parties and early evening cocktail hours. He was something high up in the United Nations, diplomatic to his lying cheating philandering backbone.

'Mud in your eye, mud in your eye,' sang Lil, in cockney.

She drank her wine faster than was good for her, faster than her erstwhile paramour would have found seemly. She was defiant now, having no-one to please but herself. She was free, with no-one to answer to, but I wasn't sure whether she wanted to be free, whether she knew what she was going to do with all this freedom now she had it.

I felt that I should know, should guess at least, but I wasn't yet very practised at being intimate with people. I didn't know the right questions to ask. It was something to do with my father, I supposed, genetic, inherited; or perhaps it came from always being on the move, not standing still long enough.

I thought that her heart was breaking, but I didn't know how to help her, so I just drank my wine quickly too and tried to look as if we were all in it together.

'Sod them,' I said. 'Bastards.'

'Bastards,' said Lil, in sudden delight.

The Italian hadn't liked her swearing either, so unfeminine, so not done, all right for him to do the dirty word, but not all right for her to say it.

'Bugger and damn them,' she said.

'Yes,' I said, thinking this must be good. Let her be angry, she should be angry, she had a right.

'Ha,' she said, banging her glass down on the table and walking round the room with quick uncoordinated steps.

I watched her. I felt that I should do something, dance or sing or hang upside down from a light fitting.

'I know,' said Lil suddenly, making strange windmill gestures with her arms.

Soon she would start breaking valuable pieces of china and throwing heavy objects out of the window.

'What?' I said, foolish and a step behind.

'What we should do,' said Lil. She drew herself up and looked at me squarely. 'We should go out and get drunk and take drugs and go to bed with unsuitable men,' she said in triumph, as if no-one had thought of it before.

'You have been going to bed with unsuitable men,' I said, surprised and tactless.

She gave me a dangerous look, as if it were I that had been running five women at once. She looked fierce and untamed, a million miles away from European salons and canapes made with salmon roe. I was lost in admiration. I had been trying for the fauve school since I was in grey serge and knee socks, but I didn't know anyone who could achieve it so effortlessly while wearing a sailor suit.

'Much much more unsuitable,' she said, spacing her words out with meaning. I could almost hear her putting each one in capitals, scattering them with dramatic emphasis. 'MUCH MUCH more.'

'It's a perfect idea,' I said, enchanted.

It was. I wanted to go to bed with unsuitable men too. It had such a brave rebellious ring to it. Unsuitable. Wouldn't do in polite company, not the right sort to take home to Mother, a bad lot, a bad hat, no future there. Everyone will warn you against them, but what do you care? Why not just spit in the eye of convention, run with the devil, walk with the beautiful and damned?

'Why not?' I said, putting up my chin and what the hell.

'I know a place round the corner,' said Lil.

She was the kind who always knew a place round the corner, it was one of the things I liked in her.

She smiled at me again, in a final kind of way.

'Let's do it,' she said.

4

So we put on our lipstick and gathered all our cash together and went to a place round the corner to find danger and trouble and unsuitable men, and the first person I saw when we walked in the door was Jack.

'Bingo,' said Lil. 'There's the dealer.'

I wasn't sure which kind of dealer she meant, so I just nodded and tried for a worldly look. Lil had been round the block one more time than I had, and it was at times like this that it showed. I had been round some blocks, whole states even, but I had never got close enough to the street to learn the language. All the people I ever seemed to have met had been poets and dreamers and revolutionaries, the kind who still thought it was possible to change the world, who wandered through life looking for a new Utopia.

'Jack,' said Lil. 'What's happening?'

She reached up and touched her cheek to his, a fleeting acknowledgement of greeting, we know the score but we're not telling. It seemed symbolic of something, some shared knowledge, like a masonic handshake or a secret agent's cigarette.

Jack had that same look he'd worn the night of the South American's party, not giving anything away, not one thing. I wondered if he'd been born like that, or whether he'd worked for years to perfect the impression that wherever the iceman was, he wouldn't be long in coming.

I tried not to look at him, but I couldn't help it. I tried for a sly corner of the eye not really taking any notice effect, but I would have needed dark glasses to pull it off, that film star number, not caring if there was any sun or not.

He was still wearing his black jeans, and one of those bikers' jackets that look as if they have been slept in and worn in the bath and used for unnatural acts. He had that general look about him, as if unnatural acts came easy to him, all in a day's work, and don't let's pretend we haven't seen it all before. There was a strange stillness as well, not watchful quite, but as if he were accustomed to – what? – wariness perhaps, watching his back.

I shook my head crossly. I thought I should stop reading all the books and live a little. He was only a man in dark clothes, it wasn't so complicated. It might just have been the mood he was in that day.

But of course (of *course*) it all shouted unsuitable, yelled it from the rooftops, put it up on advertising hoardings all over the city. It was prime time. If danger and trouble and living on the edge were really what we were in search of that evening, this man didn't have to say a word to tell us that we were on the right track.

'Nancy,' said Lil, in introduction. 'This is Nancy. Nancy, this is Jack.'

I thought of the Czechs. I thought of Greta Garbo. I thought of Rita Hayworth in *Gilda*. (They go to bed with Gilda and they wake up with me; it wasn't only the Russians that could do tragedy.)

'Hello,' I said.

I wished I could think of more, but I couldn't. I said it nice and slow, at least, with meaning. There might be more to me than met the eye, you never knew.

I didn't hold out my hand, because I knew he wouldn't

shake it. I just stood, and waited to see what would happen, as if I wasn't so very interested.

'So,' said Jack.

I remembered his voice now, coming back through the starling chatter of the evening crowd. Low and flat, all over again, not trying a yard.

'Nancy,' he said.

I stood my ground. It was all I had. There was a pause.

There didn't seem to be any more. Then, suddenly, it was all right, because it was a bar, and it was seven o'clock on a Saturday night, and two men I knew came strolling out of the middle distance and asked me where I'd been and why I never called and why I wasn't drinking bourbon with them. So there, I thought, so damn there, Mr Jack Mr Leather Mr No conversation, watch me go, and I went to the bar and invented a flirtation and hoped he was noticing.

'Well,' I said to my saviours. 'And isn't it swell to see the both of yous?'

It was. I liked them – Jimmy and Ned, too much cash and not enough sense and always there when you needed them.

'Isn't it just?' said Ned.

'A drink for the lady,' said Jimmy.

I recovered myself, and looked around. It's always nice to know where you are.

Well, it was a bar, a curious beached ocean liner of a bar, echoes of art deco and what were you singing when the Titanic went down, low lighting and high visibility, with dusty mirrors and chrome bar stools and dark aquamarine ceilings. It was camp and seedy, sleaze with class, the kind of place you could come and slum and get off with people with three aliases and PO boxes for addresses, or put on a party frock and cut glass with your accent and end up at a Roman villa for the weekend.

It was the kind of place where anything could happen,

and probably did, most nights. It wasn't quite the sixties (for which I had a yearning nostalgia), not quite heiresses running off with lorry drivers, but the idea was there. There was nothing much left to fight against any more, everything allowed, live in sin all you like, social dictates and genteel niceties just dinosaurs now, but in places like this you could still feel that somehow, somewhere, there were blows being struck.

Not that anyone said as much, and sometimes I thought it was just me. It wasn't as if there was a movement, or a cult, or a sect. There were no leaders or gurus any more, no Jack Kerouac or Timothy Leary to lead us out of the desert and into the land of milk and honey, no Aldous Huxley to open the doors of perception, although perhaps we were looking for them.

Having found my bearings, I turned back to Jimmy and Ned, and smiled. I was pleased to see them. I had met them at a new restaurant I'd gone to review, and as soon as they heard I was new in town they had taken it upon themselves to introduce me to all the late-night places I could ever need to know. Because of them, I was starting to learn where to find jazz on a Thursday and ska on a Friday and a drink after hours any day of the week. They were the best pair of ambassadors you could wish for.

Jimmy went back to the thirties, immaculate and dandy, trousers pressed into knife-edge creases, hair oiled back, double-breasted suits and wide lapels and co-respondant shoes. It was a sort of bogus aristo gangster look, Al Capone meeting the Duke of Windsor and going on the tear, thick chalk pinstripes with blood red linings, fivers falling out of his pockets, singing East End all the way to the bank, dodgy motors and everything off the back of a lorry. In fact, couldn't you guess, Jimmy really came from one of those old and venerable families who did rather well at Hastings.

His mother had never been east of Belgrave Square in her life.

Ned was his opposite, way out at the other end of the sartorial scale, dressed in that double bluff hippy drag: fringed suede jackets and lizard skin boots and bright blue round sunglasses. They were very much the thing, those glasses, there was even an expression for them doing the rounds. Seeing the world in blue, that's what people said, do you see the world in blue. But Ned had really been raised on pie and mash in the Isle of Dogs, come from thieving cars and forging giro cheques to make a pile in a dubious futures deal.

'What do you think of the whistle?' said Jimmy, in his studied barrow-boy accent.

I once asked him where he'd learnt it, but Jimmy didn't give away trade secrets. Ned said that he'd watched *The Long Good Friday* in his formative years.

'Smart,' I said.

'Wide,' said Ned, who should know.

Jimmy smirked, sure of which effect he desired, and shrugged his shoulders a little to show off the beauty of his tailoring.

'So,' he said. 'What's the story?'

'Saturday night,' I said, as if surprised that he hadn't noticed. 'We're going out and behaving badly.'

'You never behave badly with us,' said Ned, trying to look as if it mattered to him.

'Self-preservation,' I said, which wasn't strictly true. You have to be able to see the abyss to be afraid of the fall, and my eyes weren't that wide open, not yet.

'Blah, blah,' said Ned, looking pleased. Everyone likes to think of themselves as a little dangerous, from time to time. 'Absolute pushovers, we are,' he said, opening his eyes at me.

'Pussycats,' said Jimmy, looking soulful and innocent and

as if he'd just pulled a bank job. 'Just waiting to be led astray by a pretty face.'

'Not this pretty face,' I said, looking inadvertently over at Jack.

He did have a pretty face, a mournful last night's beauty, fatally ravaged by time and trouble.

'Who is that man?' I said, not meaning to. I didn't want to know, really I didn't. Just making conversation, passing the time of day.

Jimmy and Ned laughed and shifted their feet and exchanged knowing looks.

'Dodgy,' said Jimmy, who always had the inside track. 'No good for you, princess. Carve you up into little pieces, that one. Sell you to his grandmother in small plastic bags, all in a day's work.'

Ned nodded, sage and corroborative.

'Candyman,' he said. 'Little too fond of the junk.'

I thought that was rich, coming from Ned. He had an old Fender Stratocaster in his bedroom and liked to sit up nights drinking bourbon and playing Jimi Hendrix guitar solos. He said it broadened the mind. He said it was very important to broaden the mind. He said everyone should do it more often.

'What sort of junk?' I said, as if I wasn't really interested.

'Anything you can name,' said Jimmy. 'Up, down, sideways, round the houses. Doesn't look after his health.'

He looked disapproving and pinstriped superior. Jimmy didn't have much brief for pharmaceuticals. He had taken a disprin once and thought he was John the Baptist for five hours, not quite the second coming, but too close for comfort. These days he stuck to sour mash whisky and ate green pickles and cocktail onions for a headache.

Ned thought this was an affectation. I once had to stop him from spiking Jimmy's drink with two panadol and a shot of Benylin. I was fond of Jimmy. I didn't want him ending up in Oxford Street with a sandwich board telling people he had been sent to earth to save their souls.

'Someone should tell him,' said Ned, shaking his head in sorrow.

Jack, I thought, must be a true degenerate to get that disapproving tone. Ned didn't disapprove of anything, except the vice squad.

'Hello,' said Lil, appearing out of the crowd. 'What's with you two?' she added, kissing Jimmy and Ned. 'Corrupting the innocent?'

Jimmy looked regretful.

'We try,' he said. 'Honest we do. But everybody knows everything already.'

'Dark days,' said Lil. 'What can you do?'

She gave me a conspiratorial smile and took my hand.

'I'm taking Nancy away,' she said. 'So you'll have to console each other.'

'Girl's talk,' said Jimmy, old woman that he was. 'Lipsticks and B-cups.'

'G-strings and dick size,' said Lil, with the dangerous look she was using that night. 'Don't think we don't.'

'Checkmate, mate,' said Ned, laughing at Jimmy's face. 'Get out the Baby Bio.'

'Please,' said Jimmy, pained drawl and all. County background will out from time to time, however many flash whistles you dress it up in.

'Now then,' said Lil, taking me into the Ladies. 'Now we're talking. Time to powder our noses.'

I watched as she took out a small wrap and unfolded it. Jack the dealer had delivered, all right.

'Business,' I said, as if I knew, which I didn't.

Grade A narcotics weren't exactly my neck of the woods. We had looked down on that sort of thing in my downtown days, lofty citizens of the world that we were, regarding it as part of the capitalist conspiracy, the province of Upper East side trust fund babies, with their BMWs and members only, houses in the Hamptons and button-down collars, trying to show that they were more than cardboard cutouts by taking a little wander on the wild side, bankrolled by Daddy and generations of robber barons.

But if Lil wanted to corrupt innocent youth I wasn't going to spoil the party. You don't acquire worldly wisdom sitting at home warming your slippers in front of the fire, not last time I looked. I thought I should get out into the world and get dirty. I thought it was time to grow up and shock people.

'Yes?' said Lil, holding out a rolled ten pound note.

'Yes,' I said.

Out in the crowd, which suddenly seemed lighter and brighter and more promising, Jack was standing where Lil had left him. There was everyone walking and talking and flirting and trading indiscretions, the constant flux of the young and the brave getting their kicks, drinking and teasing and backing themselves into corners, movement everywhere you looked, trends being set and habits endorsed and secrets discovered, cries and whispers in the air, and in the midst of it all, one still lone figure, by himself, staring at the wall.

If I had been cynical I might have thought that he was stoned or bored or boring or just plain pretentious. But I had never been able to do cynicism with any conviction. I liked to think I could, because it always sounded good, heavy with sophistication and having seen it all before. I considered it a great compliment if anyone told me not to be a cynic, but it was nothing more than a pose, skin deep only. I still looked on the bright side, believed in horses and carriages and love and marriage and clouds and silver linings. I joined the dots and came up with the wrong picture, every time. How could Jack not seem a romantic figure to me then? He was textbook stuff.

I watched him for a while, hoping that he might sense it and turn, catch my eye, but he didn't. His fascination with the middle distance remained, unwavering.

'Please,' said Lil, who wanted to have fun. It was her party after all. She was the one trying to forget. I was just along for the ride.

'Are you going to stand there all night?' she said. 'We have a room to work.'

I shook my head. There were other men in the world, and this bar was full of them. We had cash in our pocket and time on our side, a hundred possibilities to shoot at.

'What,' I said, turning away and concentrating on the promising, 'are we waiting for?'

It was late when I woke the next day. It felt late, as if I had missed something, a train or a boat, and I sat up with a start, disorientated, thinking perhaps I was abroad and should order a cab to take me to the airport.

Then I saw that it was my white walls and my bare bedroom and my clock on the table and it was one o'clock in the afternoon. Last night came back in a rush, as if someone had turned the television on. I wished they hadn't. I wished I could go away somewhere quiet, an island, or a little house by the sea, until it had finished.

I remembered it all now, horrible insidious memory, not letting me get away with a thing. Lil and I had taken more drugs, feet firmly on the slippery slope. There had been tequila shots, my idea, of course. I had found a boy at the bar who smiled at me, which I took for encouragement, and I bet him that I could do three in a row. I won.

After that, I became aware of the conviction that I could do anything. Waves of omnipotence washed over me as I stalked the room, ten foot tall, Queen of the May. I was going to show Jack, that was it. I was going to show him how witty and pretty I was. I was going to show him that everyone in the room was in love with me. And they were, they were, the world was in love with me, and I was in love with the world, and we were all going to have a ball together.

I remember talking about sexual technique with a man called Mack, and about the strange inhibited nature of the English with two boys in torn jeans and ponytails whose names I never caught, and then I danced for a while with Ned, and then the place closed up and we went back to someone's flat and drank some beer and a slight dark man sat down next to me and told me that he could see the sadness in my eyes and I suddenly felt tragic and misunderstood, quite by myself in an uncaring world, and I told him my life story, and let him take me home.

He had a mole next to his mouth, which made me think of Robert de Niro, and a slow sorrowful way of looking at me, and he kissed me for what seemed like three years and then took me to bed and executed a great many astonishingly practised sexual acts before he fell asleep.

I moved my head a fraction. He was still there, tidily sleeping, taking care not to snore. He looked less like Robert de Niro in the afternoon light, and older than I remembered. I had no idea what to do with him. I hadn't done a one night stand for a long time, having decided that meaningless sex really was meaningless, and dangerous besides, in this day and age, living under the shadow of the virus.

I felt terrible. My mouth was dry and old and my skin felt like paper and my head ached and my bones were crippled with angst. I couldn't remember where my feet were. The goddess of the night before had resolved herself into a mere frail human after all, and it hurt all over. I wondered if I just lay very still it might pass.

The man beside me stirred, muttering in his sleep.

Alarmed, I ran into the bathroom, locking the door behind me. Every part of my body was pounding. I tried to concentrate. If I could manage to clean my teeth and wash my face and have a bath, I might be able to start the day.

'Just don't ask me how I'm feeling,' said Lil, her voice carrying weakly down the telephone line. 'Just don't. It would be wanton cruelty. Wanton.'

'Never again,' I said, not knowing quite how many times it had been said before. 'Never ever again.'

'Well,' said Lil, who had a practical streak running in her. 'Not for a few days, anyway. Give the body time to get back to beautiful.'

'Talking of which,' I said, trying to sound offhand, 'I have a man in my bed.'

'I didn't like to ask,' said Lil. 'But there were rumours.'

'Oh dear,' I said, cringing under a wave of angst. 'What shall I do with him? I can't remember how it works.'

'Cowardice,' said Lil. 'Don't even toy with the idea of being brave. Are you dressed?'

I looked down at myself. I supposed I was dressed. I had clothes on, anyway.

'Yes,' I said.

'Well,' said Lil seriously. 'Leave a note telling him to let himself out and call a cab and we'll have lunch. I'm in too much pain to go back to sleep, so we might as well hold our heads down in public.'

I smiled. I had never been very good at confrontation.

'I'll see you in half an hour,' I said, and disconnected.

We ate big plates of spaghetti without taking our sunglasses off. Around us, most people were doing the same. There was that careful disintegrated hum of post-party conversation, everyone taking care not to speak too loudly in case they had a relapse.

'I've drunk a pint of water and six alka seltzer,' said Lil, 'and still I feel like a ship that went down with all hands. I'm going to ask for my money back.'

'I should,' I said. 'Stand up for your consumer rights.'

Lil took her sunglasses off for a moment, then thought better of it and put them back on.

'Did you have sex all night?' she said.

'I think so,' I said. 'It seemed to go on for a long time.'

'Impressive,' said Lil. 'Considering.'

'He was,' I said. 'I felt like giving him an Oscar or a Grammy or something.'

'And nice?' said Lil.

'Oh, very,' I said. 'You know, one of those ones who won't let you do any of the work. I just lay back and watched the floor show.'

Lil laughed.

'And you still don't know what his name was?' she said.

I looked her very straight in the eye.

'Not a clue,' I said.

'Really,' said Lil. 'Aren't we just a pair of old sluts? Sex and drugs and rock and roll. When are we going to grow up and get real?'

'Not yet,' I said. 'Please say not yet.'

'It's all right for you,' she said. 'You've got five years on me. I know people who used to do three in a bed and all night raves and now they're talking about Cow and Gate and trips to the zoo and having to get home to pay the babysitter.'

'Lil,' I said, suddenly alarmed. 'You're not getting broody on me, are you?'

She pushed her spaghetti away and lit a cigarette and twisted her mouth up into a smile.

'Of course not,' she said. 'Not me. Just a random observation from the front line. Even a nineties woman has to have a minute off, from time to time.'

'I won't tell,' I said. 'Anyway, why can't we just behave badly and not think about the consequences for a while longer?'

'There's no such thing as a free lunch,' said Lil.

I smiled at her, not believing it.

'Come on,' I said. 'That's why they invented credit.'

5

Monday, I went back to the office, like a normal person. I was recovered, just a little shaky on my feet, like a patient recuperating from a bout of influenza. Louey gave me a look, and left it at that. I was grateful. He was good to me, Louey, better than I deserved.

The office was busy, as usual. It had that steady white buzz, the comfortable sound of success, machines and telephones and talk, ideas rising into the air-conditioning like smoke. I smiled at everyone, made myself a cup of coffee, and sat down at my desk, trying to look as if I wasn't really late. I should have known better.

'Well, well, well,' said the art director, drawing up a chair and looking me hard in the eye. 'And what have we been up to this weekend? If a girl might know?'

'Violet,' I said, hoping for clemency. 'Please.'

Violet, delighted that her shot had hit sure to the bullseye, lit one of my cigarettes and blew uncaring smoke all over me.

'Ha,' she said. 'Well, well. Tell everything to auntie.'

Violet was one of those people that you couldn't believe really existed. Or at least, I couldn't. She looked like a little china doll, all rosebud mouth and lollipop eyes, the most delicate thing I ever saw. She tripped into the office every day on her tiny feet looking like nothing so much as Holly Golightly on her way to Tiffany's – little black dresses and wide Cecil Beaton hats and chiffon scarves and alligator shoes.

Her father had been a would-be rock star who had spent the sixties mourning the hits that never were. He had finally given up the dim lights and the moan of the crowd, joined a hippy commune and spent the rest of his days wondering where all the flowers had gone. Violet's mother had been his only groupie, and when the dreams of stardom fell to dust, she ran off to look for a Rolling Stone.

Reports came occasionally from unreliable sources, that she had been seen singing backing vocals in a rock festival in San Francisco, or following a Zen master in Nepal. Other rumours filtered through over the years, that she had stolen a set of matched emeralds from the hotel suite of some society dame and set up a nightclub in Ibiza off the proceeds; that she had become the mistress of a mafia boss and was living in style in Palm Beach; that she had married an oil baron and settled in Texas, but no-one really knew.

So Violet had been brought up, motherless, on lentils and pulses, in a cloud of incense and Moroccan black. She broke out as soon as she was old enough, left the hippies, who waved vaguely goodbye and told her to give peace a chance, and hitched her way to New York. The first thing she did when she got there was to change her name, from Dandelion.

'Dandelion?' I said, when she told me this.

'Well,' she said. 'You know. That was my Pop for you.'

She found work designing sets off Broadway, those arty hippy days hitting pay dirt, moved into a loft in Tribeca, before it was a fashionable area, and slept around to beat the band.

'It was the thing to do,' she always said, without apology. 'You know how a girl doesn't like to let her public down.'

Tiring of Manhattan, she moved to London, and just to

keep people on their toes, she executed a perfect and unexpected *volte face* and married a staid thirty-five-year-old banker, who worked for the oldest stuffiest firm in the city, lived in a large solid house in Kensington, and was known to be a hard man to hounds. Rolling out the double barrel, she called it.

Then she met Louey, and now here she was, staring at me with those killer eyes, wanting to know everything. I drank my coffee, playing for time. Violet kept looking.

'Oh, don't,' I said. 'I'm doing my best.'

'Obviously you were,' said Violet, flashing about her powers of observation, which we all knew were considerable, she didn't have to show off about it. 'Was it beautiful for him too?'

'I didn't like to ask,' I said, giving in. 'Is it that obvious?'

'Some things a girl just knows,' said Violet. 'I may have a ring on my finger, but I never forget the signs.'

I smiled, sheepish. I remembered when I had done my first one night, in the days when I thought that only fallen women indulged in that kind of thing. I was just turned twenty, and he had been my birthday present, practically gift-wrapped. I remembered walking away the next morning, into the unforgiving sunshine, in my last night's clothes and my last night's face, not even with a pair of dark glasses to hide my shame, unable to find a taxi, convinced that every passer-by knew what I had been doing. Afterwards, I told myself that no-one could tell, not really, but perhaps there were signs. Violet seemed to be able to see them, anyway.

'Of course, you're right,' I said.

Violet was always right. She had the wisdom of the ages sewn into her suspenders.

'It *was* Saturday night,' I said, as if that made everything better.

'Ha!' said Violet, hooting with delight.

She liked it when people behaved in an irresponsible manner. It gave her a vicarious pleasure, now that she had settled down.

'I don't miss those bad old days,' she told me once, 'but I like hearing about other people's.'

She lit another of my cigarettes. Senseless smoking and a heavy caffeine habit were the last indulgences she allowed herself. There was nothing of the misplaced puritan in Violet. She might have left her wild past behind her, where it belonged, but she held a firm belief that too much self-deprivation was bad for the soul.

'So,' she said, twitching her tiny little button nose at me, like a bloodhound on the scent. 'Where did you find him? Who was he?'

'In a bar,' I said. 'I didn't ask his name.'

It was true. By that time of the evening, names had seemed obsolete.

Violet blew out a startled plume of smoke. 'Well,' she said. 'Life on the edge. Sex with a stranger, I'm impressed. I didn't know anyone did that any more.'

'Neither did I,' I said. 'It must be a stage I'm going through.'

'Stage, schmage,' said Violet. 'Everyone feels they have to prove a point sometimes. It happens to the best of us, and I should know.'

She was right, of course, right on the money. It had been that restless dangerous feeling, the one that says, Look at me, I can behave badly and damn the consequences. There had been a pleasing kind of irrationality about it, some nice defiance. Watch me throw caution to the winds, and don't I do it with style?

'Yes,' I said. 'That was it. That's what it was.'

'And how was it?' said Violet, who always liked to know. In her disgraceful youth, she used to keep a little black book with a list of her conquests in it, giving them marks out of ten.

'Oh,' I said, sighing, faintly regretful, I wasn't sure for what. 'You know. Very accomplished. He was older. It showed. He knew all the buttons to press.'

'Ah,' said Violet, nodding. 'A pro. Ten points for technical ability. How about artistic interpretation?'

'Probably an eight,' I said, considering. 'He said some pretty things.'

He had said some pretty things, all the right things. It was just that I had a strange feeling that he had said them before.

'A high scorer,' said Violet in satisfaction. 'Nice to know there are still some about. So what was missing?' she added. She was clever at reading between the lines, it was one of her great talents. 'No soul?'

'Perhaps,' I said. 'It wasn't so much that his soul wasn't in it, I think it was mine.'

'Ah yes, of course,' said Violet, nodding sagely. 'The great mid-twenties crisis. That awful moment when you realise that the days of your careless youth are really over and meaningless sex is meaningless after all and all you long for is the comfort of a nice double bed after the hurly burly of the chaise longue. It comes to us all. The moment when you realise that nothing but love will do.'

I nodded slowly, thinking maybe she was right. She was right about everything, we all knew that.

'Perhaps,' I said, 'that's what it is.'

Violet took one last nostalgic draw on her cigarette and put it out with a careful kind of finality.

'Well,' she said, suddenly breaking out the irreverent smile that always caught me unawares. 'You can always call Dateline.'

*   *   *

I told Louey I wanted to do a series of pieces on Notting Hill, for my August section.

'I'm thinking ahead,' I said. 'I'm still doing July.'

I was pleased with July. Since we were supposed to have our finger on the pulse, we were always telling people where the new things were. Problem was, any old rag could do that, since all the new places sent out sackloads of publicity flyers and invites and promotional items every month. So instead of just telling everyone where they should be going or what they should be seeing, I had sent the grandest of the art critics to the opening of the latest all-night rave club, and two thrash guitarists from the Next Big Thing to see an experimental dance group, and a physics student who lived on baked beans and spent all her spare time going on anti-vivisection marches to a swank new restaurant where people were already going to see and be seen. I thought this was quite a good idea, and anyway, it made me laugh.

'Yes,' said Louey, tapping his teeth with a pencil. It was a little habit he had. I sometimes told him that he should give up the day job and take it up professionally.

'Notting Hill,' he said. 'Why not?'

'So many angles,' I said. 'The post-eighties shift, of course, a microcosm of that . . .' I liked using words like microcosm, it made me feel like a professional.

'Yes, yes,' said Louey. 'Of course. Nice and topical. Welcome to 1990.'

'And the sociological aspect,' I said. 'All those public school types changing their accents and getting out the crystals. Trustafarians, they're calling them now.'

Louey gave a quick sly smile, the one that women went foolish over. This was the kind of joke he enjoyed, even though he knew he shouldn't.

'Good,' he said. 'Nice.'

'There's a fashion story as well,' I said. 'Return of the

seventies, that's all up there too. All those little pixie things wandering about in their hot pants and their skinny rib jerseys showing off their skinny ribs.'

I gave a small snarl of derision. Just as we had started to believe in the return of the bust, they invented the superwaifs, who looked about twelve and a half and had thighs the size of my little finger and before you knew it it was the return of the stick thing and we all had to look like Jean Shrimpton again.

'Yes,' said Louey, tapping his teeth faster than ever. 'I never really saw the point of flared trousers myself.'

'No telling,' I said, which we both knew there wasn't. 'Then we could do something on the artistic side, the new Bloomsbury, that kind of thing, all those novelists and screenwriters living up there. It's like shooting fish in a barrel, ever since Martin Amis.'

'Yes,' said Louey happily. He held the slightly controversial view that London Fields was a better novel than War and Peace. 'Good, good.'

'And I thought we could do an opinion piece,' I said. 'Death of the front line, a bourgeois ghetto and all that.'

'And all that,' said Louey, who could remember the days when the All Saint's Road really was a no-go area.

'There's the drug angle too,' I said, a little hesitant now. I didn't really want to go through Saturday night again, I wasn't sure my constitution was up to it. 'I don't know if you want anything on the rave culture and the acid revival.'

'I don't think so,' said Louey, putting his pencil down. 'We don't want to frighten the horses.'

I rang up Lil. I needed a guide, and I thought she qualified. The fact that she was intimate with Jack had nothing to do with it. None of this had anything to do with Jack. No no no. Not one thing. I was just doing my job, that was all.

'What are you doing?' I said. 'Are you working?'

Lil was a gilder. Her parents had wanted her to be a doctor or a lawyer, but she said she couldn't stand the sight of blood.

'Not today,' she said. 'I just finished my last commission. I'm reading Nancy Friday and thinking about dirty sex. I never knew so many woman thought about doing it with dogs.'

'Nice,' I said. I supposed it was one way to get over a broken heart. 'Shall I come and take you to lunch? If you can tear yourself away from all those dalmatians for five minutes, that is.'

'Flush, are we?' said Lil, who thought financial security meant having more than three fifty pound notes salted away under the mattress.

'Expenses,' I said, sounding important. 'I'm on a job.'

'Sexy,' said Lil. 'I've always wanted to be put down on expenses. Why not?'

'Just the two of us,' I said. It sounded like an old song I'd heard somewhere. Just the two of us, we can make it if we try. 'Just girls together.'

'It'll be a conspiracy,' said Lil.

I knew she was still hurting from the Italian's infidelity and she was working it off in defensive anger and bullish couldn't care less, to stave off the despair that none of us thought we could afford. Conspiracy was right up her alley, just then. Us against them, *contra mundum*, sod them all if they can't take a joke.

'Of course it will,' I said, taken with the idea myself. A conspiracy, now there was a noble cause.

'Just what I need,' said Lil, which was as close to admission as she would come, just then. 'Clever.'

'Thank you,' I said.

We met at a place near Lil's flat. I arrived first, trying my best not to look self-conscious. It was such a neighbourhood place, and not my neighbourhood. I was aware of curious eyes watching me across the room, wondering who I was, where I fitted in. Right of them, of course, since I was wondering exactly that myself, although I didn't think of it like that. I might be curious as to who I wanted to be, but it wasn't for anyone else to ask. It was my secret.

I was dressed right at least, old moleskin jeans and a ribbed white vest and a new age crystal on a leather thong around my neck and one of those Chinese balls that chime when you put them to your ear.

I tilted my chin a little, to reassure myself, and went to sit at a corner table, just as if I knew my way around and didn't care less what anyone else thought. The players were out, on the game, showing off their intimate knowledge of the ropes. It was the kind of place where they all knew the barman, calling their orders across the room with sure ostentation. I just smiled nicely and asked for coffee. Then I let a measured pause go by, to show I wasn't intimidated, and opened my early copy of the *Standard*.

Lil came in on a breeze. She was dressed as an urchin today in a striped matelot shirt, narrow trousers cut off ragged at three quarter length and old white plimsolls. For a final dashing element, she had added a careless handkerchief tied round her neck. I wouldn't have been at all surprised if she had hired a mongrel for the day, to follow her about in a soulful way and complete the effect.

She crossed the room with a jaunty stroll (she was a method dresser, living the part) saying hello to people as she went, marking out her patch. No doubt that she could tell me all I needed to know.

'Well,' she said, sitting down. 'Here I am.'

'You are,' I said, in appreciation. 'Has *Les Miserables* been auditioning for a new cast?'

'What do you think?' she said. 'The waif look. I thought of it before bloody Kate Moss was even a glimmer in her dad's eye. I did consider a tight belted trenchcoat and dark glasses, the female spy, you know, but I thought it might give the game away. We don't want everyone to know it's a conspiracy.'

'Of course not,' I said. 'We'll bluff it out.'

I didn't ask her how she was. She had that strained staring look about her eyes that wrote its own sad story. She had been doing her weeping in private, and that was how she liked it. I wasn't going to encroach. There were plenty of other things we could talk about.

We got more coffee.

'I'm not really eating, just now,' said Lil, which was her way of telling me how she was feeling. 'So what's all this job, then?'

'A commission for August,' I said, to give it a status it didn't have. For some obscure reason I didn't want to tell her that it was all my own idea. 'Louey wants a Notting Hill section, so I thought I'd do a little research. Just preliminaries, you understand. I'm still finishing July. I just need to get into the area, for starters.'

'Yo, front line,' said Lil. 'Nice work if you can get it. So what do you want, cards of introduction? You can feed the locals,' she added. 'They're quite friendly.'

'Pointers,' I said.

Lil threw her arms wide, expansive as the day she was born.

'All you have to do,' she said, 'is ask.'

That was the beginning of my enchantment with Notting Hill. If there was such a thing as the new Bohemia, if that was what I thought I was looking for, it was there that I found it. It wasn't quite Paris, not quite café life and sidewalk tables and copies of *le Monde* and sweating out a *vin chaud* for three hours, not quite the Coupole and the Dome and the Deux Magots. The ghosts weren't there, I suppose, the great dead names that still stalked the boulevards and drew the faithful. No Ernest and Fitz, talking about why the rich are different, no Cocteau and Sartre, no *Bout de Souffle*.

But there was something there, all the same, that thing of sitting all day, finding a table, taking some coffee, waiting to see what might happen. There was life in the streets, and music running through it, reggae and rap and old calypso, spilling out of the record shacks and dub vendors, which infected even the whitest inhabitants. People sat on their stoops and traded news, stood on street corners and passed any time of day they could think of, wandered through the market looking for plantain and christophene and okra and tomorrow's gossip.

All this, this wash and flow of people and talk, spilled off the streets and indoors – two places in particular, that I got to know, the Corner, the bar where I had gone with Lil that first night, and 21, where we had had lunch the next day. I suppose they both had real names, but I never knew them. Everybody just said Let's go round the Corner, or down to 21. I liked that. It gave me a sense of being on the inside, knowing the lingo.

There was a seductive informality to it that you didn't find in my neck of the woods, not in Chelsea, not any more, not since Mr Jimmy shut down the drugstore. There, in the expensive exclusivity of SW3, people called each other up, days in advance, and made dates for lunch or dinner, serious assignations written down in careful society hieroglyphics in hide-bound diaries. They would meet for two courses and take a little wine and trade a little chat and then depart, saying We must do this again soon, such fun darling, just the very thing.

North of the park those niceties were rarely observed.

People ran into each other, just passing, on the off chance. They would sit for a while, and move on as easily as they had come. I was charmed by this. I loved the idea that the lack of regular hours meant that life could be lived as a party. I was delighted by the *soi-disant* village that Notting Hill had become, that knowing slice of London extending from the Gate itself up the two diagonal arteries of Ladbroke Grove and Kensington Park Road to west and east, dissected by Westbourne Grove and rising up to the Golborne Road in the north. Beyond that lay the badlands, the real poverty rather than its fashionable approximation, the crack houses and the girls taking to the streets to support their habits, the frightening part that liberal white consciences preferred not to see close up, symbolised by the high brooding presence of Trellick Tower.

In the village everybody knew everybody, and their business. Walking down the street, Portobello in particular, but Lancaster Road or All Saint's or St Luke's, it didn't make much odds, you could guarantee on running into two or three people you knew, and they would have just bumped into another two or three, and that was how the jungle drums kept beating, to a rhythm older than time. It was spurious in a way, this *faux* village green bonhomie, because really that was the mile of the lost and the lonely, a lot of people putting out and dressing up, desperately making connections which might not otherwise have existed, to hide the fact that, when the sun set and the twilight closed in, they all went home alone.

Of course, I didn't think of myself as lonely, any more than the rest of them. It was one of those forbidden words, worse than any expletive. Only the very brave even mentioned it, and even then it was with a little quizzical laugh, as if you didn't quite mean it, not really, not *you*. No, no, I was proud of my freedom, that's what I called it. I could do as I pleased, I answered to no-one. A free spirit, that's me, watch me fly. I didn't put my fascination with this new community down to any stirring need. I didn't need anyone, thank you very much. I was young and dauntless and unfettered. I didn't give *that* for rules or convention. It was enviable, being me. That was what I said.

6 ∫

Lil and I took to lunching most days, for the next couple of weeks. It suited us both. There was my initiation, for a start, business lunches to swell the expense account. I got some ideas, made some notes, met some people, took in some local colour. And for Lil, it gave her something to do, to take her mind off her poor aching heart.

I met people. It was easy to meet people up there, which surprised me. They seemed so alarming from the outside, assured and intimate and knowing the moves, but all you needed was a passport, and you were in, over the border, immigration waived. Lil was my passport. My fractured background helped, too. I wasn't another poor little rich girl trying to fake it, I was a genuine gypsy, a drifter, and that counted for a lot. I hadn't had the home counties and ponies to ride and ribbons in my hair. I had had packing cases and aeroplanes and learning a new language every two years.

And now I was starting over, with a whole new population to discover, a cast of hundreds, and not a suit to be seen – everyone was a cartoonist or a novelist or a sculptor, when they weren't being a waitress or a shop assistant to pay the bills. There were actors and playwrights, singers and songwriters, disc jockeys who specialised in rap or scratch. There were a lot of bands being formed, thrashing away in the dark basement clubs that clustered round Ladbroke Grove, heavily fashionable but still unsigned, followed by a loyal minority. They all had outlandish names, like Goats on Acid, The Junior Disprins, Pimps and Needles, Dr Love and the Garter Belts, Eat Me And Shout About It.

There were Indie bands, and seventies retro, and house specialists, and then the real die-hards, defiant in the face of the love and peace trail, owing a heavy debt to punk and the Pistols, nostalgic for the days when Johnny Rotten was a boy and the most complicated thing in life was getting into a pair of bondage trousers – nice boys at heart, still trying to shock their mothers. It might not have looked pretty and it certainly wasn't going to make anyone famous, apart perhaps from a fleeting fifteen minutes of infamy, but it was rock and roll, the real kind, angry and dirty and for the kids.

Nobody ever appeared to have any money, but wealth and security didn't seem to figure large in anyone's grand plan, not yet anyway, not while they were young enough to go without. Stretch limos and dancing girls had lost their cachet, and fame and riches could go hang, because everybody knew that money don't buy you love. Once you got the cash and the furs and the yachts you had sold out, from totemic rebel to fat cat in one easy leap, and no turning back.

All anyone seemed to want was enough to pay the rent and buy a few rounds of drinks and a set of threads, and whatever substance it was they dabbled in. There might be some desirable extras, like a motorbike or a guitar or a ticket to India, but beyond that there wasn't much to wish for.

I soon settled into a hard core, Lil's inner circle. These were the people who had been her set before the Italian took her off into his uptown world, and she returned to them as easily as if she had never been away. There was a kind of impermanence to life up the Grove that allowed for this: people were always flying off to New York or Los Angeles to be film stars or screenwriters or rock icons, and sometimes they stayed away, but most often they returned to the fold, their brief desertion never held against them.

I liked the hard core. I had never had a gang, a tight little group, even when I was younger, because we were always moving on, and just as I started to belong to a set I had to leave it. So it was a kind of revelation to me, Lil's little circle. They took me in very quickly in that easy come easy go way that people had then, and I was one of them, and there weren't too many questions asked, and we went everywhere together.

There was Dexter, who was half Irish and kind of handsome in an easy blond way. He played rhythm guitar in one of the few bands that actually had a deal and put out real singles and could be heard on national radio. He had a sweet soulful way with him, his real love was jazz, and the blues, and we were all secretly impressed because he had once jammed with Ray Charles when he was only eighteen and he never talked about it. He was always in love with brainless girls who never returned his calls.

There was a girl called Willa, new out of drama school and trying to make her mark. She had that elfin look, small and pretty as a picture, her hair cut short to her head, and she made up for it with a big loud mouth that made sure that no-one ever dared pat her on the head and asked her what she was going to do when she grew up. She lived on a diet of coffee and cigarettes to keep her weight down, because she said that all casting directors were sexist bastards who thought talent spelt eighteen-inch waist.

'What about bleeding Rubens?' she said a lot. 'What about sodding Miriam Margolyes?'

She went around with a slight bespectacled writer called Davey, who had a quiet intense look about him and an occasional stutter which he used as if in apology for his great cleverness. He had had a novel published and another in progress and he wrote reviews for the heavyweight papers and serious periodicals and people who knew said that he was going places. He was as far from Willa as one could imagine, but together they proved the theory of opposites attracting, going everywhere in a pair, the most perfect friends anyone could imagine.

'It's *platonic*,' Willa said. 'Hasn't anyone heard of the sexual revolution?'

I saw a lot of Ned and Jimmy at that time, too. They had just moved into a flat together in the Portobello Road and were running a series of one-off club nights, so they were always about, giving out flyers and flirting with people and drumming up business.

I learnt to hang out, just as if I had been born to it, and I collected material for the magazine, and Louey said the Gate section was shaping up nicely. And all the time I was looking out for Jack, just with half an eye, mind, nothing serious, but I didn't see him, and quite soon I forgot about him, or so I told myself. I had other things to think about, after all. I had work to do and people to meet. I had a life out there.

After a while, I really did forget. Almost, anyway. I was taken up with my new life. And I was pleased with my work. August was going to be a big summer of love issue. Denny, the music editor, who had once actually spoken to Joe Strummer and never really recovered, was so inspired by this that he was devoting his whole section to the summer festivals, now that everyone wanted to go and sit in fields again and smoke grass and talk about Woodstock. My Notting Hill pieces were going to fit in just fine.

I had an idea of Portobello as a kind of dream factory, where anything was possible. As the yuppies were gasping their death rattle and people were realising that it was possible to achieve things without wearing red braces and Cutler and Gross spectacles, there was a feeling of hope in the air, a thought that there was more to life than a portable telephone and a filofax.

Mrs Thatcher seemed finally to have gone completely berserk; there were rumblings in the corridors of power, and everyone felt that she couldn't last long. Far away, in America, I had just seen her as a bossy matron with no dress sense who liked sucking up to presidents quite a lot and talking as if Britain still had an empire (she *wished.*) In her own backyard, people spoke her name like it was the worst swear word they could think of.

'Thatcher,' they said, spitting it out with fury, counting on their fingers – miners, nurses, NHS, DHSS, teachers, homeless. Even Louey went a bit rabid on the subject.

'The lunatics,' he said, 'can't even take over the asylum any more, since they're shutting them all down.'

As she tottered madly from one disaster to the next, the youth on the streets, one step ahead as usual, started rubbing their hands for change. I thought that all this was captured in Portobello. I wanted to show it as a global village, where the divisive us and them which had run rampant in the mid-eighties boom was being swept away, and everyone, whatever their colour or sexual preference or taste in music, could rub along, cheek by jowl, and find their place.

Louey said I was just an old idealist at heart, and I agreed with him, but he said I could run with it. He said we had had enough doom and gloom and we might as well have a bit of upbeat in your face boys keep swinging to cheer everyone up after England got thrashed in the World Cup. I said how did he know England were going to get thrashed in the World Cup. Two Words, he said. German Efficiency. There wasn't much arguing with that, so I went back to my new issue.

All Louey made me promise was to fit in one cynical grouchy voice among all the Dr Feelgood. He said he was quite happy to leave reality to the Guardian, for August at least, but we did have some kind of reputation to protect. Since he was the most reasonable person I knew, and I was still on three months trial, I promised I'd find him someone who made Simone de Beauvoir look like Doris Day. He seemed pleased.

'July looks great,' he said.

The proofs had just come back, and they did look lovely. Violet had done a crazed layout for me, and the copy read fine, although we'd had a bit of trouble with the guitarists, who had obviously spent their youth listening to Deep Purple albums rather than mastering the rudiments of written English. They had also, unexpectedly, decided that experimental dance was where it was at, and spent all their time dragging their thrash friends off to the ICA to watch it, which was causing the usual patrons – round spectacles, natural fibres, wholefoods and left wing sensibilities – something of a shock.

The best part of all was that the physics student had had too much wine at the swank restaurant and allowed herself to be picked up by a man in an Armani suit.

'Of course,' she said, when she called to tell me this, 'I didn't know it was Armani, otherwise I'd never have let him. The truth is he's so good at sex that I didn't even mind when he told me he'd got a Porsche. It's just a bit tricky with the comrades.'

Louey said I should give it all up and start a dating agency instead, which I said was all my eye until Denny told me that one of the thrash guitarists had been seen taking the dance group's choreographer out to dinner.

'I'm glad you like it,' I said.

'I do,' said Louey. 'You're doing all right.'

I gave him a quick smile, trying not to show how pleased

I was. Such small praise was all milk and honey to me. I thought of all those exams I had passed, all those straight A's I had won, sitting up late with cups of black coffee, cramming facts into my head, and not once had my father told me well done.

I had done everything I could to impress him and none of it had ever worked. He seemed to take it for granted that I would shine. I think it was that he was so clever himself it would never occur to him that he could have fathered a dunce. Everything he ever produced achieved rave reviews. I was just another critical success on his long list, nothing to write home about. It was taken as read.

'So,' said Louey. 'What are you doing now?'

'Louey,' I said. 'It's Friday. I'm yours.'

He smiled. Fridays, it was just us, but he always asked, as if I might have spent the week hatching some secret plan that would exclude him. In those dark moments of self-doubt that struck at three in the morning when I couldn't sleep and I lay in bed asking what I was doing all by myself in a city full of strangers, I wondered why he minded. He had plenty of people to see. His answering machine was always humming with messages, the little red light flipping merrily with the promise of places to go. He didn't need me.

I asked him once, but he just said that I needed someone to keep me out of trouble. I didn't believe that. Louey had never kept anyone out of trouble in his life. He was one of those who believed in changing the things we can and leaving the things we can't and having the sense to see the difference between the two. He knew all about people going to hell their own way.

I pressed him a bit. I don't know what I wanted him to tell me. Eventually he just said that I reminded him of his lost youth, and that was all I could get out of him. He could be stubborn, Louey, when he put his mind to it.

'Come on then,' he said now. 'Let's go to that new place

in the Portobello Road. I'll buy you some champagne to celebrate how good you are at your job.'

'Too kind,' I said.

'I certainly am,' said Louey.

When we got there, the joint, as they say in the old country, was jumping.

'What do we think?' said Louey, who always asked my opinion, as if it mattered to him.

'Nice,' I said.

There was a whiff of incense in the air, and not an upright chair to be seen. It was all banquettes and alcoves and deep sofas to sink into. I liked it.

Jimmy and Ned wandered across the room, arm in arm, just to confuse people.

'Hello, Duchess,' said Jimmy, kissing me.

'Nice date,' said Ned, looking at Louey.

'Date?' said Jimmy. 'No-one tells me anything.'

'And you wonder why,' said Ned, with meaning.

Jimmy thought discretion was one of the seven deadly sins. Only one thing worse than being talked about, he always said, and that was not being talked about. Ned said that was a sad excuse, and that it didn't wash with him.

'It's not a date,' I said. 'It's my boss.'

'Well,' said Ned, shaking Louey's hand. 'The main man.'

'So they tell me,' said Louey, dry as a bone.

Jimmy started to laugh. 'And there we were, Dilly,' he said, 'thinking you made up all this work business just to throw sand in our eyes.'

'You didn't,' I said, indignant. I was proud of being a working woman. I thought it lent me gravitas and a certain dignity. I wanted people to know that I was capable of more than hanging on men's arms and being a slave to my hormones.

'Our very own mystery woman,' said Jimmy. 'That's you.

Come out of nowhere. We thought you were on loan from the CIA.'

'You wish,' said Ned. Jimmy was very big on conspiracy theories. He thought everyone was a spy.

'Not me,' I said. 'I'm just trying to hold down a regular job and keep my head above water.'

Jimmy looked forgiving, as if it really wasn't my fault.

'Come on then, Jim,' said Ned.

'We're going round the Corner,' said Jimmy. 'People to see.'

'Have fun with the boss,' said Ned, kissing me goodbye.

They headed off into the street, men with a mission. I looked at Louey, and gave a little shrug.

'They never could sit still,' I said. 'Sofas would be too much for them.'

Louey got me champagne, just like he said he would. He was a man of his word. I felt I didn't deserve it, but I knew better than to say so. We ate chicken sandwiches and gherkins in our fingers. More people arrived, giving the place the once over, seeing if it would do.

'How do you know people like that?' said Louey.

'Jimmy and Ned?' I said. 'They picked me up, I suppose. I don't know how I know people like anything. I just go on a wing and prayer.'

Louey laughed. 'Following that river where it flows,' he said. 'Why not?'

'Don't you come over all Zen with me, mate,' I said. Sometimes I felt I had to defend my youth and inexperience. Louey was thirty-five last birthday and made a point of not taking anything on its surface value.

'They're just a couple of regular Joes,' I said. 'It's nothing sinister.'

'It doesn't have to be,' said Louey. 'You can come down off your high horse. I'm not your judge and jury.'

I knew I was being touchy. I knew he didn't mean anything by it. It was just that he had ten years on me, and at times it made me feel like I was back in pigtails. I had left more places than most people ever go to, and that's enough to give anyone a veneer of sophistication. I knew that it could fool some of the people, some of the time, but Louey took an awful lot of fooling.

Most of the time I liked that in him, but there were moments when I got scared that he could see right through into the dark empty spaces that lay underneath. It made me feel vulnerable. I wasn't very good at vulnerable. You can't afford to fall over if you know there's no-one there to pick up the pieces.

'I know,' I said. 'I know you're not. Don't get me wrong.'

'I won't,' said Louey.

He wouldn't, either. That was something I knew I could trust in him. I didn't have to explain myself to Louey, and if I did, it was nothing he didn't already know. There was something reassuring about that, I thought, some comfort. Half of me might have wanted to be an enigma, to live a secret life that people could only guess at, but the other half, the more prosaic half, the half that was just human after all, only really wanted to be understood.

Louey, seeing we had done with that one, laughed and changed the subject.

'What happened to your tall dark stranger?' he said. 'Did you ever see him again?'

'What is this?' I said. 'Twenty questions?'

'Just making conversation,' said Louey. 'Just clicking my teeth.'

'Yeah, yeah,' I said, giving him a look. I wasn't sure I wanted to talk about Jack. I wasn't thinking about him anyway, I had plenty more important things to occupy my mind.

Louey sat, waiting.

'I did, actually,' I said.

'And?' he said, doing that trick he had with his eyebrows.

'Oh, stop,' I said. 'There is no And. No dice. Anyway,' I said, 'he doesn't look like the type who's going to carry me off into the sunset.'

Louey laughed, although I didn't see it was so very funny.

'What?' I said. 'Have I got spinach on my teeth?'

'The sunset,' he said. 'Is that what it is?'

'I don't know,' I said, mildly defensive again. 'It could be fun, you never know.'

'The last of the great romantics,' he said, still laughing.

'Thank you,' I said, with dignity. 'At least I'm not a hardened old cynic, like you.'

'You'll learn,' said Louey, who knew better than to take offence, 'in time. It's quite easy, when you get a feel for it.'

7

Later, as we were drinking coffee and talking idly about whether we should go on anywhere, a strange thing happened. At least, I thought it was strange.

A group of people arrived, and as they stood in the doorway, looking round for a place to sit, I saw that one of them was a girl of such startling beauty that I had to look twice to check she was real.

There was a small pause in the general conversation as everyone took her in, a tiny lull in homage to that kind of bone-deep beauty that you don't see very often in real life, the kind that is always somehow a surprise. She smiled quietly to herself, as if honour had been satisfied, and then she looked straight at Louey, and she walked over and sat down next to him and put an arm behind his head, and kissed him full on the mouth.

She didn't say anything, not Hello how are you fancy seeing you here, not one thing. She just sat back for a moment, and looked at him with eyes like headlamps, and then she leant over and whispered something in his ear and laughed. I was astounded. It was so intimate it was almost indecent. I wondered why she didn't just start undressing him right there and get it over with.

I cleared my throat. Louey turned, as if he had forgotten I was there.

'Oh, Nancy,' he said. 'This is Eva.'

Eva looked over at me for a moment.

'Hello,' she said, arching her eyebrows at Louey as if to say Is this the best you could do?

'Nancy works with me,' he said.

'Really?' said Eva. There was some underlying hum of laughter in her voice, as if she thought this was a good joke.

'Really,' I said, just too loud.

I wanted to say something witty and razor-sharp, but I couldn't think of anything. I'd always believed that great beauties never have any confidence in their looks, all that jazz about Audrey Hepburn being convinced her nose was ugly, but this one seemed to have skipped that chapter. She just sat, like a cat basking in the midday sun, looking at me like I was a poor relation.

She still had her arm around Louey's neck, claiming him. She whispered in his ear again, and he laughed, and then she leant back and gave him a suggestive flash of her great luminous eyes, and then she laughed too, all throaty and melodic. I wondered how much more of this I was going to be able to take.

It wasn't that I wanted Louey for myself. The chemistry wasn't there. I sometimes wondered why not, and felt some faint regret, but I didn't really mind, because he was my friend, and that was more important.

I didn't want to be the one whispering in his ear, but I was jealous all the same. I felt it kick in my stomach, with an inadequate fury. I had a kind of clichéd outrage. Who is this woman? I wanted to say. I wanted to say, Who the hell does she think she is, sitting there, with her hands all over you? I wanted to say, What about *me*? Only five minutes ago it had just been Louey and me, because Fridays it was always just us, and now I was invisible. I felt as if I had been left out in the rain.

Eva, having dismissed me, carried on with her serial monopoly. I wanted to stamp my foot and throw a tantrum. I wanted to throw something, mostly at her head. And just then, just as I thought I was going under, I was saved.

Dexter walked out of the crowd and fell on my neck.

'Nancy,' he said. 'Thank God. A still note of sanity in a sea of lunacy.'

I felt like kissing his feet. I felt like weeping. I felt like going down on my knees in gratitude.

'Dex,' I said. 'I'm so pleased it's you.'

'I wish I was,' he said.

'This is Louey,' I said.

Dex took his head off my shoulder.

'The boss man,' he said, 'for real. Well, well.'

Louey said hello. I felt like I'd equalised in the eighty-ninth minute. I was about to say, And do you know Eva, but Dex beat me to it.

'And,' he said, with a little laugh, 'if it isn't Edna. I thought you were still doing your thing in West Hollywood.'

Eva looked put out. I wanted to clap my hands and sing Hosanna.

'I thought your name was Eva,' I said, innocent as springtime.

Dex laughed.

'That's her stage name,' he said. 'Eva Storm has more of a ring to it than Edna Boles. It's a long way from Balham High Street to Sunset Boulevard.'

Eva looked as if she was about to start grinding her teeth. Louey started to laugh.

'Edna,' he said. 'You never told me that.'

I didn't say I wonder why. I knew about restraint.

'Are we drinking?' said Dex. He was holding an open bottle of wine. 'Here,' he said. 'Have some of this. Cost me a bleeding fortune. It's been breathing for half an hour, but I don't think the lady is going to show.'

'Oh, Dex,' I said. Dex cared more about music than clothes, and it showed. Tonight though, he had made an effort. His shirt was new, and his hair was brushed. 'And you looking so smart.'

'Yeah, yeah,' he said. He had learnt to be philosophical about these things. He had to. It had happened before.

'All dressed up and nowhere to go,' he said. He had this voice he did sometimes, when he was feeling defensive, a half falsetto, unlike his normal self.

'Don't it make your brown eyes blue?' he said.

'Some people,' I said crossly. 'No manners.'

Louey laughed. Eva was busy sulking. Dexter took my hand and kissed it.

'That's my girl,' he said. 'You tell them.' He poured out his expensive wine.

'Come on then,' he said. 'What shall we drink to?' He looked over at Eva. 'How about those old South London days?' he said.

I had hoped that Eva might get bored and go back to her friends, but she seemed to have set her sights well and good on Louey. I wondered if she used to sleep with him, before she went off to the bright lights and the Hollywood Hills, and she felt like rekindling an old flame, or whether they hadn't got that far and now she wanted to make good the omission. Whatever it was, I didn't much care to sit around watching it being played out. I had Dexter now. I was visible again. I thought it was time I retired gracefully from the field. Besides, if Louey wanted to have sex with the most beautiful woman in the universe, who was I to stop him?

'Come on, Dex,' I said. 'I'm restless. Let's go round the Corner and see Jimmy and Ned.'

'Anything you say,' said Dex. 'I'm all yours.'

I looked at Louey.

'Do you want to come?' I said.

Louey started to say something, but Eva got there first.

'Stay and talk to me,' she said. 'It's been too long.'

She put her hand on his arm and gave him another go with her big staring eyes. I thought she should stop watching so many soaps and get a bit more original.

'We'll leave you to it then,' I said, giving them a nice big sunny smile. 'Come on, Dex.'

'See you,' said Dex. 'Give my love to Malibu. Give my regards to the Stallones.'

'Come *on*, Dex,' I said.

'What was all that, then?' said Dex, when we got outside.

'Nothing,' I said. 'What? Nothing.'

'Something,' said Dex.

'Just not my thing,' I said. 'That's all.'

Dex laughed and put his arm around my shoulders.

'She's all right really, our Edna,' he said. 'She used to be quite a laugh in the old days. She got a little taste of the big time is all, and it went to her head. We got a lot of talk about lunch with Jack and dinner with Sly.'

'Ha,' I said. 'I bet we did. She is very beautiful, though,' I added, fairly. I could afford to be fair, now my feet were back on dry land.

'Many many lights on,' said Dex. 'Few people at home. Not like you.'

I looked at him. I was surprised.

'Not like?' I said.

'No,' said Dex. He was calm and certain, as if he'd given it some thought. 'Plenty of people at home with you,' he said. 'All there, hiding behind closed doors.'

I wasn't entirely sure what he meant by that. I thought maybe one day I'd ask him.

'Well,' I said. 'What do you know?'

We had reached the Corner. There was noise and lights and people. I pushed open the door.

'Come on,' I said. 'My treat, since you saved me.'
'I did?' said Dex.
'You did,' I said.
'Glad to be of service,' said Dex.

It got late, but Dexter said he wasn't tired, so we went back
to his place and listened to old Van Morrison albums. Dex's
flat was tucked into the corner of a long terrace behind
Westbourne Park Road. It was six flights up and there
wasn't a lift, but it was worth it, because there was a fire
escape that went out of the bedroom window up to a flat
bit of roof, where you could sit and listen to the distant hum
of the city and look at the sky at night.

'Wow,' I said, when we got there. 'This is perfect.'

I looked out over the trees and the streets and the houses
and the cars, tinged with purple and orange from the street
lamps. It was all quiet down there. Everyone had gone to
bed. It seemed like the only people awake in the whole wide
world were me and Dex, and Van the Man, growling away
in that way he has.

'You've got pots,' I said, looking at them. They were big
old terracotta pots, planted with geraniums and busy lizzies
and sweet-smelling jasmine.

'You bet,' said Dex. I was surprised by that, too.

'I can't grow anything,' I said. 'Do you talk to them?'

'Of course,' said Dexter, with dignity. 'You have to treat
them right.'

We sat side by side, leaning back against the chimney
stack, smoking at our cigarettes. I thought the girl who'd
stood him up was a fool.

'Who was she?' I said.

'She's from New York,' he said. 'She's an actress.'

'Another one?' I said.

He looked shifty. I had seen him take on this look before,
whenever the subject of women came up. Willa and Lil

teased him dreadfully. They said he was a masochist, just begging for pain. Whip me, beat me, make me feel cheap, they said, every opportunity they got.

'She's good,' he said. 'She's at Regent's Park.'

'So where was she tonight?' I said, building up a little righteous indignation. I hated the thought of him with his new shirt and his expensive wine, looking at his watch, knowing she wasn't going to come.

'Maybe she got the day wrong,' he said.

It was half-hearted, a vain stab at handing out the benefit of the doubt. We both knew she hadn't.

'It's not right,' I said. 'You shouldn't do this to yourself.'

'I don't mean to,' he said. 'I don't go out looking for kicks in the teeth.'

'Who does she think she is, anyway?' I said. 'You're worth more than that. You know you are.'

Dex smiled at me, through the darkness.

'What?' I said. 'I'm serious.'

'I'm not laughing,' he said, laughing.

'I mean it,' I said. 'You're handsome and funny and talented. She doesn't deserve you.'

'In a perfect world,' said Dex. He stopped laughing. Van got to the end of his song. It was very still. The air was warm and sweet with the scent of the jasmine. 'It just isn't as perfect as you want it,' he said.

I thought for a moment that he was going to kiss me. I thought for a moment that I wanted him to. Then a police car screamed down the road, sirens breaking the quiet, and Dex laughed again and lit another cigarette and the moment passed. Afterwards, I looked back and wondered if it would have made everything different. I wasn't sure.

8 ∫

When I did see Jack again, I wasn't expecting to, and I took it as Fate. That was it for me, really. I didn't really do God, it all seemed to me to be bogus and pointless and a great cosmic con, the religious kick, but if I did believe in anything it was Fate.

I had gone up to 21 one Sunday to meet Willa and Davey and Dexter. We had been late the night before and everyone was feeling jaded.

'Let's have caffeine frenzy and lots of cigarettes and see what happens,' said Willa.

Lil was away. She had a strange secret life which she sometimes went into, some old Eastern Europeans she had found somewhere who lived in a Gothic folly deep in the country and held bridge weekends. The fact that Lil even played bridge always amazed me, it seemed the most unlikely game for her to enjoy, and for a long time I suspected that the ancient Lithuanians were her Bunbury, that in fact she was sneaking off for illicit meetings with a married man. She always swore that there was nothing more sinister to it than three no trumps and that I was being fanciful, but I continued to have suspicions. I liked to think of people having secret lives. I had always wanted one myself, but I wasn't quite sure how to do it.

I arrived at two, papers tucked under my arm, cheap

market shades on, in a short print dress that was very much the thing that summer. The real devotees wore those flimsy floating numbers with thick platform soles, Doctor Martens for the most credibility, but I couldn't quite carry that look, so I settled for discreet little suede numbers that didn't say anything much. I liked that Romany child look, my hair plaited long and black down my back. I had inherited my father's dark looks and fine planed face. People often thought I was Spanish, or from the south of Italy. I liked that too, although there were days when I wished I'd been born small and blonde.

'People,' I said. 'How is it?'

'Getting better,' said Willa. She had three cups of espresso lined up in front of her, and was drinking her way through them with concentration. 'How we suffer for our art.'

'No one said it was going to be easy,' said Dexter. He gave his crooked smile, nicely philosophical. Dex believed in rolling with the punches.

'How's the theory, Dave?' I said, sitting down.

Davey was always coming up with new and pointless theories, which he put into practice with dauntless optimism. Like many people of academic brilliance, he was lost when it came to real life. His new idea was that a hangover could be avoided by drinking the same thing all night.

'It's not the quantity,' he had decided. 'It's the mixture.'

The night before he had put his theory to the test by ordering frozen Absolut vodka all night and drinking it with the reverence usually reserved for Catholics with the communion wine.

'Um,' he said, clearly suffering. 'Not marvellous.'

'Poor Dave,' said Dexter, trying to look sympathetic.

'It's like communism,' said Davey, finding time to defend himself. 'Beautiful on paper, but hopeless in real life.'

'Listen to our Dave,' said Willa fondly. 'Mr political

pinko, right on. He must have been marching again. It's all cheeseball to me,' she added obscurely.

No-one bothered to question her. Half the time none of us knew what she was talking about. I'm not sure if she knew herself.

'Have to get your cred somewhere,' said Dexter, who admired Billy Bragg. 'Can't spend your whole life reading the *Stage* and waiting for your picture in the paper.'

'Willa can,' said Davey, with admiration.

'Talking of papers,' said Willa, taking this compliment square on the chin, 'we've had an idea for you, Nancy, for your Gate exposé.'

Willa, who, true to her calling, liked dramatising everything, regarded my idea of a Ladbroke Grove number as some frontline kind of investigative journalism, a sort of grooving Roger Cook. She was very taken with this notion and offered her assistance at every turn.

'We've had Watergate,' she was fond of saying, 'now we can have Gate Gate.'

'Oh yes?' I said, with only a faint degree of scepticism. Last time Willa had come up with a good idea, she had picked up a likely candidate in the market for me to interview, perfect for a piece on local colour, she had insisted. It turned out that her prize was in fact a Guatemalan exchange student with a scant grasp of English who lived in Cockfosters and had come in for the day on the tube.

'Yes,' said Willa, not even blushing. She was never put off by failure.

'For the sleaze factor,' she said. 'You know the deal, the sordid underbelly of the city, life on the mean streets cheek by jowl with the suits in Georgian terraces. The real stuff. Talk dirty.'

'Does it speak English?' I said, unable to resist.

'Yeah, yeah,' said Willa, dismissive of such trifles. Linguistics were nothing to her, her mind was on higher things. 'It's this character I know, real sleazoid McCoy, but classy, you know?'

'I know,' I said, trying to keep up.

'He's ideal for you,' she continued. 'Right up your alley. One of those big-time drop-outs, left school in an ambulance with a bottle of Jack Daniels in one hand and a pot of Dexies in the other.'

'Dexies?' I said, really mystified now.

'Dexedrine,' said Willa impatiently. 'Speed speed speed. Boy racers. Hard to lay your hands on, these days,' she added, with regretful nostalgia.

'Anyway, his Pop was one of those outward bound explorer types, no known emotions, always trekking across arctic wastes or disappearing into the dark continent to live with native tribes, coming home with one foot hanging off from frostbite or a bone through his nose.'

'Sounds like half the people you know,' said Davey.

'Ha, ha,' said Willa. She liked telling stories, and this was one worthy of her. She could rise above interruptions, it was her job. She gave Davey a look, and turned back to me.

'So,' she said, 'then his mother ran off with some touchy feely Yank creation to an island in the West Indies to run a water ski station, or I don't know. So Little Lord Fauntleroy gets packed off to one of those gothic public school institutions, cold baths and morning runs and don't ask what in the showers, and before you can say multi-dysfunctional he's learnt to roll spliffs the size of a baby's arm and is dropping anything he can get his hands on. I mean *please*,' she said, appealing to the table. 'This is not real life, this is motion picture.'

I often thought that life was one long motion picture to Willa. She wandered around with the slightly expectant air of a screen idol waiting for the director to say Cut.

'Happens every day,' said Dexter, who had seen more of the world than we had. 'Stranger than fiction, old fruit,' he said, in the Norman Wisdom voice he did sometimes. I had asked him once where he learnt it, and he just said that his Mum was Norman Wisdom's number one fan. Dexter was one of the few people I knew who actually talked to his mother. Willa and Lil both refused to speak to theirs, on principle, and Davey said he'd tried once and given it up as a bad job.

'Yeah, yeah,' said Willa, who didn't believe a word of it. She only liked her own version. 'So, anyway, the minute he's had his stomach pumped, he high tails it up here to score and that's that. Daddy gets last minute guilts and pulls a string or two so his little not-so-darling lucks into a job with some record company, and before you can say Brian Jones he's off on the road with some Spinal Tap heads who happily employ him to get all their drugs.'

'You don't have anyone like that in your band, do you, Dex?' I said, interested.

Dexter shook his head, dignified beyond his calling.

'Nah,' he said. 'I don't intend on checking out in some motel room face down in my own vomit. Too seventies.'

'The seventies are making a comeback,' said Davey, who had a naughty irreverent streak in him, quite at odds with his bright young don spectacles and post-Oxbridge haircut.

'Not for Janis Joplin,' said Dexter, who liked to think he knew how to learn from other people's mistakes.

'So then what?' I said to Willa. I was enjoying this story, it was better than *Listen with Mother*.

'Well,' she said, putting her head on one side and stealing one of Dexter's cigarettes. 'There was a kind of vague period, abroad, you know. Dodgy deals. Delivering hot cars from Detroit to Fort Worth, middleman in some Italian property scam, all the usual suspects.'

I wasn't sure what was usual about it, but I knew better than to ask. Willa waved her cigarette around, in her element.

'Then,' she said, 'he landed up in Morocco as chauffeur to some fake European princess babe, but as Keith Richards once said, things happen in the back of a car, and he has to skip the country when Il Principe shows up and finds his wife having it all off with the hired help.'

'My,' I said. 'Pistols at dawn. Horse whipping in high places.'

'All that,' said Willa, as if it happened every day, just as regular as you please. 'So it's back to London, and old guardian angel working overtime, he finds himself an upmarket squat. The owner, who is a shady character himself, gets knifed two weeks later in a fight over some woman, leaving no will or next of kin, so praise the Lord, we have ourselves a boffo pad with all the trimmings and no questions asked.'

'Nicely, nicely,' I said.

'You can say,' said Willa. 'All purple walls and stuffed with fogey antique gear hot off the back of half the lorries in town. So then, get this, have we heard it all before, he tries to get this band he's managing off the ground, complete wipe-out, next thing he's running an after hours club which gets smashed up by the mob and the police in the same twenty-four hours because he's refused to pay his protection money, so what do we have? Flash apartment, but no credit left, Daddy's off up some mountain in Sumatra and doesn't want to know, and suddenly it comes to him, in a blinding flash of light, blow those trumpets, he stumbles on his vocation – Bingo, get those scales out, call in your contacts, get dealing. No one can imagine why he didn't think of it before. He's a legend by now, everyone knows him. I mean, even Thunders came to score off him, when he was in town.'

'Thunders?' I said, losing the plot one more time.

'Johnny Thunders,' said Willa. 'You know. He was with the New York Dolls, before the Heartbreakers. Big time dope fiend, hello Sister Morphine, let's have a party. The ultimate rock and roll suicide, except he's still walking and talking, living proof of the living dead. He invented punk, that's all.'

'He did not,' said Dexter, who was a purist and still had all his Pistols albums. 'You can't say that.'

'Watch my lips,' said Willa, feisty and not to be crossed. The third espresso was kicking in nicely. 'If Malcolm Maclaren hadn't met the Dolls in New York there would *be* no Sex Pistols.'

'Maybe, maybe not,' said Dexter. Punk and destiny were the same thing in his mind, both of them stronger than us and impossible to resist.

'Blah, blah,' said Willa, who had never conceded a point in her life.

'Dexter once played with Thunders, at the Lyceum,' Davey told me. 'I remember it.'

I was surprised. I couldn't picture Davey at a hard-core rock gig. He looked as if Shostakovich was about the heaviest metal he ever got.

'He was a wanker, really,' said Dexter. 'He was unconscious for the sound check, the roadies had to carry him in feet first. We thought we'd have to go on without him. Thirty seconds before the gig was due to start he woke up, strapped on his guitar, spat at the audience, and played a perfect set.'

'Ah,' said Willa, with a little shudder. 'Now that's rock and roll.'

'So what about this legend, then?' I said. 'This dealer to the stars?'

'Well, isn't he perfect material for you?' said Willa. 'Look, here he is now.'

And I looked towards the door, and there was Jack.

9

I often think, that of all the illusions we labour under, the one of trusting your instincts is the most dangerous. Especially when it comes to matters of the heart. There is this spurious idea put about that when you meet your one and only you will know, at once, without hesitation, unshadowed by doubt. Even in the cynical know it all of 1990, learning from the mistakes and divorces and paternity suits of the baby boomers and before, there were still people who talked of eyes meeting across a crowded room, of lightening striking, of *coup de foudre*, every cliché strung across the romantic scale, still holding credence from those who should know better.

Of course I was one of the credulous, unreconstructed romantic that I was. My ABC came straight from the tempting pages of Shelley and Byron, I thought Scott Fitzgerald was misunderstood, I cried every time I read that line from *The Wasteland*, about I, Tireseus, who have foresuffered all.

When Jack walked into the restaurant that day, he looked at me properly for once, for the first time, and he smiled. I don't know why he did it, maybe he had got out of bed the right side or just won a premium bond, but he did smile, his sullen wasted face lighting up, sunshine chasing away the shadows, and why ever he did it, it seemed as if he was smiling at me, for me, because of me.

So I smiled back, and that was when the bolt came gliding in from the blue, as if someone had turned on a switch. I felt it deep in the base of my spine, and at the ends of my fingers; I was shaken by it, this revelatory shock, and I thought, this is it, this is what they all talk about, this is how I know. That was what my instincts told me, in that moment, and I believed them. How could I not?

Jack came inexorably towards me, and sat down and said hello and acted like a normal person, or as near as he ever got. I stared at him mutely, wondering if I should ever be able to speak again.

Lucky for me, none of this showed. I don't know if it's an advantage or not, but I had one of those faces that give nothing away. I could be dying inside, and all the world would see was an opaque serenity, a flat stillness, reflecting nothing. The eyes might be the windows to the soul, but on mine, the blinds were all drawn. My father laid claim to some distant Iroquois blood, so perhaps that was where it came from.

So there I was, with all this confusion raging inside me, and everything on the outside seeming ordinary as you please, just another Sunday, nothing to write home about. Jack looked at me with his pale washed-out eyes.

I took out a cigarette, concentrating hard on lighting the right end, casting my eyes down to the flame, hoping that I might look just a little mysterious.

'Jack,' said Willa. 'This is Nancy, you must be polite to her.'

'Nancy,' said Jack, easily. 'We met before.'

We met before. He seemed so different now from the taciturn creature that I had seen that night with Lil.

'We did,' I said. 'I remember.'

'So,' he said, smiling some more. I couldn't tell whether it was at me, or whether that was just the expression he was using that day. 'You're the one who is going to make me famous.'

I felt suddenly furious at his ability to incapacitate me so completely. Who was he, anyway? Who the hell did he think he was? I felt angry and dirty. I wanted to tell him that I didn't care about making him famous, I just wanted to make him.

I laughed out loud, wondering what he would say if I told him, and instead I said, collected as you please,

'It depends.'

Then I looked right back at him, challenging him with my impenetrable black eyes. So there, buddy, I thought, you're not the only one who knows how to make the earth move.

'Depends on what?' he said, as if he wanted to know.

He looked a little surprised, as if he was used to people rolling over and begging every time he opened his mouth. Not this baby, I thought, this chick takes some work. I might be a sucker for a pretty face, but that was my secret.

I arched an eyebrow at him, just to show him who was boss. Then I took a draw on my cigarette and blew some smoke in his eyes. Then I laughed again, a careful secret laugh, at my own private joke. This was a performance, this was the stuff that Oscars were made of. I might roll over, but I surely was not going to beg.

'On you, of course,' I said, as if wondering why he had to ask.

'On me?' he said, lost.

I smiled a measured smile. I had him now. I was up and running.

'Why yes,' I said, waving my cigarette in a couldn't care less kind of way. 'It depends on whether you are worth it.'

Willa looked astounded. This was obviously not the accepted way to address a legend. Davey laughed up his sleeve. Dexter ordered another cup of coffee.

'I might,' I added slowly, 'be able to use you.'

Then I looked at him again, harder this time, throwing down the gauntlet like they used to in the old days. Let him work out just what I meant by that. If he knew so much, he could figure it out all by himself.

'But you must,' said Willa. 'It would be criminal not to. He's perfect for your purposes.'

Jack and I looked at each other, and laughed, and I think we both knew then that whatever we did or said next wouldn't make much difference. There is always a moment when you know, when inevitability takes over, and it's no longer a question of if, or whether, but just when.

I looked away, at my watch, gave a little stage start, and invented an appointment out of the air.

'Oh, dear,' I said, not in the least bit regretful. 'I'm late. I must run.' (Running for my life, of course, but I didn't know that yet.)

I took a card out of my pocket and gave it to Jack, who regarded it with bemusement, as if it were some obscure equation for calculating the speed of light.

'There,' I said. 'Why don't you call me and we can discuss it? My deadline isn't until next month.'

And on this note of perfect composure, I kissed the others, said I'd see them soon, told Jack it was nice to meet him, and breezed out of the restaurant, not even bothering to look back to see if anyone was watching me go.

I went home after that, just another lazy Sunday afternoon. The sun was shining, hot and yellow, and the kids were out on the street, doing their thing. I drove back slowly, looking about me. I felt a strange shift of perception, as if something momentous had happened, but I wasn't sure what it was.

The walking talking Sunday crowds filled the pavements, not going any place in particular. They looked new to me, different, as if I were in a foreign city, driving on the wrong side of the road. I found myself surprised that I knew the way home.

Back in the flat, it was just me. I felt restless, the flush of victory fading from me. I might have performed with daring, I might have gone out on a roll of drums, clutching my academy award – I don't owe anyone for this, I won it all myself – but fallible creature that I was, I wanted the telephone to ring.

I watched it a little, knowing what a cliché I was. Then I hated it for a while, just like girls do. I walked round it with small vicious steps. I tried ignoring it, mistress of the double bluff, but it knew better, in its bland plastic smugness. I restrained a sudden atavistic urge to smash it against the wall, to shatter its knowing passivity, to assert my own living breathing will to power over its inanimate disdain.

Say what you want about the onward march of sisterhood, and we are marching, yes we are, banners held high, it's the small battles that still prove the problem, the guerrilla warfare, the jungle combat. We might have been given the key to the executive washroom, but when the telephone doesn't ring we're right back to corsets and skirts covering the ankle.

This reflection made me angry, which helped. I put some Hendrix on the record player – there was something about that crashing anarchic guitar which always made me feel better. I turned it up so loud that I wouldn't be able to hear the telephone, should it deign to ring, which of course it wouldn't, I knew it wouldn't, I wasn't born yesterday. I turned it up loud enough to fry the neighbours, which gave me an obvious and perverse satisfaction. I stamped around the empty room and sang a little backing vocals and wondered if I had missed my vocation.

'Foxy,' said Jimi, all hard breath and unfettered sexuality. 'You *know* you're a little heartbreaker,' he told me, as if he had the inside track.

Somewhere, dimly, a bell started to chime. I let it. After a while, I picked up the receiver.

'Louey,' I said, 'I'm busy.'

'You live in a big house,' said Jack. 'With just one telephone.'

I really hated him at that moment.

'I think you must have the wrong number,' I shouted. 'This is 6770.'

'I know it,' said Jack. 'Turn the man down.'

'Who is this?' I yelled. 'I live next door to a policeman.'

'Your neighbourhood degenerate,' said Jack. 'Perfect for your purposes.'

I laughed, which was the beginning of the end, and turned the music down.

'Do you have a name?' I said. I was damned if I was going to give everything away. 'Or is it just a man called Horse?'

'Jack,' he said. 'We met at lunch.'

'It was a long time ago,' I said. My heart was beating so loud I could hardly hear what he was saying. I wanted him to ask me out so I could say no.

'So,' he said. 'It's time for dinner. What do you say?'

My principles deserted me, fleeing for the hills without a backward glance, the rats.

'Anything for Art,' I told him. Some things you just can't fight. 'And don't say Who's Art.'

'Who's Art?' he said.

We met at one of those small dark anonymous restaurants that you only ever go to once. It surprised me, I don't know why. I think I expected him to take me to one of those crowd places, 21 or somewhere, somewhere he would be surrounded by his own kind.

It was all strange. He was on time, waiting for me, which I guessed, and later knew, to be unusual for him. And he was dressed tidily, or the nearest he ever got, in soft black velvet trousers and a purple shirt. He had that fresh-watered expectant look of a small boy who has been allowed to stay up and eat with the grown-ups.

I was wearing hot pants and a psychedelic T-shirt that looked as if it had shrunk in the wash. I had even put my hair up, despising myself as I did it. But there were so many intimations hanging in the air already that I thought the only thing to do was add to them. I thought it might faze him a little, take him aback for a moment, give me an edge. And apart from anything else, there really isn't any point in dressing as if you're going on a Sunday school outing when you know you're going to dine with the devil.

'Hello,' I said, sitting down slowly, just to let him get a good look.

He looked. 'Hello,' he said, and he smiled, as if he was pleased to see me.

Maybe he was pleased to see me. It wasn't an unknown phenomenon. I wondered what we were going to talk about. He was a stranger to me, after all, even if I did know his entire life story.

'So,' I said.

I made a business of getting out my cigarettes, looking for my lighter. He had one sitting on the table in front of him, but he made no attempt to use it.

I didn't mind so much. I had met men who lit your cigarette and stood to attention every time you came back from the Ladies, and in my limited experience, they were generally up to no good, covering their nefarious intentions with silk-smooth charm and gentlemanly behaviour. If people had nefarious intentions, I'd much rather they were upfront about them, so at least you know where you stand.

'So,' he said, watching me. 'Tell me what you want to know.'

'Know?' I said.

'For this magazine,' he said. 'For Art.'

'Oh,' I said, trying to gather my wits and concentrate.

I had forgotten for a moment the ostensible reason for this meeting. I had a few nefarious intentions of my own, and I had been letting them carry me away. Bad bad bad. Quite soon I would be allowing him to catch me at a disadvantage, and then where would we be?

'Well, yes,' I said, trying to look businesslike, which wasn't so easy, considering my dress.

'The magazine,' I said. 'Of course.'

I took a pull at my cigarette, playing for time. Jack waited, watching me.

'Of course,' I said again, abrupt and modern and mistress of my own destiny, which was a real joke, if only he had known. If only I had known.

'Of course,' he said gravely, waiting with interest for me to get to the point.

The point deserted me.

'Oh, fuck it,' I said, giving up.

I had never been very good at playing games, and it didn't look as if I was going to start learning now.

'I can't think about work,' I said. 'It's outside office hours. Let's drink some wine and have fun and we can talk about it tomorrow.'

He laughed, which was nice. I felt a little thrill of achievement in the back of my neck.

'You laughed,' I said.

'It happens,' he said.

'Maybe,' I said, suddenly brave and not giving a damn. 'Can we have some claret?'

'I know sod all about wine,' he said.

'Yeah, yeah,' I said. 'But you know what you like. Use a pin. It's not neurosurgery.'

I had this feisty streak in me which surfaced under pressure. I was pleased to see it coming out now. There were days when I went dumb and shy, and couldn't remember how to do it, when I thought I was pointless and useless and feckless and hopeless and I might as well pack it all in and go and farm sheep in the West Country. Violet said that happened to the best of us, from time to time. She said it was what Holly called the mean reds. I didn't know what it was called, but I didn't like any of it. Thank the angels, it wasn't happening now. I felt brassy and bold all of a sudden, shiftless and heedless and ready for anyone.

'No,' said Jack.

He gestured at a waiter, who shuffled over with an enquiring look.

'The lady wants some wine,' he said.

The waiter, who had snow-white hair and eyes that went in different directions, regarded me with one of them. He nodded with decision.

'I bring,' he said.

Jack looked at me, still and solemn.

'He bring,' he said.

'So he do,' I said affably. 'Lady, I like *that*.'

I gave him the kind of look which suggested that if he was going to be in luck, she sure as hell wasn't going to be a lady tonight. No Sister Sarah for you, buster.

Jimmy had told me once, in a moment of late-night indiscretion, that the secret of being irresistible was to look as if you liked really dirty sex. So I looked at Jack some more, and I thought of latex and rubber and manacles and dressing up in nurse's uniforms. I suppose the desired effect was to produce instant smoulder, ready to burst into flames at any moment, but it just made me laugh.

'What?' said Jack.

'Just thinking,' I said, trying to retrieve the femme fatale, who had strolled off to let some Left Bank bounder light her Sobranie. Maybe I just wasn't built for sophistication.

'Was it dirty?' he said.

'What? Me?' I said, trying to look affronted. 'Why would you think that?'

'You had this dirty look on your face, just for a moment,' he said. No doubt he was puzzled. Give me a minute and I might just intrigue him, after all.

'And there I was,' I said, 'thinking I was impenetrable.'

'Mysterious ways,' said Jack. 'People say it's nice.'

I wasn't sure what he meant, but I didn't like to ask. I thought I was plate glass beside him. The waiter arrived with a bottle.

'Here's my wine,' I said in relief. 'I think I'm light-headed from thirst.'

'Must be,' said Jack.

'Don't you think?' I asked, as if he might know. I certainly didn't. I didn't know what was going on.

'Is good,' said the waiter, his wayward eyes regarding both of us at the same time. 'Drink.'

It looked like the best advice either of us would get all evening, so we took it. There's something reassuring about a good glass of red wine, when all else is shifting about you.

'Is good,' said Jack, seriously. 'Drink.'

10 ∫

It's a good expression, fool for love. Maybe I was more foolish than most. I remember thinking that when he kissed me first, later that night, in his strange stolen apartment, and I remember thinking it even more when I got up the next morning and crept away before he woke.

I knew I was being a fool, but I couldn't help it. It would have been better if I hadn't known about him, if I thought that he was just another lost soul looking for salvation. But I did know. I knew what he did for a living; I knew that he skimmed the fine line between alluring and dangerous. I knew that he inhabited a world I didn't understand. I could see the rocks, shadowy under the surface, and still I dived in. I'm not making excuses. There aren't any excuses to make.

But I couldn't help myself. I felt as if I were in the grip of some greater force, too strong to resist. And for all that, I didn't want to resist. He was so tempting. He was temptation walking and talking and doing all the things that other people talk of in low disapproving voices. I'm like Oscar Wilde, like that. Temptation gets me every time.

Perhaps it had something to do with the fact that he *was* so unsuitable. No-one was going to make him Chairman of the Board. He was never going to retire at sixty with a nice engraved watch and a golden handshake. It was debatable whether he was going to make it to sixty at all. It didn't take a rocket scientist to tell you that he was a bad lot.

But there is a reason that bad lots are such an enduring feature in romantic fiction, that nice girls are forever throwing themselves away on rogues, that mothers are still taking time out to warn their daughters against the perils of running off with a cad. There are plenty of reasons, too, many to count. There's excitement and risk and steps in the dark. The promise of redemption, too, that's still going. An accountant is always going to be an accountant, but a bad boy, now there's a challenge. If you love him enough, you might make him good. And this dangerous myth keeps its credence because some bad boys do turn good, after all.

The problem is, no-one notices that the ones who change were just good boys pretending to be bad. They don't change, they revert. The leopard, he don't change his spots, but the sheep in wolf's clothing, he can put on a new jacket and everyone goes all misty-eyed and talks about what love can do. Kiss that frog, why don't you, and just watch to see if he doesn't turn into a prince.

And then there's the romance of it, too – the angry young man, the wastrel, trapped in a world that doesn't understand him. It's not bad behaviour, Ma, it's rebellion, a battle against a society that doesn't understand about people who don't fit in, don't play by the rules. It's a noble cause, a heroic last stand. I know you wouldn't let your daughter marry a Rolling Stone, but without them we'd all end up with the gas man.

So you can say it was folly, and it was. You can say I went in with my eyes shut when they should have been open, and I did. Wrapped in all my youthful optimism, all that muddled romanticism that I had learnt so well from my books, I marched in, brandishing a cherished conviction in the possibility for change. It was the hope for change that made everything worth it, for me, that made the strange dance of life worth the steps, because if people didn't change, and things didn't change, and ideas didn't change, we would all be lost. I should have been a real revolutionary, it would have been easier. I think it would have been less tiring to try and change the world. But I just wanted to change people. My mistake, my folly, was not going with Jack, it was thinking that I could make him different. What I didn't know then was that you can't make people different, whatever you do. They have to do it themselves.

I didn't know any of this at the time. All I was aware of as we sat in that dark little restaurant, the world shrunk to the size of our table, was a rising tide of elation. I was filled with excitement. I started drawing strange hieroglyphics on the tablecloth with my fork to try and distract myself. I set up the salt and pepper as goal posts and played a little game of penalty shootout with one of my peas.

'Oh dear,' I said, as it went straight down his shirt. 'Missed.'

That made him laugh, too. My attempts to impose myself on the situation didn't seem to be coming off, although at least I seemed to be confusing him. I was certainly confusing myself.

We exchanged a little information, skirting round the dangerous parts. I told him about my father and always moving on and living in New York and working for Louey. He didn't tell me very much in return. He didn't seem the kind that talked about himself so very much. He listened, and asked a question every so often, and then he dropped some startling sentence into the pot and left it there to stew, without elaboration. I was talking about South America, where we'd lived when I was thirteen, and a strange nostalgic look came over his face, and he said,

'Poker games.'

I stopped, mid-sentence.

'Poker,' I said foolishly.

'That was South America,' he said. 'Five card stud with freedom fighters. The louder the shelling the higher the stakes.'

I thought for a moment he was making it up, but I could see he wasn't. He said it without fanfare or braggadocio, just mere matter of fact, as if he was talking about going down to the pub for a pint of bitter. I wanted to ask him more, but he said, 'What then?' so I didn't. I didn't want to seem like I was prying. I didn't want him to see how much I wanted to know.

And later, when I was talking about New York, he said, deadpan as you please,

'I ran numbers once, on the lower east side.'

I didn't know what to say to that either. It sounded like something people did in *The Sting*; it needed a Scott Joplin piano rag to go with it. I felt a sudden flash of anger. Why couldn't he go to Brighton for his holidays, like a normal person? Why couldn't he cut his hair and go to bed at a reasonable hour?

'Nice neighbourhood,' I said, some snide edge sliding into my voice. But he looked at me again, and smiled, and I wasn't angry any more.

I knew suddenly what it was, part of it. He was exotic, that was it. Not so much in the way he dressed, or the way he talked, not in the way that Jimmy or Ned were. With them it was all on the outside, dressing up, remembering how clothes could make man.

It was different with Jack. It was the true sense of the word – having a strange or bizarre allure, beauty or quality. That's what it said in the book. That's what he had, that strange allure, that curious quality, the kind that you can't explain, if someone asks. I felt it tugging at me, as I watched the shadows move in his face. It was like a lone voice calling in the dark, calling just to me, for me alone.

We drank single cups of espresso and then we went for a walk. It was his idea. That surprised me too, just when I thought I was past the age of amazement.

We walked round the wide white residential streets behind Pembridge Crescent, Sunday night quiet. It was still warm, and the sky was clear. There was even a new moon, just as if I needed that, on top of everything else.

'This is where the fat cats live,' said Jack, easily derisive. 'Getting their kicks from living so near the front line.'

Perhaps he was a revolutionary after all, a streetwise Marat, all dressed up in hip threads and nowhere to go.

He looked at me, an evil glint in his eye.

'Shall we,' he said seriously, 'ring all their doorbells?'

Eventually, we came to his door.

'So,' he said. 'Do you want to come in?'

'For coffee?' I said. 'Or do you want to show me your record collection?'

'Yes,' he said.

That took me right back.

'Well,' I said, trying to sound as if it meant nothing to me. 'That would be just dandy.'

He took me upstairs into a dark purple room. More plum, perhaps, than purple, that deep shined colour of the outside of an aubergine (what we used to call eggplant, in the Village, I never knew why).

It was extraordinary, that room, another surprise on the evening's little list. The floorboards were lacquered black, covered with a venerable Persian rug, and it was crammed with furniture, arranged without thought.

There were long ornate sofas and an empire day bed

covered in gold damask, the kind of thing Madame de Stael used to lie about and be clever on. A chandelier hung from the ceiling, a mass of intricate crystal drops, refracting the light into a thousand spinning splinters.

There were marquetry tables, and ebony cabinets, and a statue of Robespierre on a marble plinth, with a high carved Indian mirror for him to admire his incorruptibility in. Whoever this villain had been, the one who Jack inherited this place from, his taste had been grandiose but unformed. There was no unity to his interior design, no common denominator – it was just big expensive old stuff, odd bedfellows thrown together and rubbing along.

Sitting on and among this incongruous finery was all the paraphernalia of a young bachelor rebel on the loose. Dirty glasses, empty bottles, crushed Marlboro packets, cigarette papers, full ashtrays, incense burners, discarded items of clothing.

Jack gave me a beer without asking, and we sat cross-legged on the floor, and looked at his record collection.

Right at the front was an album called Johnny Thunders Bootlegging. I turned it over. It gave me a start. There was a blurred black and white photograph of a man with dark hollow eyes and dark hollow cheeks, just like Jack. I read down the list of song titles – *In cold blood, Personality crisis, You can't put your arms around a memory* – and then, right at the end, in big capital letters – *WIPE OUT*. I remembered what Willa had told me.

'The man himself,' I said.

Jack nodded. 'Thunders,' he said, his voice reverential. 'God.'

I really should have known *then*, but I didn't have the knowledge. I knew that I was wading into treacherous waters, it was just that I had no idea quite how treacherous they would be. All the signs were there, staring me in the face, but I was too ignorant to read them right.

'God,' I said. 'I see.'

I didn't see at all, but I didn't want him to think that I was a little know-nothing, from the right side of the street, scrubbed behind the ears.

'Why God, exactly?' I added, trying to sound analytical.

'He didn't sell out,' said Jack, as if surprised I should have to ask.

I knew what that meant, at least. I had heard that before. Dexter held the same disdain for those musicians who got a little success and cashed in, from a back street squat and Oxfam jackets to designer suits and dinner at flash restaurants and trips to the opera and staying at some crumbling aristo gaff for the weekend. Buying class, Dex called it. So I recognised the sell out jive – the biggest insult you could pay anyone in that neck of the woods. You could sell your sister into white slavery and people would call it enterprising, but if you sold your soul out to the bourgeois ideal there was no remission.

'So what did he do?' I said.

'He stayed true to rock and roll,' said Jack.

He took out an old New York Dolls album, dusted it with the back of his sleeve, and laid the needle carefully on the vinyl.

'He followed his calling,' he said.

The jarring notes of the first track roared out of the speakers, as if daring me to say different. I didn't say different. I didn't know different.

I learnt a lot about Thunders in the next few weeks. I learnt that he liked to mime jacking up on stage, that he was once arrested at an airport before even reaching customs, for stealing the valium from the aeroplane's first aid box, that his first drummer died in a bath in Chelsea.

His first band, the New York Dolls, spent their time in Max's Kansas City bar and a joint called Nobody's with

Truman Capote, Andy Warhol and the Velvet Underground, wearing platforms, pearls and fishnets – subterranean sleazoid flash, said the *Melody Maker*. The band insisted they were just a bunch of kids looking for a good time, and it was commonly held that the only way to get laid in those days was to be part of their entourage. The staider press called them transvestites, drug addicts and perverts, but this was the kind of thing the Dolls took as a compliment. They had a hysterical female following, led by a fifteen-year-old called Sable Starr. 'She was a weird chick,' Johnny once said. 'But kind of nice. She's crazy but she's cool, you know.'

It was rock and roll, the real dirty version, no quarter given. Thunders was too fast to live, too young to die. Johnny himself told the papers, 'I'm not a professional drug taker, I just want to make them dance.' But as one astute observer noted, his life was like a warning television documentary. Kids, don't try this at home. But they did, and when Thunders returned to New York at the beginning of the eighties, he didn't stay long. There was no-one left to play with. 'All the kids I used to hang out with,' he said, 'are dead or in jail.'

When the Dolls fell apart, Thunders formed the Heartbreakers – a band described in the music papers as great, hot and anybody's. Billboards across the city advised fans to *Catch them while they're still alive*. It wasn't that much of a joke. Plugged into his needle, even Johnny knew that he was playing with fire. There was a line in *Chinese Rocks*, his ode to heroin, that said it all – I found I was happy to die, he rasped in his damaged Queen's drawl, Chinese rocks was the reason why. But somehow, he did survive, against every one of the odds. There were endless rumours of his death, but each time he reappeared, stumbling onto any stage that would take him, thrashing at his guitar, sneering at the audience as if daring them to believe that he would still be there tomorrow.

This was Jack's hero. At first, when he told me some of this, I thought it was affectation, some kind of adolescent hangover, like saying fuck in front of people's parents. Later, when I knew him better, I thought I understood. It was quite simple, really. It wasn't the junk so much, the mythology that goes with buying your dreams in chemical form. Thunders might be out there, by himself, digging his Chinese ditch, disdainfully courting death while others packed it in, got themselves born again, but it was more than brinkmanship.

I think what it really was for Jack, was that here was a man, who said anything and did anything, and *didn't care*. He didn't make excuses, he never apologised. He wasn't just a part-time anti-hero, he saw it all the way through, shocking and startling and not giving a damn. It might not have been clever, and it never looked pretty, but it was the real thing. And apart from anything else, whatever example he set the kids, he did make them dance.

Sitting then, in Jack's strange darkened room, I didn't know any of this. I'd like to think that if I had it might have made a difference, but I'm not sure if it would. He looked so pale and lost and lonely, sitting on his Persian rug, surrounded by another man's things.

Everyone said, afterwards, that they never knew what I was doing with Jack, and most times I agreed with them. It was hard to explain. He wasn't love's young dream, that was for sure, and his redeeming features were difficult to find. But for me, then, he was perfect. He was out of reach and ready to save, and if I could find a mission then perhaps I could convince myself that I was worth something after all.

'What?' he said, looking at me with those sad pale eyes. I wanted to touch his face.

'Nothing,' I said. 'Just thinking.'

I was just thinking, some confused version of why I was here at all running through my head, none of it making any sense.

'I should go,' I said. I knew I should go. That was the only certainty I had to hold on to, just then. I knew I should go, but then he kissed me, and I was lost, and I stayed.

11

'Did you have insomnia last night, or is there something you want to tell me?' said Louey.

He had brought me a Danish for breakfast, just like he did every morning. There was a curious domestic side to our friendship: we had breakfast together each day, and then I drove him to work. Louey didn't drive. He said that the motor car was the root of all modern ills.

'Please,' I said. 'It's Monday morning.'

I was running on four hours sleep and the realisation that I had taken a step in the dark and I didn't know what happened next. It was all I could do to remember how to make a cup of coffee, let alone answer questions.

'So it is,' said Louey. 'Who is he?'

'How do you know it's a he?' I said, playing for time.

'Stands to reason,' said Louey. It should have been his catchphrase. He believed in reason, and followed it to the right conclusion every time.

'Circles under the eyes and a distracted air,' he said. 'A certain lack of co-ordination mixed with a cat that might have got the cream but isn't quite sure yet. You don't get that sitting at home watching the late show.'

'And there I was,' I said in resignation, 'thinking I was impenetrable.'

'Not you, sweetheart,' said Louey. 'Your face is a book in

which men may read strange things, if you will forgive me for paraphrasing.'

'It was strange,' I said.

Louey drank his coffee and regarded me with his level eyes. It always struck me as odd that he was so interested in my life. I wasn't used to it.

'So,' he said. 'Do you want to tell me, or shall we just draw a discreet veil and pretend it's another day?'

'Eat your Danish,' I said.

Driving down to the river, stuck in intolerant rush hour traffic, Louey smoked a cigarette and waited.

'It's the one from the party,' I said at last. 'You wouldn't approve.'

'What's not to approve?' said Louey. 'I'm not your mother.'

'He's not very suitable,' I said.

'Suitable for what?' said Louey.

'For anything,' I said. 'He's irresponsible and he doesn't have a job and he's far too familiar with illegal substances.'

'Sounds like a riot,' said Louey. 'But is he nice to you?'

'I don't know yet,' I said. 'I only met him properly yesterday.'

'Moving fast,' said Louey. 'It may not be wise but it can be fun.'

I wondered suddenly whether he had slept with Eva that Friday night. I had never asked him. I had wanted to, but I didn't want to sound like the thought police.

'I'm not sure,' I said. It had been fun, I supposed, but I wasn't sure how much it was going to cost me. 'I'm not sure if I know what I'm doing.'

'Always a good start,' said Louey. He looked over at me, smiling. 'It's not nuclear physics,' he said. 'It's just sex. You've got a few years yet before you might want to settle down with a grown-up who can meet your emotional needs and fill in a tax return. You might as well take your risks now. You won't be able to later.'

'Why not?' I said, interested. I liked it when Louey came out with his small pieces of homespun wisdom. They were never what I expected.

'Old bones take longer to heal,' he said. 'And if the worst comes to the worst, I can always go round and duff him up.'

At my desk, there were messages and pieces to read and letters to draft. I tried to concentrate. Louey was right, it was just sex. There were more important things to think about. I tried to think about them. My mind was chasing itself in circles, not helping me. I wondered if he would call. I wondered if I wanted him to call. I wondered what I would say to him if he did.

They ought to warn you, or at least give out a handbook for the uninitiated, helpful hints for beginners. I shook my head crossly. I should know *something*. I should have picked up some shards of wisdom on my travels. I had seen more than most, after all. I hadn't been so very sheltered, not cossetted and coddled and wrapped in cotton wool and told everything would be fine if I ate my greens and went to bed early.

I tried to remember what I had done in these situations before. It all seemed too distant, just something that happened, while I stood by and watched. There are people who say that every time is like the first time. It did feel like the first time. I felt shaken up, dislocated, as if everyone else about me was marching in time and I had lost step.

'Nancy? Pieces.'

I looked up, bringing my eyes into focus.

'Bob,' I said, stupidly. 'For me?'

Bob laughed. He was my assistant. Assistant, if you please,

I must be grown up to have one of those, this surely must be proof of adulthood and ability to deal with anything. He was twenty-two, tall and laconic and aware that he reminded people of a young Gary Cooper. Despite the times, he was investigating his burgeoning sexuality to its limit, like an explorer in search of lost tribes and anthropological revelation. He didn't suffer from regret or remorse and he carried a pack of rubbers with him wherever he went. It was just sex, he said. He left the hearts and flowers for others, who were better at that kind of thing than he was.

'Not my alley, all that,' he liked to say.

'Not yet,' I told him. 'Your time will come.'

'Maybe,' he said.

Bob didn't believe in arguing. He had no politics, but he was liberal at heart, allowing everyone their own mind. He sat happily on the fence, seeing both sides of every story.

'Love,' he once told me, 'is complicated. Messy. I don't know how to do it. Better stick to what I'm good at.'

I wondered if it could ever be that simple. I didn't think so, not for women anyway. Men have a kind of linear view of the world, looking straight ahead. They can concentrate on one thing at a time. So for them it can be just physical, like a good lunch. For us, lunch is never enough.

'Nancy?'

I looked up. Bob was still there, watching me with amusement.

'Yes, yes,' I said, trying to sound efficient and on the case. Bob broke out his lopsided Gary Cooper smile. I wondered if he'd started out like that or whether he'd practised for years in front of *High Noon*.

'Get laid last night?' I said. I knew about attack being the best form of defence.

He smiled more than ever, knowing I didn't have to ask. It was like the sun rising in the morning.

'I was about to ask you the same question,' he said.

I opened my eyes very wide. I wondered if my theory of impenetrability had always been misplaced, or whether it was just lately. Perhaps it was all slipping as I got older.

Bob, having got his answer, pointed at the sheaf of paper he had put in front of me.

'I need this for tomorrow,' he said. 'I need it for yesterday, but we'll make allowances. Can you read?'

'I can read,' I said, glad at least of one conviction as the world shifted about me.

'Nicely, nicely,' he said. He gave me a look which was the closest he ever got to penetrating and went back to his desk.

I turned to my work. Everybody was doing it, for heaven's sake. Birds did it, and bees, and educated fleas. Bob did it every night. It couldn't be so complicated.

At two o'clock, someone started playing Bob Marley in the street. Louey and I were finishing our lunch – pastrami on rye, cigarettes and black coffee, a hangover from my downtown days. The strains of *Natural Mystic* came floating through the open window. I smiled. Louey tapped his teeth with a pencil.

Violet came in, without knocking. She never knocked. Lucky we had nothing to hide.

'There are two men outside,' she said, 'with balloons and a ghetto blaster, holding up the traffic.'

'There goes the neighbourhood,' said Louey.

We crossed to the street side and looked out. Jack, holding a large bunch of many coloured balloons in one hand and a cigar in the other, was standing on the pavement. Behind him, a small rag-tag figure in outsize thrift shop rejects and purple Lennon spectacles was hefting a stereo system. I shook my head, laughing. This wasn't what I had expected.

'There she is,' said Jack, pointing.

Across the road, people were looking out from behind discreet net curtains, curious. Passers-by and men in motors stopped to see what was happening. A group of children on their way to the river gathered round Jack, gazing up at the balloons. I thought maybe they were too much, kind of Gene Kelly corn, but this was a rearguard action. I was smiling all over my face, I couldn't help it.

'Is that *him*?' said Louey.

'Yes,' I said.

'Is that who?' said Violet.

'Just a character I know,' I said. I hadn't told her about Jack. Until last night, there hadn't been so much to tell. Now, I didn't know where to start.

'Character is right,' said Violet.

'Happy birthday,' Jack yelled.

'It's not my birthday,' I said loudly, to make myself heard over the music.

'Bad call,' said Jack. 'Come and have a drink anyway.'

I started to say yes, without thinking.

'Not,' said Louey, in my ear. 'Respect yourself. You're busy.'

'He's right,' said Violet. 'Hard to get is the only way. Not that I can talk,' she added fairly.

They were right. I knew they were right. Besides, I needed time for reflection. For something, anyway. Just time.

'I'm busy,' I said, trying not to sound regretful. 'I have work.'

I have work, you see. I have other things to think about. Last night is last night, it was swell, but I have a life to think about.

'I *told* you,' said Jack's companion.

Jack stood his ground, unfazed.

'We'll be in the pub,' he said, pointing. 'We'll wait.'

'Until six?' I said.

'Of course until six,' he said, as it surprised there might be any doubt about it.

He turned and walked away, sketching a little salute in the air as he went, followed by the sound technician and a stray band of children.

The office gave me looks and went back to their desks. I could almost see the question marks floating above their heads in small cartoon bubbles. Of course, they were far too urban and knowing to ask anything. Conclusions might be drawn and speculation indulged, but only in the privacy of their own boudoirs.

'What's he going to do next year?' said Louey. 'Join the circus?'

'Below the belt, sunshine,' said Violet. 'Go and talk to your pot plant.'

'Yeah, yeah,' said Louey, sticking his hands in his pockets. He went back to his office and shut the door with quiet ostentation.

'Men,' said Violet, 'will be boys, whatever you try to do about it.'

I wasn't sure exactly which one she meant, so I said nothing. She followed me back to my desk, sat herself down, and offered me one of my own cigarettes.

'Have a gasper,' she said.

We smoked for a while. I was still smiling like an idiot. Violet watched me with interest.

'Is it?' she said, after a while.

I turned up my palms at her, knowing nothing. It sometimes seems to me that the only knowledge you gain as you get older is the extent of how little you know. Sometimes I wondered if I would ever be sure of anything ever again. And me, with all my expensive education.

'I don't know,' I said truthfully. I smiled some more. 'It's just a man.'

'Oh, dearest,' said Violet, with a small nostalgic sigh. 'It's always just a man.'

She put out her cigarette and stood up, looking down at me for a moment. Then she laughed.

'Those balloons, though,' she said. 'I see how you can't resist.'

I arrived at the pub at six-fifteen. I had considered not going at all, but I was curious. That was my story and I was sticking to it. I wasn't very good at playing games. I hadn't had enough practice. Besides (of course, can't you guess?), in my ardent misguided idealistic soul I believed that if it was right it was right and no game on earth would make the blindest bit of difference.

There was an argument going the rounds at that time, about playing the game. Those who were in therapy and read all the books said that deep down the cave won out every time and at heart all men wanted to be hunters. Willa headed this contingent.

'You *have* to give them something to chase,' she said, loudly and to anyone who would listen. 'How*ever* much they like you, if they don't think you are a *prize*, nothing will work. Blue riband or bust, see? Give yourself away too easy and the subliminal voice will tell them it can't be worth it. What are you going to do – buck two thousand years of conditioning?'

Willa went to Hampstead once a week for enlightenment and cups of tea.

'Of course I don't lie on a couch,' she said in derision. 'Get real.'

Therapy was just kicking in now that the diamond perfection of the eighties had passed and we were allowed to admit to flaws. Violet, ahead of the crowd as usual, had been going for years. I was jealous. I longed for a voice of reason to call my own, but I was frightened. I was afraid that if I took the lid off my Pandora's box I might never be able to put it back on.

There was a faint feminist slant to the debate as well, a view that the hard-to-get school fostered self-respect.

'See,' said Willa, over many cups of strong coffee, 'if you give yourself away too easy, it means that deep down you don't believe you're worth so much. Have me now, I'm not worth jousting for. Get it?'

The other side argued for instinct – if it's wrong it's wrong and if it's right it's right and you might as well find out sooner rather than later, save time and money and emotional wear and tear.

Since neither theory seemed infallible, and we were at the age when it was hard to tell whether exceptions proved or disproved every rule, the argument continued with heat on both sides, no-one willing to give any quarter. It wasn't an exact science, after all, no lab rats and men in white coats. It wasn't $E = MC^2$.

The pub was full when I arrived, King's Road types showing off their flash gear and packs of grunged-up Sloane Square refugees trying to lose their accents in the mêlée. Jack and his friend sat in a corner, pint glasses crowding the table in front of them. They seemed to have ditched the balloons.

'It's a lady,' said Jack, as if he had never seen one before. He stood up and pulled me against him, kissing me hard on the mouth with a kind of defiance, as if asking what anyone was going to do about it. No-one took any notice. The earth shifted a little, was all, but it could have been that I was reading Hemingway that week.

'Hello,' I said, all blinding wit and snappy comeback. I could feel that foolish smiling coming on again. Jack's face was very close to mine. He smelt of incense and patchouli and cigarette smoke. I thought suddenly of last night, of lying beside him, feeling his skin stretched soft and fine over his shoulder blades, and I looked away, not wanting to betray myself.

'This is Kid,' he said, gesturing at his companion. 'Don't take any notice of him. Nobody does.'

Kid blinked heavy eyelids at me, slow and solemn, and said hello.

'Don't take any notice of me,' he said, nodding slowly. 'Nobody else do.'

I sat down.

'Have some Guinness,' said Jack. He pushed a pint across the table.

'The black beer,' said Kid, nodding again, as if at some esoteric wisdom. Under his coat he wore a T-shirt in rasta colours with a black power salute printed on the front. Perhaps he was another one waiting for the revolution. Perhaps he was just taking time off from plotting the overthrow of the bourgeois hegemony.

'What are you doing?' I said to Jack.

'Doing?' he said. 'I'm just waiting on a lady.'

'I'm not waiting on a lady,' said Kid, with sudden animation. 'I'm just waiting on a friend.'

He looked about, as if startled by this rash speech, and slumped back into his corner, contemplating his beer with gloomy interest.

'Don't hold your breath,' said Jack. He laughed silently, his shoulders shaking.

I wasn't sure what to do next. I lit a cigarette and wondered what might happen. I supposed I should make polite conversation, but I didn't know what to say. I felt I should remark on the weather or the state of the government.

'How did you know where I work?' I said, just to hear the sound of my own voice.

Jack regarded me with a kind of sorrowful indulgence. I knew that look. Louey used it, most mornings.

'You gave me your card,' he said.

'I did?' I said. That seemed long ago too, back in the days when I had some surety to cling to. 'I did,' I said, remembering my virtuoso exit. 'Yes.'

'Yes,' Jack said.

Then he looked at me with those indecent eyes, and I knew exactly what was going to happen next.

12

'You're *what*?' said Lil.

I looked at her. 'Don't make me say it again,' I said.

'I don't believe you,' said Lil. 'You're making it up, to take my mind off . . .' She paused, almost giving herself away. 'Other things,' she said.

'I wouldn't do that to you,' I said.

'Jack,' she said. 'Of all people. You're *going* with Jack. It's too much to take in.'

'I don't know if I'm going with him,' I said. I didn't believe in presumption. 'I'm sleeping with him, is all.'

'*All*?' said Lil. 'What more do you want? An audience?'

I smiled. I was enjoying myself. See Ma, I'm not such a good little girl after all.

'It's not such a big deal,' I said, hoping it was. 'People do it all the time.'

'Not with Jack,' said Lil. She had this doom-laden voice she did sometimes. If you closed your eyes you could believe you were out with Peter Cushing. She was using it now.

'I thought he was your friend,' I said.

'He is,' said Lil. 'I've known him for ever. Everyone has. He's a dealer, for Christ's sake.'

'So what,' I said, 'do you want me to do? Go out and find myself a nice chartered accountant?'

'There is the middle ground,' said Lil. 'People say it's nice.'

'My point exactly,' I said.

We were eating in 21, prawn gumbo and hot sauce, soul food. It was still early and the place was half empty, just a few punters abroad, drinking San Miguel and waiting for the evening to start.

'Where is he now, then?' said Lil. She looked around suspiciously, as if expecting to find him hiding behind a pillar.

'I don't know,' I said.

I didn't. I had left his apartment that morning and gone to work and there had been no call, no serenade at my window, no six o'clock rendezvous. That was all right. I needed a moment to get used to the newness and strangeness of it all.

'You don't know?' said Lil.

'I'm not the kind who drops everyone flat the moment a man walks in the room,' I said, with dignity. 'I'm eating with you.'

'Yeah, yeah,' said Lil. She laughed suddenly, giving in. 'You're crazed, did no-one tell you? Didn't your mother ever warn you about men like that?'

'My mother never warned me about anything,' I said.

She hadn't. She had sent me to school and given me frocks to wear and then run out of ideas. Her life had never been checked by trouble, so I'm not sure that she would have known what to warn me against.

'No,' said Lil. 'Figures. So,' she said. 'Is it?'

'I don't know,' I said. 'It's only been two days.'

'Ha,' said Lil. 'That's all it takes.'

'Lil,' I said, trying to keep my voice level and scientific. 'I'm trying to be rational about this. I don't know what it is. It's too early to tell. It could be anything. It could be nothing.'

Lil looked like she knew better, but she didn't say any-thing. She was right, of course. I knew what it was. I had known from the moment I saw him that Sunday afternoon. I had known from the moment I met him at that South American party. He was the one I wanted. He touched something in me that no-one else had guessed at. All the signs were there, staring me in the face. I was walking on air, I was swinging from lamp-posts, I was all lit up inside. It was love, all right. But that was the most frightening word in the English language, so I couldn't admit to it. Not yet.

Lil smiled at me with some faint sorrow. She could read the signs too. She had been there before, and she had the scars to show for it.

'Just watch yourself,' she said. She paused, searching for answers. 'Eat your gumbo,' she said, at last.

'Got to keep body and soul together,' I said, pushing a prawn around my plate. I wasn't hungry. Loss of appetite, another sure indication.

'Food,' said Willa, arriving with Davey on her arm.

She sat herself down and started on my dinner. Her diet meant she wasn't allowed to buy food, but she could eat other people's. It was one way of doing it.

'Gumbo, prawns, hot sauce,' she said, as if reciting a mantra. 'Yes, yes, yes. Feed that soul.'

'You don't have a soul,' said Davey. 'Everyone knows that.'

'Ha, ha,' said Willa, her mouth full. 'Sold it to the devil, dirt cheap, on the never never, and still I don't get a job.' She waved her fork in the air, to illustrate her point.

'Five auditions this week,' she said. '*Five*. Wiggling my ass off in front of a crowd of dyspeptic menopausal film directors, promising them the key to eternal bliss and all the trimmings, and what do we end up with?'

I shook my head, not knowing.

'Diddley squat,' said Willa. 'Fanny Adams. Jack shit.'

'Sounds like a nice bunch of guys,' said Davey. 'You should have let one of them take you home.'

'Funny,' said Willa. 'You're the one should be in pictures. Don't let your daughter on the stage, Mrs Worthington. I should give it all up and go back to the farm.'

Lil laughed. Willa had never been to the country in her life. She didn't even know where it was.

'Let's have some drink,' said Davey abruptly.

'What's with the prodigy?' said Lil, watching him head off to the bar.

'Block,' said Willa. 'He got halfway through the new book and realised he was telling the wrong story. Don't you hate it when that happens?'

'Sounds like my life,' said Lil.

'Sounds like *my* life,' said Willa. 'I told him to get drunk. It can help. Look at Hemingway. Look at Eugene O'Neill.'

'Just look at them,' said Lil.

Willa finished off my gumbo.

'Actually,' she said, with sudden candour. 'That was really what I wanted to do, so Dave said he'd keep me company. He's good that way.'

Davey came back with three beers and Dexter.

'Dexter's life is over,' said Davey, setting the bottles down with care. 'So I told him to join us.'

'Charming,' said Willa.

'What happened, Dex?' said Lil.

'She went off with a man in a Porsche,' said Dexter, trying to look manful and failing.

'Bitch,' said Willa. 'Bitch bitch bloody bitch.'

Dex had given up on his New York actress, since it turned out she was doing it with her leading man, which was a better career move, and had moved on to a French model called Dominique. She was one of those women who promise trouble from the start – grecian profile, perfect bones, broken accent. Life for her was a journey from one mirror to the next.

We had all warned him. He had brought her to 21 one lunchtime, where she had pouted prettily and picked at a salad and left early because she had a meeting with Herb Ritts or someone.

'Dex,' Willa had said, crossing her eyes at him. 'Does it know any words over one syllable? Every time she opened her mouth I thought her brain was going to fall out, right splat into her Caesar salad.'

Dex looked wounded.

'It's just her English isn't very good,' he said.

She had dallied with him for a while, letting him take her out to the smart restaurants and flash clubs which form the natural habitat for people who live by their faces, never returning his calls, torturing him with talk of other men. There had never been any doubt that when she tired of playing with him she would cast him aside and break his poor trusting heart. I think even he had known it would happen, but there was some strange dauntless optimism in him that kept him hanging on when all hope was lost. He always thought that a miracle might happen, a change was going to come, and the sunset would beckon.

'It's OK,' said Dexter now. He shrugged, with that fatalism he had learnt so well. 'I don't suppose she was right for me anyway.'

'Not if she wanted to ride in a Porsche,' said Lil. 'Promise you won't ever drive one of those, even when you are rich and famous.'

'I promise,' said Dexter solemnly. He still drove the Ford Cortina he had bought before he ever cut a record. It wasn't to prove anything. He liked it.

'So what's with you, Nancy?' said Willa, suddenly. I had been hoping she wouldn't notice. 'Have you been having sex while the world crumbles about our ears?'

'And there I was,' I said, playing for time, 'thinking I was inscrutable.'

'I can do inscrutable,' said Willa, her face wiped of expression. 'But it took me three years to learn it. No-one gets this way without sweat and tears.'

'She has,' said Davey, looking at me. 'Who is he?'

Davey liked asking questions, which always surprised me. I would have thought that the purist in him would have disapproved of gossip. Willa said that he spent so much time surrounded by people who didn't exist that he had to ask about what real ones did, just so he felt some kind of connection with life going on around him.

'If you live in your head,' she said, 'you've got to find out about the world somehow. We do all his living for him. That's why he likes me, because I go out and get dirty. I'm not a poet.'

I supposed it was the same thing with my father. He never ventured far into the world, either. Sometimes, when I was struggling to make sense of things and come to the right conclusions and work out what it all meant, I almost envied him. I thought it must be restful, not bothering with real people, just surrounding yourself with nice fictional characters, who always did what you wanted them to.

'Come on,' said Dexter. 'You can't leave us hanging like this.'

'Watch her,' said Lil.

'Just a man,' I said.

'Oxymoronic,' said Willa, who had read more books than she gave herself credit for. 'Return to Go, do not collect two hundred. Starter for ten, fingers on the buzzers, no conferring.'

'It's not English,' said Davey, 'but how it rolls off the tongue.'

'Don't you pull rank with me, Einstein,' said Willa. 'My school was a hard one.'

They all looked at me, waiting. I felt like telling them why I wanted the job.

'Jack,' I said. 'I'm sleeping with Jack.'

'Jack who?' said Davey.

'Jack?' said Dexter.

'Jack Jack?' said Willa.

'Jack,' I said. It was gratifying, in a way.

There was a silence. They were all looking at me again. I wondered if I'd failed the interview.

'Stop,' I said. 'It's just sex.'

'Blah,' said Willa. 'Not. Not looking like that, it's not. And I should know.'

'Nancy,' said Dexter. 'Didn't you skip the intermediary class? This is strictly for honours students.'

'You can talk,' I said, defensive. I gave myself a little credit.

'Jack from lunch?' said Davey. 'The dangerous one?'

'On the button,' said Willa. 'You win the big cigar.' She turned to me. 'Has this been coming on for some time,' she said, 'or did you just wake up one morning and decide to end your life?'

'Willa,' said Lil, warning.

'No,' said Willa. 'I think we should be told.'

'Willa, please,' said Davey.

'I've been there, you see,' said Willa, ignoring him. I stared at her, shaken.

'With Jack?' I said, stupid with jealousy.

'Not with Jack,' said Willa. 'So near as makes no difference. They're all the same, those ones. Sweet and hopeless and lost the plot. But you can't find it for them. They won't let you. They chew you up and spit you out first. They're ruthless. Take my word for it. Skip the country, turn lesbian, take the veil – anything to get out while your head is above water.'

'Shut up, dearest,' said Davey. 'We have the gist.' He

looked at me with his clever eyes. 'I know I don't know much about these things,' he said, 'but I think she's right.'

'She is,' said Lil. 'I hate to say it.'

I was suddenly furious. How dare they come and stamp all over my joy with their big clumsy boots. Just because they were having a bad day didn't mean they had to wreck everyone else's good one.

'You don't hate to say it,' I said. I kept my voice low and even. I didn't want to shout.

'I'm very sorry that I haven't hitched up with Prince Charming,' I said, 'but he didn't show on time. I'm sorry that I'm such a disappointment to you. They were all out of perfection, but fucked-up was on special offer.'

'Nancy,' said Lil. 'Don't get upset. We just want to warn you, that's all.'

'Oh, yes,' I said. I looked at them. 'And you're all doing so well in that department.'

It was a cheap shot. I knew it was a cheap shot, but I couldn't help it.

'I'm going now,' I said. I stood up and put a tenner carefully on the table. 'Thank you for all your support,' I said, and then I walked.

Out in the street, I stopped. I didn't know where to go. I thought of Jack, but it was too early for that. You can't start crying on someone's shoulder after only two days, even I knew that.

Anyway, what did they know? Sitting there, preaching at me, as if I was just out of school, as if I had failed all the exams. They weren't the ones sleeping with Jack. They had the gall to write him off without a second thought. Forget him, he's a loser, he's not the one for you, he's got disaster written all over him. How did they know that? People change. It happened all the time. Nothing is set in stone. Who is to say who is right for someone and who isn't? Who is to say what will work and what won't? The history of the world is built on unlikely couples. Look at Arthur Miller and Marilyn Monroe. Look at Napoleon and Josephine. It wasn't living by numbers.

Dexter came up behind me and took my arm.

'Go away,' I said. 'I'm angry and I'm bitter and I don't want to talk about it.'

'Don't be difficult,' said Dexter. 'It doesn't wash with me. Come and get a drink.'

'I'm not going back in and eating humble pie,' I said. 'I'm not going back and saying I'm sorry and you were all right.'

'Of course you're not,' said Dexter. 'Don't shout at me, I'm too fragile. We'll go somewhere else.'

'Why?' I said.

'No need to get analytical,' said Dex.

We went to a bar down the road. It wasn't anywhere special. It was just a room where people went to sit and be left alone.

'This is where I come when I want to be anti-social,' said Dexter.

'Great,' I said. I wasn't going to back down too easily. I had righteous anger burning in me, after all.

Dexter, taking it on the chin, sat me down and brought me a bottle of beer.

'What about all this weather we've been having?' he said.

I gave him a dangerous look. 'Patronise me and I'm leaving,' I said.

'Aw, come on, Mrs,' he said. 'Don't shoot me, I'm only the piano player.'

'Yeah, yeah,' I said, but I laughed. Seeing it, Dex smiled.

'See,' he said. 'It can't be all bad.'

*　　*　　*

We sat for a long time, avoiding the subject. We talked about whatever happened to rock and roll and whether grunge would take off and if we thought The Inspiral Carpets were all they were cracked up to be. We talked about where we would be in ten years time and what we would do with a million dollars and who we would be for a day, if we could choose.

Eventually, inevitably, we got around to the point. I brought it up. I thought I did want to talk, after all.

'I'm sorry,' I said. 'I'm such a double standard. All those girls I told you weren't good enough, and now I get the same thing and I don't like it one small bit.'

I looked at him, wondering if he was going to hold it against me, but he was smiling, in that easy way he had.

'It doesn't matter,' he said.

'I can dish it out,' I said, 'but I suppose I can't take it.'

'Theory and practice,' said Dex, carefully. 'Very different.'

I smiled at him, grateful that he let it go. He believed that all our houses were made of glass, that we should all be careful where we threw our stones.

'Do you,' I said, 'ever know, really know, if it's the right one? How do you tell? Is there something everyone else knows and I don't?'

'Nah,' said Dex.

He was growing philosophical now. It was that time of night. It was late, and the crowd that had filled the place when we arrived had dissipated, leaving behind it small groups of serious drinkers, gathered closely round smeared table tops, drowning all their sorrows and trying to guess at the secrets of life, or at least who they were going to go home with.

'Nobody knows,' said Dexter. 'There is no trick to it. It's all just a guess.'

'Dex,' I said. 'Come on. There must be times when

you're sure, when you know, when you make the right decision.'

'Guessing,' said Dexter. I wondered if he would say that if his French model had resisted the Porsche. I wondered what he would say if he was settled and happy, instead of waiting in bars for girls who never showed.

'Watch them,' he said, gesturing widely at the room, 'waltzing up that aisle, promising in front of their God and their peers to love honour obey, worship with their bodies, in sickness and health, till death do they part. *How do they know*?'

He stared at me, almost angry, as if I were the one who had started the whole charade in the first place, as if Adam and Eve had been my idea.

'I don't know,' I said, shaking my head. 'I don't.'

'You see?' said Dexter. 'You see? That's the point. It's all a big guess. They hope, they pray, they cook and garden and get a better job to pay the mortgage and read dirty books to keep bedtime interesting, but they don't *know*. There are no guarantees. Sometimes you just stop loving someone. You just stop.'

'Dex,' I said. 'Don't. It's not that bad.'

Please don't let it be that bad. Please don't let me be wrong. Please don't break my dream.

'I'm bitter, I admit it,' said Dex. 'My girl went off with someone else. I blew it. I chose the wrong one. And it's not just me. People do it all the time. And you know what everyone says? They say, you should have known better. Why should you? Why?'

'Someone must know something,' I said. 'Otherwise no-one would know anything. If you see what I mean.'

'Oh, yeah,' said Dexter. 'In around ten, fifteen years, we might know something. We might learn something by then.'

He smoked hard on his cigarette, looking out across the room, as if wondering whether he would last that long. I watched him. I had never seen Dex get serious before. I thought all he cared about in the world was his rhythm guitar.

'You know,' he said, 'how we learn?'

I shook my head. No-one had told me the secret of eternal wisdom. It wasn't on the curriculum, not the one I'd studied.

'How?' I said.

'From doing what we're doing now,' Dex said. 'Which is the result of knowing nothing. Do you know why Willa got so angry with you tonight? She did the mission deal, found herself a poor little boy lost, brushed him down, kissed him better. And just as it was getting really sweet, the telephone goes dead and it's goodbye happiness, hello loneliness. That's why she's by herself now. Self-preservation, see? She's got Dave, and they can be friends, and she can call him at four in the morning when things aren't so good, and he's never going to leave her. She wasn't being cruel, it's just all too close to home.'

'I see that,' I said. I thought I did. 'But every case is different. And anyway, you can't learn from other people's mistakes.'

'Not unless you're very clever,' said Dexter sadly.

'Drink up,' I said.

For all the knocks, I still had my bubble intact. I was still buoyed up on the euphoria that comes with the promise of proving to be different. I had more of a challenge now, that was all that had changed. I had the possibility to prove them all wrong.

Dexter smiled at me. I kissed his cheek.

'I'm buying,' I said, brandishing a note at him. 'It'll be all right. No-one said it was going to be easy.'

'The problem is,' said Dexter, some strange dying sadness in his voice, 'that someone did.'

*　　*　　*

I called Louey when I got home, like I did most nights.

'How is it?' he said, like he did most nights. Except this night was different, because things were changing and there was Jack.

'It OK,' I said.

'Are you sure?'

'Oh, Louey,' I said. 'When was the last time you were sure of anything?'

He laughed, but then he would.

'Some time around 1979,' he said.

13

'Have you heard?' said Violet, on Wednesday.

'No,' I said, 'It don't mean nothing.'

It did, but it was all right. Two days was all right. Three was borderline. Four and I'd declare my life officially over.

'Has he?' said Louey, Thursday breakfast.

'What?' I said. 'What? Eat your Danish.'

'Just curious,' said Louey.

'No,' I said. 'Just no. It's a free country.'

'Ha,' said Louey. 'Don't make me laugh.'

'I won't,' I said.

Dex called at lunchtime.

'How's it going?' he said.

'You know,' I said. He did know, better than anyone. 'I watch and wait.'

'He didn't call.'

'Not yet,' I said. 'I'm not bothered. I'm not sixteen years old any more.'

'That's what they all say,' said Dexter.

Thursday night, Jimmy and Ned took me out.

'We hear we missed the boat,' Jimmy said, over the telephone. I didn't ask how he had heard. Jimmy kept his ear closer to the ground than anyone I'd ever met. He prided himself on it. 'Too late, too lost.'

'Yeah, yeah,' I said. 'The other one plays jingle bells.'

'Can we be second best for the evening?' said Jimmy. 'Be a dilly. Ned's bored with babes.'

'So what am I?' I said. 'Chopped liver?'

'You know words we have to look up in the dictionary,' said Jimmy, reproachful. 'Some people never know how to take a compliment.'

'I'm touched,' I said.

'See you at eight then, Duchess,' said Jimmy. 'How can we wait that long?'

'Beats me,' I said.

I watched the telephone vaguely until six, but nothing happened, so I dropped Louey off, just like normal, went home, changed my clothes, told myself it didn't matter, and went out. It would be fine. Jimmy and Ned were enough to take your mind off anything, had I needed my mind taking off anything, which I didn't, much.

They were waiting for me at the Corner, Jimmy in racing green pinstripes, and Ned, as usual, looking as if he could never quite forget Woodstock.

'New beads,' I said, looking at his necklace. 'Very nice.'

'Isn't she a dilly?' said Jimmy.

'I should hope so,' I said. I suddenly felt impatient, I wasn't sure for what.

'Come on, then,' I said. 'Let's do something.'

'Imperious,' said Jimmy, in approval.

'Touch of class,' said Ned. He pulled a wad of notes out of his back pocket. Ned didn't care for plastic. He liked the reassuring feel of real dirty money between his fingers, crumpled with the promise that it had passed through many hands before it got to his, that it would pass through many more once he had done with it.

'Readies,' said Jimmy, who knew better than anyone what a bit of cash could do. 'The world is our oyster.' He sat up straight, and faced me.

'So, Pearl,' he said. 'Dealer's choice. What's it to be?'

'Crawl,' said Ned, like a little boy off to the zoo. 'Say it's a crawl.'

'Why not?' I said.

Jimmy got first call.

'Down the boozer,' he said. 'And no mistake.'

He led us along Portobello and under the flyover. Groups of dubious characters, ready for business, gave Jimmy a wide berth, but nodded with speculation at Ned.

'What?' said Ned. 'You think I was born yesterday? Rip-off city.'

'Hey, man,' the hawkers said, in reproach, their tender feelings cut to the quick. 'No way, man.'

'Way,' said Ned.

'Come along, dear,' said Jimmy, in the uptown voice he reserved for dealing with low life. 'I'm getting bored of this conversation. It lacks originality.'

He led us down a side street, past crumbling white terraces that had once been genteel, their bourgeois façades scarred with graffiti and the evidence of police raids.

'Now then,' he said, stopping at a pub. 'Here we are. After you, Princess.'

He held open the door, like the gent he was, and we were in.

'Ah, James,' said Ned, looking about in deep appreciation. 'Now you are talking.'

'A real public house, I think you'll agree,' said Jimmy, pleased.

It was. Windows smeared with dirt let in yellow late-evening sunshine, shot through with rising dust and thick smoke from the Woodbines smouldering in a dozen ash-trays. The carpet, which might once have held a hopeful pattern, was brown and matted with years of abuse, and gave off that particular heady smell of ancient beer slops. Heavy-set men, paunches straining at synthetic shirts, nursed pint glasses in thick hands, faces set in bulldog determination. There was no high fluting evening chatter, no exclamation, no fluttering laughter, just the low rumble of disconnected remarks and the hollow clack of snooker balls hitting off each other from the pool table.

It was the kind of place where a man, knowing where he stood with his pint of John Bull bitter, could escape from his wife or girlfriend or mother, and drink off the strains of the day. There were no women, apart from two old girls in worn herringbone overcoats who sat, immaculately upright, handbags clutched on their knees, looking straight ahead with dull disinterest, small glasses of sweet sherry on the table in front of them. They looked as if they had been there forever. I had seen a photograph once, in a book about Soho in the fifties, just like this, down to the ill-fitting unseasonal coats and the lifeless eyes, that terrible glazed look which is the last defence against a world that didn't turn out as they planned.

Jimmy and Ned leant on the bar easily, as if they were part of the furniture, as if entirely unconscious of looking as out of place as a pair of tigerlilies in a Beckenham window box.

'Orchidaceous,' I said.

'It talks dirty,' said Jimmy. 'Just fancy.'

Ned waved a folded ten pound note at the barman, who regarded him with a wearied resentment. I had the feeling that you would have to come here every night for five years before you would be considered a regular. There was none of the romanticised pub tradition of rosy-cheeked landlords polishing up glasses and offering people their usual and joshing with the customers. This was strictly the barbed wire school of establishment, lucky to get a drink without broken glass in it.

Ned, who'd had a knife in his sock since he was seven years old, stared the barman out for a while. I often thought that half the reason Ned dressed as he did was so he could surprise all the people who took him as soft. He loved breaking from love and peace back to the mean streets, from *Blowing in the Wind* to *Raging Bull* with one flicker of his eyelids.

The barman, recognising the threat of GBH when he saw it, withdrew his offensive stare and asked what he could do.

'Three pints of Guinness,' said Ned. 'If you *wouldn't* mind,' he added, with that insolent politeness that petty officials use when they call you Madam.

I thought he minded very much, but I knew better than to say anything.

It seemed that urban realism was the theme for the evening. After we left the pub, pleased to be alive, Ned took us to a pool hall down near the dead lands behind the Harrow Road. The ceiling was low and there were no windows, the only light coming from those suspended above the tables, which made for a pleasing chiaroscuro, straight back to *The Hustler*. Jimmy Cliff rumbled from speakers the size of the Empire State Building.

'Mash it up,' said Ned happily, slapping hands with the players, who regarded me with languid curiosity. 'We're going to teach the lady how to shoot.'

This was considered a very good joke, pool being one of the things that girls didn't know about, like football terminology and what a big end was.

We bought three tins of Red Stripe and chose a table. A small group of spectators gathered round to watch.

'Nancy,' said Ned, grave as a toastmaster. 'This is Junior, Ken, Hollis.'

We shook hands with formal solemnity.

'Your break, Duchess,' said Jimmy.

This occasioned more laughter. I smiled with girlish deprecation, as if I were used to being the best joke anyone could imagine. Junior, who was a head shorter than the rest, lent me his cue with politely held hilarity.

I was up first. My four self-appointed advisers lined up behind me to show me what to do.

'Here,' said Jimmy, pointing his finger. 'Just aim here and shoot.'

Ned chalked his cue with nonchalant expectation. I opened my eyes as wide as the day the pod went pop.

'There?' I said.

'There,' said Ned, settling back to enjoy the show. I gave him the benefit of one more skittish smile, and then I took him to the cleaners.

'Where did you learn how to do that?' said Ned, as we left.

'Catalonia,' I said.

'Catalonia?' said Jimmy.

'That's where we lived when I was fifteen,' I said.

'I told you she's been around, this one,' said Jimmy. 'Didn't I tell you that?'

I had been around, I supposed. We had moved to Spain from the hot dusty plains of Argentina, to a converted monastery on the top of a mountain, looking out over a blue bay and a harbour filled with fishing boats and a tiny insular town where Dali had once painted. We ate lunch at five and dinner at midnight and everyone had that curious distant look in their eyes that comes from a misspent youth.

I was inspired by this, just entering into my years of teenage rebellion. I cut my hair into spikes and put three rings in each ear and spent all day in backstreet dives with faded dissipated men who had come to visit for three weeks in 1968 and never left. They were all artists, although I never saw them paint anything. They taught me Catalan argot and the finer points of snooker. It was an education, I suppose.

'Serves me right,' said Ned. 'Never underestimate a babe.'

'You can underestimate a babe,' said Jimmy. 'Now this,' he said, taking my arm, 'this is a woman.'

'Is that what it is?' I said, hoping he was right. It was about time.

We went to another pub, even dirtier than the last, where two apes tried to pick a fight with Ned ('Are you *looking* at me?'). Later, we grew hungry and stopped for greasy tortilla in a crowded basement run by two ancient Cubans. Jimmy and Ned were impressed because I talked to them in inaccurate colloquial Spanish.

'What were you jawing about?' said Jimmy. 'Castro and Che Guevara?'

'All this weather we've been having,' I said.

Then we went up to Soho. The streets were crowded and the night was warm and people were sitting out at pavement tables and everything was all lit up and it felt like being abroad. There was a feeling of excitement in the air, as if something strange and new and remarkable were about to happen.

We took a break in the Bar Italia, where the pavement tables were crowded with hipsters drinking double espresso and trying to decide where to go next.

'I've got it,' said Jimmy. 'A little place I know.'

We took a taxi. 'You'll like this, Nancy,' Jimmy said. 'It's a quality gaff.'

It was a quality gaff, I suppose, if you're talking in relatives. Marble floors and mirrors everywhere and low lighting and little slips of paper as you walked in saying you were a guest of Roy, whoever he might be.

'Just a nod to the coppers,' said Ned. 'If anyone asks, it's a private party.'

'I see,' I said. I didn't, but it was too late at night for questions.

Jimmy dipped into his pocket and bought us a round.

'Plush seating anyways,' he said. 'Small mercies grow large at this time of the evening.'

Many middle-aged gents in shiny suits and heavy jewellery bought drinks for girls they'd never met before.

The girls, smiles switched on to order, asked for champagne, by the bottle. They had that hard-edged slightly used look about them, something mannish, like drag princesses who haven't got the make-up right.

They were pros, and they knew it. They gave me looks to prove it, dismissive and patronising, with a warning edge, telling me it was their turf. I felt a sudden urge to go to the bar and see how much I could get for my body, on a good night. I wondered what the going rate was in this place. These looked like girls who took American Express, gold card, natch.

'Roy,' I said, 'sure does have a lot of friends.'

'Ssh,' said Jimmy, only just joking. 'These are big time hoods. You want to keep your profile nice and low in here, or you won't come out with your kneecaps intact.'

Ned snorted, but it was a halfhearted attempt at derision, just to show that he wasn't intimidated. He could recognise types like this at forty paces, the sheen on their suits hardly hiding the flint hearts that lay beneath. It was low life, all right, the real kind. Don't rock this boat missus, because there aren't any lifebelts handy.

'Well,' I said, impressed. I was always impressed by the

real McCoy. It reminded me how little I knew and how much I had to learn. It was like a lesson in sociology: protection racket on your right, illegal gambling on your left, and here's one I prepared earlier. 'You don't say.'

'He do say,' said Ned. 'You'll be all right though, since you're with us.'

'Lucky for me,' I said, 'that you boys know so well how to show a lady a good time.'

Just out of the blue and when I was thinking of something quite else, Jack came to our table and sat down, without being asked. He kissed me. I felt weak and unsurprised.

'Look at you,' he said, 'checking out the real sleaze.'

'Are you referring to us?' said Jimmy.

'You appreciate it,' said Jack.

Jimmy smiled. It was true.

Jack drank my champagne and held my hand. I was transported.

'So,' he said. 'Are you going to come out tomorrow?'

'Why not?' I said. Why the hell not? What was I going to do, say I was busy? It was too late in the evening for mystery.

'Nine at my place,' he said. He seemed pleased, although it could have been a trick of the light.

'It's a date,' I said. I turned away a little, trying to see if I couldn't care less. At least he could see that I wasn't sitting by the telephone, pining. At least he could see that I had more life than that.

'Catch you,' he said to Jimmy and Ned. And then he left.

'Watch him go and I'll never forgive you,' said Ned.

I looked him very straight in the eye. I was touched.

'Ned,' I said. 'I never knew you cared.'

14

'He called,' said Violet, the next day.

'Is it that obvious?' I said, knowing it was. I wasn't even bothering to try and hide it.

'Obvious, schmobvious, said Violet. 'What else you want to do, put up banners all over the city?'

'I have a date,' I said.

A Friday night date, it was too good. Friday night was made for sex, Friday night was the real date time, because there was Saturday after, and the whole weekend, and the promise of waking up the next day and making breakfast and reading the papers in bed and maybe not getting up at all. Friday night was so full of promise it was practically illegal.

Violet took one of my cigarettes and considered me.

'I'm not your mother,' she said, 'so I'm not going to give you any words of warning. We all have to make our own mistakes.'

'He might not be a mistake,' I said, too happy to take offence.

'Dear one,' said Violet, suddenly serious. 'At this stage, anyone can be a mistake. There are very few ways of telling. This is why Irma Kurtz is still in business. Just do me one favour, one small thing, to humour me in my old age.'

'Tell me,' I said. At least with Violet, I knew I wouldn't be told to go home and have a cup of warm milk.

'Get yourself a family pack of rubbers,' she said seriously, 'on your way home.'

'Why surely,' I said. 'I never go anywhere without them.'

I told Louey, straight out. I didn't know how else to say it. There was a part of me that wanted to make an excuse, but I wasn't sure what for.

'I have a date,' I said. 'Tonight. It's not going to be just us.' It wasn't going to be just us any more. Things were changing.

'That's all right,' he said easily. 'Is it the dangerous one?'

I sat up straight. I wasn't ready for another chorus of disapproval.

'Dangerous?' I said. 'Who said that?'

Louey laughed at my cross face.

'You did,' he said.

I stopped, remembering.

'So I did,' I said. I shrugged, feeling foolish. 'It's just that everyone is trying to put me off,' I said.

'It's your life,' said Louey.

I looked closely at him, to see if he meant it. He looked right back at me, straight as a die. There was no side to Louey. He said just what he thought. He thought my life belonged to me, and I thought he was right.

'Yes,' I said. 'It is. It just is.'

I wanted to thank him. He was a good friend, Louey, the best I'd ever had. I wanted to tell him, but I didn't know how. I felt weak and sentimental. I wanted to pledge undying love and tell him that I would still need him when I was old and grey.

'See you Monday, then,' I said.

I wondered if he minded. I wondered if he felt the same as I had, when Eva had come and put her beautiful long arms all over him. I wanted to ask him that, too.

'Have a good time,' he said.

There was a queue in the chemist, young girls getting lipstick and kohl, fast men in pinstripes stocking up on Alka Seltzer and Neurofen, couples furtively buying baby oil. You could tell it was a Friday. Midweek it was mums with Pampers, old ladies with crumpled prescriptions, teens asking for Clearasil and medicated face wash. Fridays were not for practicalities, because the weekend was on the way, and everyone was going to go out and get laid. I felt like singing.

The woman behind the counter was middle-aged and disapproving. I held out a large packet of Mates, and some Durex arousers, which Violet had told me were the business.

'I'll take these please,' I said, just loud enough to get everyone's attention, just so they could tell that I was a liberated woman, I bought my own protection.

The fast men looked at me with interest, the teenage girls with envy. The matron behind the counter turned red and hustled my disgusting purchases into a bag so no-one could see my wantonness. I smiled at her, just enough dirt in it to get her really hot under the collar, paid my money, and walked away. Watch me. I have somewhere to go.

I lay in the bath for a long time, and then I stared hard into the mirror, trying to see myself as Jack would. I couldn't really tell what I looked like. I was so used to my face, it was hard to be objective. My eyebrows were too heavy and my nose too long, but I liked my eyes.

They were wide open tonight, which happened when I was excited. When I felt old and cross and stupid they went small and clouded, as if trying to shut out the world, and everything else fell out of balance, my mouth too big and useless, my face bland and crooked. But when they opened up, as they did now, they brought a kind of harmony to everything else about them.

I should have looked like yesterday's news, after my late night with the boys, but the anticipation that hummed in me was saving me from that, bless it. When I was feeling plain, I sometimes read those articles they run about famous beauties giving away their closely guarded secrets – always the same, as if no-one had thought of it before – get enough sleep, drink lots of water, throw away the gaspers, eat up your greens.

Sometimes I even put myself on one of those regimens, when I was feeling at my weakest, giving into that shameful hidden female conviction that if you can make yourself thin and beautiful everything will magically come right, that you will find the key to eternal bliss, even though we all know, deep down, that it isn't for sale.

Tonight though, I just felt good. You're all right, I told myself. It's going to be all right.

I put on red lipstick, just to continue the illusion, and I smoothed my hair down until it was black and shining, and I stared at myself for a moment more.

Ready, I drew a last gasp on my cigarette, and then I took a taxi to Jack's place.

I arrived at twenty past nine, just enough late to let him wonder once or twice whether I was coming or not. I stood in the street for a minute, looking up at his lit window. People walked past, going somewhere, dates to meet, places to fill. There was a feeling of anticipation in the air, murmured discretions and secret laughter. It was time to be out on the town, and the town was there for the taking, all too possible.

Now everything was fresh and new and unexpected. Later might come the sad bad bits, the stand-ups, the let-downs. She might not ask him in after all, or she might, and wish she hadn't. He might not turn up, or be found with someone else. There might be fights and recriminations, tears and mistakes.

Later still, in the morning light, there might be a time for fear and regret, waking up in the wrong bed, dazed and feeble, make-up smeared, picture-perfect no longer; running away from a strange door before there was time to ask why, or how, this had happened, hoping not to be seen, caught out in last night's clothes with no defence. But now, all that was in the future, and the endless roll of hope over experience was putting the spring into a hundred steps as the same old dance got underway, everyone pretending that it had never been done before.

Jack's window was open, shedding light out into the street, filled with promise. I could see his shadow on the wall as he moved about the room. He had a record playing, that old Pink Floyd number, *Shine on you Crazy Diamond*. It had such a great meaningless sound to it. You crazy Diamond. Shine on.

I waited for a minute, aware of my hesitation. I thought maybe I was getting nervous, so I crossed the street and knocked on the door before I could think better of it.

I could hear him coming down the stairs, his steps heavy and hurried. He was hurrying for me. My face broke out into a great stupid smile, and he opened the door before I could take it off, so that was how he found me, waiting at his door just like I'd come to the end of the rainbow.

'Hey,' he said, and smiled right back at me, no complications or it don't mean nothing, just a boy smiling because his girl came round.

I laughed with pleasure, any game I might have tried

too late now, and we just stood looking at each other, all the chemistry exploding round us like fireworks. It was like the Fourth of July. It was marching bands and girls with pom-poms. It was the weekend.

I looked down and found myself surprised that my feet were still in contact with the ground. They looked strangely normal, just standing there on the pavement. There was something about all this that demanded Judy Garland red and the yellow brick road. I had to stop myself looking round to see if I had brought Toto with me. They should warn you, really they should. I mean, they tell you the easy bits, about the stomach going and the head spinning, but no-one mentions the lunacy, the loss of any kind of reality. Why don't they ever tell you that part?

'Come in,' he said, stepping back and holding the door open.

'Thanks,' I said, welcoming my composure, which seemed to have returned, just in time.

I started up the stairs, collecting myself. I made it to his door, thinking I was going to be able to impose myself on the situation, when he made a rearguard action, putting his face in my neck when I wasn't looking. I felt everything flying away, all rhyme and reason, anything I'd ever known.

I put my hand out to the door frame to steady myself. A little reality snapped back. I felt a latent stirring anger at the effect he had on me, hardly even trying. Or maybe it was anger at myself, letting him have this effect. I straightened up, moved away from him, into the room, paused, just to make him wonder, smiled half a smile, stood my ground, and spoke.

'So,' I said, 'are you going to offer me a drink, or what?'

He didn't touch me again, after that. He went all decorous,

just like a good host should, acting as if we were at some diplomatic reception. I wouldn't have been surprised if he had asked me if I was in town on business or pleasure.

He gave me a drink, and changed the record. That was a knave's trick too, playing *Hey Joe* to a girl when she hasn't got all her wits about her, and then sitting a polite three feet away, lulling her into a false sense of security.

Lucky I could play that game too, or so I told myself, marshalling all my reserves, who at least seemed glad to be called out of retirement. I smiled and gave small light laughs, and when I felt like it I did a little trick with my cigarette which I had learnt from watching old Lauren Bacall films late night on cable in my downtown days.

That was all right, for a while. It got us out of the flat and to a place he knew, some backstreet Turkish dive, and we ate hummous and vine leaf things and meatballs, and avoided the dangerous subjects.

We talked about me for a bit. I didn't want to ask him too many questions. Maybe even then, in my murky subconscious, I didn't want to hear the answers, just in case Lil and the rest of the doubters were right after all. I don't know.

He asked me about my job. I told him, a little.

'It's work,' I said. 'I like it. I can do it. It suits me. I like having somewhere to go every day.'

He looked at me, some strange expression on his face.

'You don't want to take a flyer one time?' he said. 'See what happens?'

'No,' I said. I didn't. I knew that much, at least. 'I've been living like that my whole life,' I said. 'Moving. My father didn't like staying in one place. It's still novelty for me, staying still.'

'So, you're going to be a career woman?' he said. I couldn't tell if he was laughing at me, or not.

'Maybe,' I said. I hadn't thought that far in advance. I

was still getting used to where I was at. 'I just like having something that's mine, that belongs to me.'

'Nothing to do with Daddy?' he said, and now I think he was laughing. I wasn't going to allow that. I wasn't just another poor little Poppa's girl, trying to get out of the shadow of her big old Dad. No, sir. I belonged to myself. It was my life.

'It's not to do with that,' I said.

I had told him about my father being famous, the first night we had gone out. I had wanted to get it out of the way. People always asked, sooner or later.

'He's a writer,' I had said. 'He wins prizes for it.'

I hadn't told him that he was a stranger to me. I hadn't told him that we had never had a conversation in our lives that had lasted more than three minutes. I didn't tell him that my father made me feel as if I were an irrelevance. I had just sat there and waited for him to be impressed, because people always were, but he wasn't.

'I never heard of him,' he said. 'I don't read books.' I was surprised by that for a moment, and then I realised that I was delighted. It was so perfect, that Jack should be the only person in the western world who didn't know who my father was, and didn't care.

'Not just that,' I said now. I shook my head. It was complicated. There were complications enough, just now, without going into all that. 'I was never going to be another literary sensation,' I said. 'I don't have it, don't want it. I wanted to do something different, so people could see I wasn't competing. I'm not competing. I just want to be let alone.'

I stopped. I wasn't sure that I had thought these things to myself, not in so many words, and now I was telling him. Somehow that seemed far more intimate and frightening than letting him take my clothes off and see me naked. I laughed, trying to show him that it was all just talk.

'It's nothing,' I said.

Maybe I was trying to convince myself as much as him. There was danger here, and thin ice, and I wanted to skate away to another part of the pond. There might just have been the thought that he would understand, from what Willa had told me of his father, but it was too soon for that. It might always be too soon for that, I couldn't tell. All I knew then was that I wanted to change the subject, and that's allowed.

'Can we have that Turkish coffee with grounds in?' I said. 'Can we talk about the weather?'

I didn't mean anything by it, not really. It wasn't a trick or a snare. But all the same, I was throwing myself on his mercy. I was telling him that I needed him to help me out. I had been doing the nothing can touch me deal for the last hour, and now I was letting him know I was touchable after all, and that's enough to throw anyone off balance.

It was just that I hadn't been able to look him in the eye for some time, and now I did, and I wanted him to kiss me so bad I didn't know what to do. I had put the ball back in his court, and it was up to him to think what to do with it. I was telling him I was human, and that's not always easy to hear.

It took him back a little. I could see it in his eyes, even if he didn't know what it meant.

He got me coffee, and watched me while I drank it, and then even that was finished and the place was closing up. We split the bill. The waiter brought us our change.

Jack took my hand, and paid me back the Spanish coin I'd dealt him.

'I was,' he said, 'going to take you out, show you those places people don't know about.'

I didn't say anything. I didn't want him to see how frightened I was. I was frightened he would ask me, and frightened that he wouldn't, and I was most frightened by how much I wanted him to. And I was frightened because I knew the answer before he had even asked the question.

'But,' he said, 'I just want to take you home.'

There it was, right in the gut. It was one thing actually doing it, but asking, that was the cards really coming out on the table. Asking like that, in cold blood, that's offering your neck for the axe. Because whatever anyone says, because of the games we're all taught to play, because of the liberties that we're told we must take in the name of self-preservation, you can never be sure of the answer. He couldn't be sure, even now, even though I had come out with him on a Friday night, even though I had let him kiss me in his hall, even though I had let him take me home before. Nothing, these days, comes with guarantees.

So, if I had been brave earlier, he was being braver back. That was the way I looked at it, anyway. I could have told him I was tired, maybe another night. I could have gone out and got a cab and left him baffled. I could, and perhaps I should. But I didn't. I thought he had come near to honesty, and that's not something you found too often in that neighbourhood.

Besides, I wanted to go home with him. I could have said no, but I didn't want to.

I realised I hadn't said anything. He looked away, at the wall.

'Will you?' he said.

I looked away too, around the empty restaurant, the candles guttering on deserted tables, the remnants of the night waiting to be cleared away. I wasn't making him wait, I just didn't know how to say it. I shook my head and turned back to him, and he was watching me, and I forgot about nefarious, and Thunders, and thin ice.

'Yes,' I said.

15

I woke early the next morning, and I was smiling before I knew where I was or who I was. It was Saturday and I was in a strange man's bed and he was sleeping beside me.

I sat up and looked down at Jack. His face was white and shadowed, his eyes underlined with black circles. He looked frail, and there was something about that fragility that touched me as no robust rude health could have. I thought he looked beautiful.

I got out of bed, hoping not to wake him, but his hand reached out and caught mine.

'Don't go,' he said, his voice muffled against the pillow.

'I'm not,' I said. 'I'm just going to the bathroom.'

There were no clues in the bathroom, no cabinet I could look through for traces of other women, just toothpaste squeezed in the middle and a tin of Sure with the top off and an old Bic razor with the blade starting to rust. I looked at my face instead, and it looked back at me, straighter than it had any right to. I brushed my teeth and tidied my hair. I leant against the wall for a while, giving myself some time. The carousel was still swinging about me, muted now, but not slowing enough to let me off. After a time, when I could put it off no longer, I went back into the bedroom. I wasn't sure what I was going to say.

Jack was awake, lying on his back, watching the ceiling.

I got into the bed, and lay beside him. I realised I was holding my breath, and let it out in a sigh.

'I thought you'd broken for the border,' he said.

'Couldn't find a cab,' I said.

I could feel him smiling. There was silence for a while.

'So,' I said, breaking it. 'What are we going to do now? The crossword?'

'Three letters,' he said.

It was strange, in the daylight, which came pale and tentative through the curtains. All the times before had been in the dark. It made me feel shy, but he touched me so gentle and so slow, as if he wanted to, that I let the fear go behind me. I was used to performing, I was used to *doing* things, as if to say, look at me, see how modern and accomplished I am. I remembered times, with other men, when it had seemed like we were two gladiators in the ring, that erotic thrill in two young hard bodies clashing with each other, and that moment after, when you lie back, sweating and breathless and post-coital and all the things you know you should be, except it feels like something is missing and you don't know what it is. But it wasn't like that with Jack. I don't know why it was different, but it was. There was some kind of passivity in it, unresisting, something easy and deliberate. I felt it, deep inside, true and inexplicable at the same time. Perhaps that's why all those sex scenes in the blockbuster novels always seem so unreal, because when it is close and right, there is no way of explaining.

Much later, we got up. Jack lent me one of his shirts. I liked that. It was one of those badges of intimacy, small proprietorial proof. Look at me, I'm with the band.

I washed and put on some lipstick and pinned my hair up on my head. Jack went to make coffee. I was surprised, when I came out into the sitting room, to find it full of people.

'Oh,' I said, taken aback. This was not what I had expected. It seemed nakedly indecent to walk out into a crowd, washed and clean and wearing his shirt.

'Nancy,' said Jack, coming out of the kitchen. He gave me my coffee. 'This is Maurice, and Mariana, and you know Kid.'

I knew Kid. I wished I could have just gone in, all streetwise and swinging, slapped his hand and asked him what it was. I wished I could have said, 'Hey Kid, what's happening?' but I hadn't been in the area long enough, so I just said hello, and tried to drink my coffee which was too hot.

Jack seemed to find nothing curious in the situation, but sat down and lit up a cigarette. Kid had his stereo with him, old Calypso pumping out the rhythm, and was sitting very close to the television, which was showing a picture of goldfish swimming round and round, aimless.

'Nancy,' he said, without looking round. 'I'm down in the tube station at midnight.'

'Don't mind him,' said the man called Maurice. 'What he really wants to know is why the coloured girls go Doo, doo, doo-doo. All night bloody long.'

He was ageless old, anything from fifty to seventy, with a long mulatto face and a dark pressed suit, three pieces, and shined lace-up shoes. He held out his hand, formal with some light trace of irony, for me to shake.

'How do you do?' he said. He had a curious old-fashioned voice, like a thirties matinée idol.

'Fine,' I said, feeling inadequate.

I felt I should break out the Oscar Wilde, start talking about the carelessness of mislaying more than one wife, but I didn't know where to begin. I wondered who the coloured girls were, and why Kid wanted to know about them.

Mariana, who had cross slanting eyes and expensive clothes, looked as if her night had only just finished. She flapped a hand at me, speechless.

I sat down, next to Jack. It was worse than being taken home to meet Mother. I wondered if this was a statutory greeting committee, laid on each weekend. Perhaps I was one in a long line, perhaps a new girl wandered out of the bedroom every Saturday morning, to be vetted and measured and given marks out of ten. Perhaps I was the cabaret. Supper was too far away to sing for, and I couldn't remember the words anyway. I thought of inventing an urgent appointment, but it would be too transparent, dead giveaway of the shakiness of my ground. I didn't want to show I was intimidated.

'So,' said Maurice, who seemed to be in the middle of a story. 'The God squad, now short on cash, go down to that cheap press in Kensal Rise to get the new banner printed up, calling on their faith and sense of forgiveness to rise about the unseemly removal of the last. It can be done on the fly, much rejoicing and waving of tambourines, praise that Redeemer, but when they get to the great unveiling ceremony – up it goes, everyone looks expectantly heavenwards – dead silence. Our dear Richie had taken one too many blues before he set the press in motion, and the famous much-heralded poster, instead of proclaiming Blessed are the Peacemakers in letters ten feet high, actually says Blessed are the Pacemakers.'

He laughed a long wheezing laugh.

'I almost pissed myself,' he said.

'What happened to the Pacemakers?' said Jack.

'Richie still owes me fifty quid,' said Mariana.

'Some of us have a pot to piss in,' said Maurice.

It went on like that for a while. I didn't say anything. I had no bearings, nothing to ground me. There was nothing to tell me where I fitted in. I had slept with Jack and I was wearing his shirt, but I didn't know if that made us an item, if I could consider myself to be with him, his girl. I hardly knew him at all, and these people had the inside track.

I let them bicker and banter around me, having nothing to add. I was on the outside looking in, not knowing any of the moves. It made me angry. I wanted to make an excuse and leave, but I thought that it would seem petulant, like a child stamping its foot because no-one is paying it enough attention. So I sat it out, stiff and furious, trying to pretend I didn't care.

After a while, Maurice decided he was hungry. It seemed that he had some sway, an unspoken leadership. If he wanted to eat, everyone wanted to eat. So we went to eat.

We walked across the street to a place where they made goat stew and spiced chicken. I was weighted down with fear and fury, scuffing my feet along the pavement, gritting my teeth to stop myself shouting out. What about me, I wanted to say. What about me? Who are the fucking coloured girls anyway? But then Jack came up beside me and put his arm around me and kissed my cheek.

'I'm sorry about all this crowd,' he said. 'I didn't know I was going to have company.'

It was a rat thing to do, because he was telling me that he wasn't taking me for granted, and that's a sure way to any woman's heart. I so wanted to take my anger out on him, but he was smiling a slow smile at me, and his arm was warm about my shoulders, and I remembered earlier that morning and how sweet it had been, and I couldn't.

'It's OK,' I said.

'OK,' he said. 'What is that?'

'OK,' I said, and it was, all of a sudden, because I was with him and the others didn't matter. 'Just OK.'

*   *   *

We ate. Jack became very animated. I watched him, wondering where this new incarnation had come from. He talked fast, chopping his hands to make a point, biting out his words.

'So they asked Lou Reed, why did all the Velvets always wear sunglasses at gigs,' he said. 'And Lou thought for a minute and said, Because we literally couldn't stand the sight of our audience.'

I remembered now, about the coloured girls. It was a line from an old Lou Reed song. The one about Candy coming from the Island, in the back room she was everybody's darling; the one about all those trannies who used to hang out with Andy Warhol. It made me feel better that I remembered.

Maurice ate his way slowly through a plate of thick stew, chewing carefully, looking at Jack with quizzical indulgence. Mariana took a cup of coffee with a shot of rum, which seemed to revive her. She picked at her food and threw out thickly lugubrious remarks which didn't seem to have much to do with anything. Kid stared into space for a while. He seemed to miss the goldfish. He came to for a moment when two tremendous Rastas walked in – rising suddenly to his feet, slapping his hand on theirs, asking them how it was.

'You can get it if you really want,' he said earnestly, 'but you must try. Oh, the Israelites.'

'Mixing his songs again,' said Jack, shouting with unexpected laughter. I laughed too. It was funny. It was strange and not what I was used to and not what I had thought might happen, but perhaps it was all right after all.

Afterwards, we walked through the market. It was crowded, Saturday families out for the afternoon, tourists searching for local colour, local colour hanging out for them to see, girls showing their legs, New Age hippies hawking crystals, old men with caps and teary eyes, sharp-eyed boys with portable telephones hanging in groups outside the pubs, talking business. It smelt of fish and incense.

Mariana and Maurice strolled arm in arm, holding themselves very straight, as if they were promenading the seafront at Biarritz before the war. Jack and I walked behind, in close step, our shoulders touching, leaning into each other, as if we were on board ship in a mild swell. Kid followed at a distance, one arm held out in front of him, chattering at no-one.

'He thinks he has a dog,' said Jack. 'Did you ever want a dog?'

'No,' I said, truthfully. 'I didn't.'

We reached the flyover, the clusters of stalls selling old discs and musty tweed jackets and pointless pieces of china, and Jack took my hand and pulled me away.

'Come on,' he said. He started to run, pulling me with him, through the wandering crowd.

'Keep on running,' called Kid, seeing us go.

'What?' I said, 'What?' But I was laughing. I knew what.

'Faster,' said Jack.

We ran through the maze of back alleys that led to his place, quicker and quicker, laughing with ragged breath. I felt a fantastic delirium, hurling myself from a high cliff, watching myself fall. And we reached his door and he fumbled for his keys, and we ran up the stairs, and into his purple room, slamming the door, and he tore the telephone from its socket and pulled all the curtains and when he opened them again it was Sunday and I knew I was his girl.

16

Monday, I went to work just as if everything was usual and nothing to be remarked on. That was what people did, Mondays. Drag themselves from bed, wipe the sleep from their eyes, feed the cat, catch the bus.

Except it wasn't usual. Everything had changed. There was no cosy breakfast with Louey, no bitching over who got the third Danish, no comparing Saturday nights. It wasn't just us any more, and I didn't want to compare. I didn't want to talk about it with anyone, not even Louey, not yet. I didn't want to talk about it because it was all magic and new and mine. I didn't want to give any of it away.

I left Jack at seven. He had smiled without opening his eyes and reached for my hand and asked me not to go. He knew that I had to go, that I would, but I liked it that he asked.

'Don't go,' he said, his voice slow with sleep. 'Stay with me.'

Stay with me.

I went back to my flat, did all the morning things, bathing, dressing, putting up my hair. I moved slowly, dreamy, unlike myself. I could feel all the places where he had touched me, could still smell the air of sandalwood and patchouli that hung about him, could still hear his voice in my head. Stay with me.

Watching myself in the mirror, I was surprised that I looked the same. I had thought that my face would have changed. It felt different. But it looked back at me, just as it had on Friday, everything in the same place. It seemed as if it belonged to a stranger, someone I had met once, years ago, and only vaguely remembered. I felt like introducing myself.

I drove through the busy morning streets, the city quick again after the languor of the weekend. It looked new to me, and familiar at the same time, as if I had come back to it after a long stay abroad, when all the landmarks are still in the same place, but you know everything has moved on a little in your absence. It looked lovely.

I crossed the Fulham road, the traffic buckling as lorries double parked to deliver supplies into the bars and restaurants. Shopkeepers were throwing up shutters, hosing down the pavement, putting out crates of fruit and vegetables. Men in suits hurried by, folded copies of the paper under their arm; harassed mothers chivvied unwilling children to school; loafers wandered into the local French caff for their first coffee of the day. I watched them, wondered what they had been doing all weekend, wondering whether they were looking at me too, and wondering.

Down at the Embankment, the river was moving and shining in the sun, bridges stretching away into the distance. I parked the car and walked up the two flights to the office. I felt I should compose myself, have some snappy answer ready to deflect any awkward questions. I had some vague idea that I would walk in the door and find a welcoming committee with flowers and applause and twenty multiple choice questions. But perversely, it was just the same as any Monday, telephones ringing, the fax chattering, people wandering about trying to settle into another week, the usual small crowd round the coffee machine.

Louey, working at his computer, waved at me from his desk. Violet wasn't in yet, but she was always late on Mondays, coming up from her country life. I could never imagine her in the country, but she swore she had taken to it like a duck to water. 'Although, of course,' she always said, 'not too much like a duck, otherwise I should be shot and eaten for lunch.'

Bob had his statutory bumper pack of alka seltzer out and two tins of Coke, to show that he still knew how to party. I sometimes thought that he would bring these in on a Monday even if he had spent the weekend on bread and water, just to perpetuate the mystique.

I got myself some coffee, said hello good morning nice day the weekend was fine, and sat down at my desk. Bob came and sat himself down opposite, wincing a little, just to show that he'd had a really rough night of it.

'Nancy,' he said. 'Good weekend?'

He didn't wait for an answer. I was tempted to tell him that I'd spent the last two days in bed, just to show him that I still knew how to do it. I sometimes thought that he regarded me as a staid old single career woman, no time for dalliance. At his early age he was interested exclusively in peachy young things, all high-pitched laughter and wide open eyes and no questions asked. I wondered what he would say if I told him I had been having sex on the front line.

'Nance?' he said. 'Are you listening?'

'No,' I said. 'It's Monday. Start again.'

He gave me a resigned look.

'And me with three days of hangover, backed up,' he said.

'My heart,' I said, 'is bleeding.'

'Yeah, yeah,' he said. 'I can see it dripping all over your desk.'

It was just another day. I would do some work, chase up late pieces, start thinking about next month's section. Bob would tell me about the three girls he was juggling, complain about his work load, ask me to ask Louey for a rise. There would be gossip spread and rumours started, speculation about rival publications, discussion about new layouts, suggestions for new columns. There would be meetings and lunch breaks, panics about last minute changes, complaints about the coffee and the vagaries of the Xerox machine. This was what people did, Mondays.

I wondered what Jack would be doing. I had no idea what his day meant, and I didn't like to think about it too much. I thought Willa must be exaggerating. I had the media-stereotyped view of his line of work. There were no flash cars, no trained Dobermen, no shiny suits, no submachine guns. It must be something he did as a favour, for friends, a sideline, just for cash, until he found himself a proper job. It must be just a stage he was going through.

Plenty of people did worse things, like molesting young children and defrauding old ladies of their savings. I supposed that he had to make a living. I had to suppose something. For heaven's sake. There are women who fall in love with serial killers. Violet's husband thought that slaughtering innocent pheasants was a nice way to spend a Saturday. We can't all be perfect.

'What?' said Violet, appearing like a genie from a bottle. 'Go away, Bob.'

'I'm gone,' said Bob, who liked to think he knew about girl's stuff. 'I'm history. I'm off like a dirty shirt.'

'Really,' said Violet. 'I don't know how you ever get laid.'

'Beats me,' said Bob. 'I just do the job.'

He gave her a sunny smile. He liked Violet. He said she wasn't half bad, for an old broad.

'So,' said Violet, to me. 'Aren't you going to offer me a cigarette? Aren't you going to ask me how my weekend was?'

Knowing there was nowhere to run, I held out my packet. Violet was like a force of nature. You couldn't fight it.

'Have a cigarette,' I said. 'How was your weekend?'

'Pastoral,' said Violet dreamily. 'The horse chestnuts are out. The roses are coming on a treat. I have a new hat for doing the borders.'

'No pop pop?' I said.

'Nothing to murder this time of year,' said Violet. 'Very restful. Reg has got bad enough tinnitus as it is.'

Violet's husband was called Reginald, a perfectly respectable old feudal name, if you liked that kind of thing. There had been Reginalds in the family for years. She insisted on calling him Reg, which drove him mad. He said it made him sound like a garage mechanic. Violet said that was silly, since he knew nothing about cars.

I wondered about her husband. I had asked her once, how she liked being married. She had been distracted and evasive, just saying that it was something to do. I hadn't asked her again. I thought it was something she might explain to me, one day, when the time was right.

She put out her cigarette, her eyes wandering about the room with calculated vagueness. I waited.

'A little bird,' she said, suddenly looking me very straight in the eye, 'tells me that you were not at home all weekend. A retreat, I expect, to recharge your batteries. Or a trip to the seaside. Cromer is very pretty at this time of year.'

I sighed. 'I was having sex,' I said, thinking that honesty was the only policy. 'Actually.'

'Don't,' said Violet, as if she'd never heard of it. 'All weekend? I thought it was Friday night, your date.'

'Vi,' I said. She hadn't had such fun for weeks. 'It went on a bit, that's all.'

'That balloon man,' said Violet. 'Tell me all about it. Was it turgid and unmentionable? Was it earth-shattering and revelatory? Were unspeakable acts committed? Did he blow up the condoms and float them round the room?'

I laughed. I couldn't help it. Violet regarded me with interested level eyes.

'It was fine,' I said.

'Fine?' said Violet. '*Fine*? You have got it bad.'

There she went again, straight to the heart of the matter, taking all the right conclusions from what was left unsaid.

'How can you tell?' I said, curious. Sometimes I wanted to take notes so I could learn to be penetrating too.

'Dear heart,' said Violet. 'My dearest darling thing.'

She always talked like this when she came back from the country. People might say that imitation is the sincerest form of flattery, but for Violet it was the best defence. She could do perfect county, with a docile smile and tinkling laugh, and it left the sporting set flat-footed, since they never knew whether she was sending them up or not. I had once asked her where she learnt how, sure that there wasn't too much la di dahling on the lower west side. 'Nancy Mitford, of course,' she said, just as blithe and bonny as maybe. 'Do sharpen your wits and concentrate. See how one can't resist.'

'Fine,' she said now, 'is a nothing answer. Means you don't want to talk about it, even with little old me. So it must be serious.'

It felt strange, hearing someone else say it. I didn't know what it was. I didn't even want to think what it was. I wanted to feel helpless for a little longer, carried along by the tide. I didn't want to think about the future, about tomorrow, about next week. I just wanted to let it be. Whatever it was, I would find out soon enough.

'Maybe,' I said. 'If you say so.'

'Darling,' said Violet. 'You don't have to tell me twice. I shall go and flirt with Bob. Who knows, I might even be able to convince him of the point of older women.'

She got up, smiled at me without resentment. She was good like that. She might have seen a lot in her life, but she never pulled rank, did that sorrowful you'll find out soon enough number. She knew all about marks and overstepping them.

'Just remember,' she said, in one of her small moments of gravity, 'if you do want to talk, I'm on the telephone.'

I made some calls. I tried not to think about Jack. From time to time, I realised I was smiling, and stopped myself. But it was summer, after all, and the sun was shining. There wasn't a law against it.

Louey bought me a sandwich for lunch.

'To keep your strength up,' he said. I gave him a look, but he was smiling, bland and innocent. Shucks Ma, I don't mean nothing by it.

'Bitch,' I said. 'I'm sorry about breakfast.'

'Don't think of it,' he said. I knew he meant it. Easy come, easy go, that was Louey's philosophy. He had a great respect for the inevitable. On bad days, he liked to listen to Doris Day singing *Que Sera, Sera*, just to get things in perspective.

'I can make other arrangements,' he said, chewing on his bagel. Penitent, I took a napkin and wiped some cream cheese off his chin.

'Thanks,' he said. 'Besides, it doesn't do to get stuck in a rut. Quite soon we would have become like an old married couple, another cup of tea dear and long meaningless silences.'

'It's not that bad,' I said, but I knew what he meant. He was telling me that it was my life and none of his business and if I was happy he was happy and that I didn't have to explain anything to him, not one thing.

'You never know,' he said. 'Eat your pastrami.'

'Yes, dear,' I said.

That was all. Everything carried on around me, just like it did every day. The small shift in – what? – status, perception, something – had been acknowledged. Everyone had behaved with decorum, honour had been satisfied. Lines had been drawn, for people not to cross. I smiled some more, and got something done, and thought about Jack.

At three, he rang up and asked me what I was doing.

'Working,' I said. 'Of course.'

'I thought of you,' he said, 'today.'

I didn't know what to say. He made all the hard things sound so easy.

'That's nice,' I said.

It sounded lame and pointless. I thought he might tell me so, but he didn't.

'Do you remember Nice biscuits?' he said.

'No,' I said. I started to laugh. 'No, I don't.'

'They were disgusting,' he said.

17

The French have a saying that happiness has no story. Trying to think what happened in those first few weeks, there isn't much to tell. I was happy. I was with Jack. I liked that so much. I liked it that we went places together, in a pair. It gave me another of those small feelings of belonging somewhere, with someone, having a place to go. I liked it that he knew my voice on the telephone, that he would call and start a conversation without even saying hello, picking up where we had left off the last time. I liked it when he put his arm about me in the street, or kissed my cheek in front of people. I liked it that he asked me not to go every morning.

I got used to being surrounded by a crowd. Jack's flat, hard by the market, was a convenient place for people to drop by to catch up on any news there was, and the door was always open. Jack was a reliable source of information, since he had no office to go to and could spend his days with his eyes open. Any dramas acted out on the streets fell into his province, and he reported it all with a meticulous detail and deadpan observation, as if he wasn't much interested, merely performing a public service.

Privacy was impossible, there were too many people packed together, cheek by jowl, knowing too much. The wide windows so touted in estate agents' particulars provided front row of the stalls for all interested parties, and in those days, everyone was interested. There was some perverse theatrical instinct there that threw domestic disputes out of doors, led to fighting in the street and kissing in public. There was no need for jugglers or trained elephants, all human life was there, for everyone to see, all the strolling players acting out their small dramas, no tickets required.

There were so many faces then, I never knew their names, and no-one seemed to bother with introductions. Sometimes Jack had enough and threw everyone out, saying that we needed to be alone. I liked that, too.

But even though there was a crowd, it wasn't my crowd. There was something anonymous about it, that old thing of company being more intimate than just the two of you alone. In the first three weeks, I found myself avoiding my own people, Lil and Dexter and Willa and Davey, the ones who might have questions to ask. I hadn't seen them since that night in 21, when they had told me how wrong I was. I wasn't angry any more, because I was right and what did they know, but all the same, there was a reluctance in me to go back and hang out just like we used to before everything was different.

So I didn't call, and I didn't go to the usual places. Jack and I went out sometimes, but to different places, the kind of hidden backstreet places that he liked, where you didn't run into half the people you'd ever met in your entire life the minute you walked through the door.

Dex called me, in the end, one afternoon at work.

'Just checking in,' he said, in his straight way. 'I thought something must have happened since we didn't hear.'

'Oh, Dex,' I said. 'I'm sorry.'

'I didn't call for that,' he said, in reproof. 'I just wanted to know if you'd heard.'

'Oh, yes,' I said. 'I heard.'

'And how is it?' said Dex.

I thought for a moment, and wondered how it was.

'It's lovely,' I said.

'So you're happy,' he said, hope and caution battling in his voice.

'Yes,' I said. I was. That's what it was. 'It's strange,' I said.

'It's always strange,' said Dexter.

It is always strange, at the beginning. I sometimes think we should go back to the old days, when there was proper courtship, when people walked out together for weeks and weeks before anything happened. At least then you know something about each other, you have some solid ground to put your feet on. We're all so impatient now, we just want to get to the main action.

Some nights I lay in Jack's bed, watching him sleep, and I wondered who he was and what I was doing with him and how it was that I knew I loved him. I wondered what it was in him that moved me.

I wanted to tell him some of this, but I didn't know how. I didn't know what he wanted, because he never asked. I wanted him to need me, but I wasn't sure if he did. There was something in him, some transient shifting thing, that made me think that if I wasn't there any more he would just carry on as he had before, nothing any different. I wanted to make myself vital to him, but I didn't know how.

In those early days, I felt the strangeness of it very much. I felt that it was curious that I could sleep naked with him and I still didn't know whether he liked spinach or if he'd ever had braces on his teeth. Most people tell you that kind of stuff, sooner or later. Most people like talking about themselves. Jack didn't.

I tried to ask him one time. We had been in a pub round the corner from his flat, with that strange amorphous crowd he surrounded himself with, and we had left at eleven, and gone back to his place.

He shut the door and headed for the bedroom.

'Wait,' I said. It came out more abrupt than I had intended, and he stopped, and looked at me in surprise.

'What?' he said.

I felt foolish, now it came to it, but I couldn't stop now. I wanted to know something about him. He wasn't going to tell me, unless I asked.

'It's early,' I said. 'Maybe we could make some coffee, or talk, or something.'

Jack laughed.

'This is what women want,' he said. 'Isn't it?'

I almost got defensive. I almost asked him what he knew about women, when he said it in that general way, all the millions of women all over the wide world, and what they wanted. I wondered what he knew about that.

'Sometimes,' I said.

'So what then?' he said. 'Do you want me to play you some discs and tell you the story of my life?'

He made it sound stupid, the kind of thing that teenagers did on their first date.

'We could,' I said. 'It might be fun.'

'Oh, Nancy,' he said. There was something in his voice that I couldn't quite catch. 'You're so funny.'

'Oh, yes,' I said, going along with it. 'Yes, yes. Bleeding Abbot and Costello, that's me. I'm just a one girl Crazy Gang. Who needs the tube, when they've got me?'

He laughed again, but he did make me some coffee, and he put an old Charlie Parker record on the player, and he sat down next to me, and we listened to the strange shifting magic sounds that crackled out of the speakers. Jack sat beside me, watching me, waiting for me to get round to it. He could do that, just sit quiet until I said something.

I wanted to know so many things, I didn't know where to start. I felt it should count, what I asked him now, be something weighty and grave, something to reward his patient silence.

'What did you want to be when you were small?' I said, at last, because that was all I could think of.

He thought that was funny too, but I told him to shut up and tell me.

'Bigger,' he said. 'An astronaut, sometimes.'

I thought of him, small and cross, looking out of his bedroom window at the moon, and wanting to be up there, not having to worry about gravity any more.

'Like that old Bette Davis line,' I said. 'Don't let's ask for the moon, we have the stars.'

'You know every film, don't you?' he said. 'You know all the lines.'

I knew all the lines. Sometimes I thought that was all I did know, and where did it get me. You can talk the talk until you're blue in the face, but most of the time it doesn't mean so very much. Not when it's all other people's words in the first place.

'When I was younger,' I said, slowly, remembering, 'I thought that they did life much better in the films. I wanted to be in a film. I wanted to be Lauren Bacall. I wanted to meet men like Humphrey Bogart and ask them if they knew how to whistle.'

'How long ago was that?' he said. 'Yesterday?'

Later, when we did go to bed, and he had fallen into that instant sleep that he did so well, I lay awake, and realised that I hadn't learnt any more. Without me even noticing, he had changed the subject, steered it away from himself. We had talked, but it had been about my life, not his.

I had told him about always moving on, about some of the places I had seen. I had told him about my first memories, of the hill country down south from Naples, of the heat and the noise and the plumbing never working very well. There was a bent old lady called Mara who dressed all in black and smelt of garlic and almonds and took me for walks. While the water grumbled yellow and unwilling from the taps and my mother wandered through the house trying to wake the plumber from his siesta, Mara took me up the long dusty climb to church and lit a candle for her dead sister. God would provide, she told me, shrugging her old stooping shoulders. I didn't understand about God, but I knew I didn't mind not having to bathe every day.

I told him about Greece, which came after that, one of those stark lost islands with unforgiving scenery and bright white houses staring in the sun. I was old enough to go to school, and I went with four other children to the local priest, who had lived in Weston-super-Mare in his youth. Every afternoon, we sat in his dark shuttered room, watching the flies buzzing fatly against the walls as he read to us from Gibbon and showed us vulgar fractions. My mother brought in sophistication from distant cities, her friends from Paris and Rome, who flew in with piles of matched luggage and exclaimed in high fluting voices about the garden and the figured Turkish furniture, shipped in from Ephesus, and the quality of the light. They lay in the sun all day, drinking small glasses of sweet yellow wine and talking idly about getting up a four of bridge.

I told him about winters in Ireland, of the rain and the bitter wind, when we sat in a strange fantasy of a house hidden high up in the Wicklow hills with a steep shadowy mountain watching over us. There was a black lake with a thin crescent of white sand, and there was a legend about it in the village, that it had no bottom. Three people had drowned in that lake, and they never found the bodies. Drinkers came in from Dublin, poets and playwrights and men with Uillean pipes who played into the night, and even my father came out of his study to hear them.

I told him that I had come as a mistake, that a child wasn't one of the things that my parents had wanted, and that once I arrived they hadn't seemed to know what to do with me. I told him that my father often didn't appear to know who I was, or where I had come from. I made it sound funny, as if it were a joke. I didn't want him to feel sorry for me. I told him about all the things I'd done to try and shock them and how none of it had worked.

I told him all this, that night, and all he told me was that he had wanted to be an astronaut.

I didn't try again, after that. I thought I should just let it ride, that he would tell me things in his own time. I wondered how much people ever did know each other, anyway. I thought I should just get used to it that he was always surrounded by other people, that I couldn't have him all to myself, that I couldn't make it into my idea of the ideal picture book romance. I didn't want to spoil it by asking for too much. I thought maybe I shouldn't go asking for the moon, not while I had the stars.

18 ∫

One of the parts I found hardest to understand was his inner circle, the real stalwarts, Maurice, Mariana and Kid, there every day. They were the strangest trio: I couldn't guess at the bond which joined them to each other, or to Jack, but they were always together.

Kid wasn't so hard, he was sweet and easy to figure, an archetypal art school drop-out, fighting hard against his comfortable middle-class background, but I was wary of the other two. There was something mysterious and difficult about them. I felt as if they were judging me, and I couldn't guess what the verdict was. They made me uncomfortable, because I had no clue what they were thinking and they were unlike anyone I knew. I felt that we were all going through the niceties, putting up a polite front, circling round each other, just waiting for the balloon to go up. And then, one day, it did.

I had gone round to Jack's place, after work. It was still at that stage when we saw each other every night. At first, we had tried to make formal arrangements, to meet at places for dinner or a drink, but he was always late, and I got tired of waiting for him on my own, so in the end it became tacit that he left the key under the mat, and I went round to his place, and waited until he came. It was never long. Some nights he was there already, waiting for me. But this night he wasn't. There was just Mariana and Maurice.

'Hello,' I said.

I smiled at them, trying not to show how disconcerted I felt. I had never been alone with them, without Jack to shield me. I had no idea what I would say. I had been working hard, finishing up the August issue, and all I wanted was a glass of wine and a pizza and to fall into bed. I didn't want to have to be clever and defensive.

'Jack's not here,' said Mariana. She was wearing a tight leopard-skin dress and heavy eye make-up. She always dressed as if she were going to a night club, whatever time of day it was.

'Silly old Jack,' she said, laughing her tight cross laugh.

'It's all right,' I said. 'I don't mind waiting.'

'Always waiting, waiting,' said Mariana, making her voice sneering and dramatic. 'You should slap him. I would. I'd slap him. I'd say, Come on time or I'll slap you.'

'You wouldn't,' said Maurice.

'I don't mind,' I said again.

I didn't know what else to say. I didn't mind so very much. It was just one of Jack's idiosyncrasies. I didn't think it meant anything. It was just one of the things about him.

'Have I upset you?' said Mariana, peering at me with her blackened eyes. She seemed hopeful, as if she wanted a scene. I thought suddenly that I didn't like her at all. I wondered why Jack did, whether there was something between them that I didn't know.

'You don't have to worry about me,' she said, seeing it. 'I'm not in love with Jack. I have a husband.'

I was taken aback. It seemed so strange, that she was married. She didn't seem like the marrying kind.

'That's how she affords all these expensive frocks and furbelows,' said Maurice. 'From her nice rich husband.'

'Not nice,' said Mariana, fiercely. 'But rich. What else is the point?'

I still didn't say anything. I wanted to ask why she had said that about Jack. I wanted to ask where her husband was. I wanted to ask why she was telling me.

She watched me. Maurice was laughing his wheezing laugh.

'I'm in love with Maurice,' she said, suddenly. 'You see.'

I looked blankly back at her. I wasn't sure what I was supposed to see. I wasn't sure what I was supposed to say. They made me feel like that, as if I were out of my depth, with no idea if I would make it back to dry land.

'Oh,' I said.

Mariana stared at me again for a moment, narrowing her cross slanted eyes. Then she sat back, and gave a shout of laughter.

'She doesn't know,' she said to Maurice. 'She doesn't see.'

'See what?' I said stupidly.

'Maurice likes boys,' she said. She turned to him and dug her long nails into his arm, watching him, seeing if he would react.

'That's the whole point,' she said. 'Nice young boys, don't you?' she said. 'Nice Moroccan boys.'

I had had enough. I felt that this nasty little scene had gone on long enough. It wasn't frightening any more, it was just stupid. It was turning into the Hammer House of Horror. All we needed was for Vincent Price to turn up and we would have had a party. I didn't know what they were trying to do to me, but I was bored of just sitting there and letting them do it. I didn't know what all this was about. Everyone liked boys, these days.

'So?' I said. 'Do you want me to be shocked?'

Mariana looked startled. She dropped Maurice's arm and

lit a cigarette. Maurice looked at me for a minute, and I looked right back. Then he laughed.

'Serves you right, Mariana,' he said. 'She'll tell you all about it, if you let her,' he told me. 'We never hear the end of it, this great unrequited love.' He hit his breast with theatrical emphasis. He didn't seem at all disconcerted that this great unrequited love was for him.

'My dear,' he said. He seemed to be enjoying himself. 'All the drama, the pathos, the heartache.'

'You're a bitch, Maurice,' said Mariana. 'You're just a bitter bitchy old queen. You should get a life.'

'Hark at who's talking, twinkletoes,' he said. 'I might be a failed artist, but at least I failed magnificently.'

I knew about that, at least. Jack had told me about that. I knew that Maurice had spent years trying to be a poet, hanging out with Allen Ginsberg in San Francisco and Dylan Thomas in the Village, getting drunk and raising hell and badgering publishers to put him into print. After that, he had gone to Tangier to write a novel, but it was never finished. And then he came back to London, and gave up.

'No-one knows where his money comes from,' Jack said, when he told me this.

I thought he must have a dark secret. He looked like the kind who would, with his thin lined face, and his watchful eyes, and his curious measured Nöel Coward patois. He always wore a dark suit, cut narrow and perfectly pressed, and carried an umbrella although we hadn't seen rain for weeks. He looked to me as if his closet was rattling with skeletons, but Jack said I was being fanciful.

'You think everyone is like a character in a book,' he said.

'I don't,' I said. I thought that was nice, coming from him, the man who didn't read.

'Maurice just didn't turn out the way he planned,' he said.

I thought it was more than that. I thought there was something strange and sinister about Maurice. I did think he was like something out of a book, but it was a book I'd never read.

He sat there now, watching me. Mariana was still staring too, as if wondering what was going to happen next. I had a sudden sense that they were just doing all of this because real life wasn't enough for them, that they had to make up something more interesting.

'Maybe Maurice is the one who is in love with Jack,' I said.

There was a small silence. Waiting in it, I felt relieved, as if we'd taken the gloves off at last. I thought I could play this game too. I had always prided myself on being a quick study.

Mariana stared at me some more, her mouth open, as if this wasn't my line, but Maurice just laughed.

'No, no,' he said. 'If there's one thing us old fags know, it's forbidden fruit.' But he gave me a sidelong look as he spoke, as if to say, What do you know about it, maybe you should wonder.

'I'm bored,' said Mariana.

'You're always bored,' said Maurice. 'You've been bored for five years.'

Kid came in, with all his worldly belongings, which wasn't much.

'It's a party,' he said, happily impervious to atmosphere. He put his goldfish video on the TV, watched for a moment, just to check that they were all swimming merrily around, and turned on his stereo, which started playing Gregory Isaacs.

'I know,' said Kid seriously, 'it's a universal tribulation. I feel it and I know it.'

'What's with the bag?' said Mariana.

'Squat got shut down,' said Kid. 'Bloody fascist regime again. Bloody police state.'

Kid was always moving on. He said that good squats were getting hard to find. He blamed the government, but in a half-hearted way, as if it were something he had learnt by rote.

He sat down and started to skin up, frowning with concentration. He made enough money to keep him in grass by selling dodgy videos and pirate tapes in the market, and said he didn't care about much else. He regarded ganja as a magic herb. He said he didn't believe that Bob Marley could really be dead.

'We'll have a smoke then,' he said. 'Where's Jack?'

'Ask Nancy,' said Mariana, cruelly. 'We don't know.'

Kid lit up his spliff and sucked in the smoke and smiled at me.

'It seems so long ago,' he said, 'Nancy was alone, looking at the late late show through a semi-precious stone.'

Kid told me that, most times I saw him. It was from an old Leonard Cohen song. Kid said my parents must have been way cool, to name me after a song by Leonard Cohen.

I wasn't to tell him any different. I didn't want to tell him that my parents didn't even know who Leonard Cohen was. My father listened to Rimsky-Korsakov all day, or Wagner, if his work wasn't going well. When I was very young, I had once smashed his whole box set of *Tristan and Isolde* in a fit of rage, and he hadn't said anything, not one thing. He had just gone out and bought himself another set. He hadn't been angry. He hadn't shouted or yelled or slapped me. He just got himself another lot of records, and played them in his study, same as he always did. After that, I had given up trying to take him on. I had just given up.

*   *   *

Later, when Jack came back, and they all left, I told him what had happened. I don't know what I expected, but he laughed.

'You shouldn't listen to Mariana,' he said. 'She hates her husband.'

'Why does she stay married then?' I said. It wasn't my fault she hated her husband. She didn't have to make me jump through hoops because she had made a mistake.

'Money,' said Jack. I waited for a moment, for him to elaborate, even though I knew he wouldn't. He never did.

'Where is he, then?' I said. I don't know why I wanted to know. I felt there was something missing, some lost part that I hadn't been told about.

'Making money, I guess,' he said.

'It doesn't make any sense to me,' I said.

Jack looked at me, and then he said something which surprised me.

'You don't have to be her friend,' he said.

I wanted him to mean, all that matters is that you're with me, but I don't think he did mean that. I wanted him not to need them any more, now he had me, but he did need them. They were his friends, from the old days, the days before I was thought of. They knew things about him I was still guessing at.

'It's not that,' I said.

'You think everyone will be your friend, if you smile at them,' he said.

I wanted to tell him I didn't think that, but I couldn't, because I knew it was true. It made me angry.

'Did you fuck her?' I said.

'What?' he said.

It was his turn at being surprised. I didn't say things like that. I was all sweetness and light. I was the one who believed in fairy tales.

'When?' he said.

'Ever,' I said.

I looked at him. His face was still, no expression in it.

'No,' he said.

There was a pause.

'Is there,' he said flatly, 'anything else?'

'Did you fuck Maurice?' I said.

He laughed this time, and I knew then that it was all right.

'Maurice,' he said. 'No. I like girls.'

'Even at school?' I said. I knew about English public schools. Violet said her husband had been at it hammer and tongs with the captain of the first eleven.

Jack laughed again, and kissed me.

'Even at school,' he said. And he kissed me some more, and I let him, and we never mentioned it again.

It was so easy at first, just to take it all as it seemed, to look no further than the surface, not to ask too many questions. It was living in a fantasy. I was dimly aware of that, that all this had nothing to do with the real world, but I liked that, too. I liked it that we didn't do usual everyday things, like going to the supermarket or walking the dog or having people round for dinner. All that seemed so settled and middle-aged, the kind of thing you do when you've given up, too worn down by time and trouble to think of anything else. I didn't want routine or security, not yet. I didn't want a nine-to-five man, who wore suits and understood about the Ecu. I was young. It was the time for danger and illusion and everything coming up roses. I didn't want to sell out, not yet.

19

Soon after that, Lil called.

'Rumour has it,' she said, straight off, 'that we're fighting. It's not true, is it?'

'Of course not,' I said.

Lifted up on my new wave of happiness, I couldn't hold grudges. Besides, I was right and they were wrong. It was all fine. It wasn't perfect, but some of the time, it was close. And I was pleased to hear her. I hadn't realised that I had missed her.

'What nonsense people talk,' I said.

'That's what I said,' said Lil, having the tact not to sound relieved. 'Just what I said. Do you want to come and eat something? I have a chicken.'

'Please,' I said. 'We're still in family viewing time.'

'I forget,' said Lil. 'So, are you free?'

'Jack's got something,' I said. 'I'm not meeting him until eleven.'

'Something,' said Lil, darkly. 'I won't ask. Come round after work, then.'

'It's a date,' I said, pleased.

'Nancy,' said Bob. 'Could you get off the blower for one moment and talk to me?'

I smiled at him, serene and attentive.

'Bob,' I said. 'I'm all yours.'

*   *   *

It seemed funny going round to Lil's again, something I used to do in the past, before things were different. Everything was different now. I felt different, almost like another person. It's hard to explain. Someone had jammed a pair of rose-coloured spectacles on my nose, and suddenly everything was tinged with pink. I hadn't thought that I was lonely before, that the world had seemed a little drab, grey, unhopeful. Looking back, that was how it seemed now.

I had thought that I was good at being on my own, that I didn't need anyone, that I could be self-sufficient, because that was what the books said, and it was the nineties, and I was a modern woman, loaded with choices, no longer hemmed in by the antiquated social mores that had trapped our mothers into loveless marriages and thankless child-bearing. I still carried that illusion with me, a remnant of what had gone before, but the great release of joy I felt having Jack, having someone, not being alone any more, made me think that perhaps I wasn't such an island after all.

I didn't worry about it too much, it wasn't as if I let him pay the bills and explain world affairs to me, so that I didn't have to bother my pretty little head with men's stuff. It was just that there was someone there, a body beside mine at three in the morning, the dark night of the soul, someone who wanted me. Everyone needs to be needed, I told myself, as if it were all rational and logical. Everyone wants to be loved.

Lil opened her door, kissed me on both cheeks, and led me inside. Her place was as jumbled as ever, hardly room to move. We picked our way over to the kitchen through a small crowd of tropical plants.

'Exotic,' I said.

They were new. Lil had never gone in for growing things

much. She liked quoting that old Dotty Parker line – You can lead a horticulture, but you can't make her think. Things were changing all over.

'Now I have no love in my life,' she said, unusually candid, 'I'm developing green fingers. Orchids don't bugger off with other women, and they always respect you in the morning. You just water them every day and never have to ask if they had a good day at the office.'

'Sounds ideal,' I said. 'You'll get cats soon.'

'Don't put it past me,' said Lil.

She gave me her fierce smile and poured out the wine. She was in blue today, buttoned up to her neck, a kind of Maoist uniform, harking back to the days of the cultural revolution.

'Nice threads,' I said. 'Up the party.'

'Don't you think?' she said. She gave me a glass. 'It's nice to see you,' she said quickly, as if embarrassed by the admission. 'It's been too long.'

'It has,' I said.

It had been too long. The days had gone by so fast, but it seemed a hundred years ago since I had sat round that table in 21 and watched everyone disapprove of my choice.

'So,' said Lil.

She wandered round the kitchen, as if unsure where to start. She opened the oven and looked inside.

'Chicken's coming along,' she said.

'So they say,' I said, and then we looked at each other and laughed, because we had never had to make polite conversation before and we didn't know how.

'How is it?' said Lil, sitting down. 'Do you want to tell me? Are you in love?'

'I suppose,' I said. 'It's hard to tell.'

'Look at you,' said Lil, 'all lit up like a Christmas tree. It must be love.'

I felt a sudden shaft of fear, as if I were tempting

fate. I didn't want to look at it too hard, in case it wasn't everything I thought it was and hoped it might be. But I couldn't prevaricate with Lil. She was my friend. I owed her.

'I don't know,' I said again, slowly, trying to be truthful. 'We don't use that word.'

'I don't blame you,' said Lil. 'It scares the shit out of me.'

I laughed, with some strange sense of relief, glad that it wasn't just me.

'It is terrifying,' I said, suddenly wanting to talk about it, for the first time.

Lil watched me with that peculiar sympathy that women can give to each other, because they've been through it all too. She, of all people, knew about giving your heart away with no guarantee that you will ever get it back in one piece.

'I feel,' I said, trying to think how to explain, 'that I've found myself half way along a high wire and I can't see if there's a safety net.'

Lil let out a long sigh, as if she had been holding her breath, as if it was what she knew she was going to hear but had hoped not to.

'Yes,' she said. 'I remember.'

'Oh, Lil,' I said, giving in. 'I'm so in love I don't know what to do. I don't know if it's Christmas or Easter. Some days I can hardly remember what my name is.'

She laughed then, because it was absurd, because it is absurd, because we all should know better and we never do.

'I don't know,' she said. 'I don't understand what any of it means. I used to think I did, that there were rules, or signs, things you could be certain of. Before the Italian.'

There was a pause, a small beat of silence. I kept my face still, trying to look as if I wouldn't judge anything she said, just accept it, because there weren't any rules any more. That was what we were all starting to find out, that all the knowledge we had so carefully garnered over the years meant less than nothing, that we were having to start again, from the beginning, that before we had just been making it up as we went along, ignorant with how much we thought we knew.

'I thought that was real,' she said. 'All the signs were there, the things they tell you to look for. I felt safe. Isn't that ironic?'

She looked at me, almost pleading. She was explaining herself to me. She had never done that before.

'I wondered,' I said. 'I never did understand, not really. It seemed such a strange life for you.'

She laughed, bitter with disillusion.

'Of course it was,' she said. 'Me, the great iconoclast. I think I was just tired of being big and strong and brave, all by myself. It was suddenly a relief, allowing myself to be protected. It was like sinking into a feather bed. He even used to talk of marriage.'

She sighed, letting the unfamiliar word hang in the air.

'I didn't let myself think about it too much,' she said, as if it were something she should be ashamed of. 'But all that time, I think somewhere in the back of my mind was the idea that I would end up in some crumbling old barn of a house in the Veneto, children all around me, fat and contented on spaghetti and olive oil. I don't know. I think I thought that was what I wanted.'

'It's allowed,' I said. 'Husbands, babies. It's not against the law. People do it all the time.'

'I know,' said Lil. 'But it was such an illusion. What would have happened? All that security I thought he would give me, and I would have ended up shackled to the kitchen sink, exhausted with child-bearing, while he went off to the city and ran his mistresses. That's the terrible thing.'

I didn't know what to say. It was terrible. I hadn't yet reached the stage of worrying about betrayal and infidelity. I was still looking for clues, listening closely for dropped hints about next week, next month, the inferred promises that there was a future to mind about. Lil had gone beyond that, started that dangerous dream of rose-covered cottages and growing old together, leaving the turbulence of early passion behind, settling into the comfort of shared memories and domestic intimacy. To have all that broken, to be left alone to start again, that was hard. It was an awful lot of pieces to pick up.

'It wasn't your fault,' I said. 'How could you know?'

'I should have known,' said Lil, angrily. 'I bloody should. I should have seen it coming, a mile off. I didn't want to see. I wanted it to be like the story books, but I think I knew it wasn't, all along. I feel like a fool. I'm starting to think that men are all the same, that they know they can cheat and lie because we always believe them.'

'It's not that bad,' I said, hoping it wasn't. It couldn't be that bad. 'There must be some good ones, somewhere,' I said. 'And he was Italian, after all.'

'Oh, yes,' Lil said. She laughed then, as if she meant it. 'I should have taken notice of what they say about the Latins, so charming and so lovely and so unfaithful. I just thought this one would be different.'

There it was, the worst admission, the one that makes fools of us all. Either you think they will be different or, more dangerous still, you think you will be the one to make them different. It's that age-old illusion, the most fatal of all, the one about the love of a good woman.

Lil shook her head and lit a cigarette. She had never told me this much about herself before, and it seemed to have left her vulnerable, not sure what to say next. The terms of our friendship had shifted; we couldn't fall back into that easy staccato chat that had passed as intimacy before.

I didn't know what to say either. I felt sad for her lost dream, and flattered that she should choose to confide in me, and inadequate that I couldn't say anything to make it all better.

'I'm sorry,' I said. 'It's horrible for you.'

'It's all right,' she said, bravely. 'It will get all right. Sometimes I'm angry, I think how dare he treat me that way. I can deal with that. The bad bit is when I miss him. Not him, exactly, but what I thought he was. There were some good times.'

'Oh, Lil,' I said. 'I wish . . .'

I didn't know what I wished. I wished that all the things they'd told us when we were small could come true, that everyone could have a happy ending, just like they said we could.

'I know,' said Lil. 'I know.' She smiled at me, resigned and rueful. 'But if wishes were horses,' she said, 'we'd all be bloody Lady Godiva.'

We ate the chicken in our fingers, with tomatoes and bread. The fading evening light came in through Lil's big windows, falling over her bare floorboards and strange artefacts and potted plants. I felt as if I were far away from everything I knew, in some hidden safe place, where no-one could find me. I felt as if the world, which had been spinning fast enough to make me dizzy, had paused for a moment, to let me catch my breath.

We stayed away from the subject of Jack for a while, talking about other things, about Davey and Willa, who had got a part in a play and was down in Kennington, rehearsing, and Dexter, who had another girl, worse than the last, Lil said, another model, six foot tall and brain the size of a walnut.

'Poor Dex,' I said. 'Heartbreak dead ahead. I miss him.'

'He misses you,' said Lil. She said it straight, taking care not to make it sound pointed, but I knew what she meant.

'I know,' I said. 'Everything seems to have happened so fast. The days just go by, and there's Jack every night, and then it's three weeks.'

I stopped, not sure what I was trying to say. I wanted to say I was sorry, because they had all been good to me when I knew no-one and I had deserted them for a man, and I despised women who did that. It wasn't exactly that I wanted to keep Jack all to myself, in another part of my life. I thought perhaps I was afraid, frightened that they would all sit in judgement, disapproving of him.

Lil smiled, understanding.

'You don't have to hide away,' she said. 'We won't shoot him. Willa feels bad about the other night. She says it's none of her business and she'll quite understand if you never talk to her again.'

'Oh, no,' I said. 'Of course I will.'

'It's not that we don't approve, exactly,' said Lil, more careful still. 'Everyone likes Jack. It's just,' she said, slowly, looking at me straight on, 'it can sometimes be a bit dodgy, with those ones.'

'I know,' I said.

I did think I knew. I thought she meant that I should be careful because he didn't have a regular job and lived in a stolen apartment and had a fractured childhood. I thought that because I knew all this I was armed, going in with my eyes wide open, that it would be all right, that I could make it all right.

And I thought, after everything, because I was so happy it must be right. I thought this was what people meant when they spoke of the real thing, when it wasn't just sex or convenience or fear of being alone. I knew, they always said, I just knew. I thought I knew.

Lil sat smiling at me. 'How is he?' she said. 'Is he nice to you?'

'Oh, yes,' I said. 'He's lovely. He's a sweetheart.'

And we left it at that, because there wasn't anything else to say.

20

I left Lil before eleven. We parted with a kind of emphasised fondness, as if we had put our friendship through a small test and seen it come through stronger than before. It added to my growing idea that I was entering life at last, not moving on or passing through, but settling, with a real job and a real lover and a real friend. This, I thought, was what people did. It was like a moving picture about modern urban life. It was everything I thought I wanted.

I drove round to Jack's place, happy and proud with the illusion that I was learning another of life's lessons. Nothing in my childhood had prepared me for other people, there had never been time, and certainly no example. My mother treated people as if they were characters in a drawing room comedy, two-dimensional, simple extremes – they were brutes or bores, angels or wits. They didn't even have names. Everyone was called Darling.

And my father, who understood complexity better than he might have wished, had no communion with it. He watched only, an observer on the sidelines, judging and refining. So I, having stopped long enough to see how much ground I had to make up, felt each stride as a victory, like passing a test I hadn't studied for.

*   *   *

Jack wasn't back. I knocked politely, waited, but the flat was quiet and empty. He had given me a key, the week before. There had been no great ceremony about it, no declaration that what was his was mine. We had been out, eating lunch, on a Saturday, with Kid and Mariana and Maurice. I was contented, eating Jack's pizza, listening to Maurice and Mariana bickering, watching Kid watch them with his unblinking incurious eyes. Jack had looked at his watch and said he had to go.

'Perhaps I'll go home,' I said.

I was careful never to ask questions like when will you be back or will I see you later. I wanted to be with him every moment, but I had more pride than to let him see that. I wanted to pretend, to him and myself, that I could take it or leave it. That was what all the books said. Play hard to get, demand nothing, retain mystery. Blah blah.

'Don't,' said Jack. 'I'll only be an hour.'

He took a key off his ring. He had a great jangling bunch of keys, hung off a long copper chain. I sometimes wondered what they were all for, he had only his front door and a car, but I knew better than to ask.

He gave me the key. 'Later,' he said. He kissed me straight on the mouth, waved at the others, put ten pounds on the table for his share, and left. I didn't watch him go. I didn't make a scene. I just put the key in my pocket, very matter-of-fact, and finished my coffee. I felt as if I'd just been given a diamond solitaire and draped in orange blossom, but I didn't say that.

Maurice shot me one of his sly looks, sidelong and benign. He was in a good mood today, avuncular, expansive. Times like this I liked him, felt as if he were fond of me in an old-fashioned old mannish kind of way. Something had changed since that strange scene in Jack's flat. It was as if something had been decided, something unspoken, a truce. I didn't feel frightened any more, always at a loss.

They weren't going to be my friends. They belonged to Jack, and it was a part that had nothing to do with me.

But there were still days, with Maurice, when he could be difficult and uncommunicative, picking up on rash statements, pretending to misunderstand. Jack was used to it and told him to stop being crabbed and crusty, but I found it disconcerting. He could still make me feel stupid and jejune, that everything I said was worthless and wasteful, and I would shut up, mutinous, and dream of clever put-downs which I knew I would never use. But today he was all smiles and benevolent wheezes, all but patting my hand.

'He's very sunny, these days,' he said, humming a little. 'Our Jack. Very sprightly.'

I laughed. Sprightly was not Jack at all, but Maurice liked to use unlikely adjectives for his subjects, it was one of his favourite parlour games, along with mixing up genders.

'She's a pretty little piece,' he would say, of a bovine cabinet minister in his Savile Row suit. 'Watch her twitch her little behind at the cross benches.'

It was old school Evelyn Waugh, Lottie Crump in her parlour – here's what's his name, knew him since before he was born, and there's the King of Ruritania, bless him. I sometimes wondered if Maurice had read Vile Bodies one too many times or whether he had arrived like that, improbably placed in the wrong era and the wrong neighbourhood.

'The sunshine of my life,' said Kid generally. He liked to agree with people. He said it brought him good karma.

'Transformed by love,' said Mariana, with a meaning look at Maurice.

I didn't say anything. Kid said it for me, quoting from an old song by the Shangri La's.

'When I say I'm in love,' he said, seriously, 'you'd better believe I'm in love, L – U – V.'

'You must be good for him, Nancy,' said Maurice. 'Comforting our boy. It's nice to see him looking happy.'

I ducked my head, pleased. It was as if I had royal approval. But I never knew with Maurice, so I just said that we all do our best, and someone changed the subject.

Afterwards, I carried it with me like a talisman, that remark. I made Jack happy. I had his key. Let the doubters take that one and run with it.

I thought of it now, as I let myself into the flat. It was another of my clues, the signs I hoarded to keep me safe. I turned on the lights, feeling proprietorial, pleased that here I was, alone in his place, treating it like home, knowing where everything was. I made some coffee, stole a cigarette from the packet on the table. Then I sat down, not sure what to do next. I was restless, lifted up with the anticipation I still felt whenever I was to meet him. I looked at my watch a bit, watching the second hand work its way slowly round. He had said eleven, I was sure. It was half past. That was all right. He was always late. He would be here soon.

I wandered about the room for a while, looking out of the window, down into the streets, where cars were passing and people walking and doors opening and closing. I had a sudden urge to snoop, to look for diaries or letters or photographs. I knew so little of his past. I wondered whether I was jealous or not, of the other women, all those ones I didn't know about. People said that you should never be afraid of the past, only the future, but there is always the lurking fear of comparisons, of being held up and found wanting by those who have come before.

I shook my head crossly. I couldn't start rifling through his drawers, not now. I looked through his record collection instead, and put on an old Small Faces album. Any record with a name like *Ogden's Nut Gone Flake* had to be worth something.

Around midnight, I started to grow angry, suspecting I had been stood up, thinking at least he could have called, instead of leaving me here to wait. The record was finished, the needle lisping sadly in the groove.

At half past twelve, I grew fearful, convinced he was with someone else, that my version of events was twisted and mistaken, that he wasn't lovely at all, but another of those lying cheating men, the ones that Lil had spoken of, who take advantage of our hopeful credulity.

By one, I was terrified, knowing he was dead, in a car crash or a house fire. I looked at the telephone, wondering if I could call the police or the hospital or the morgue. I knew I couldn't.

At one-thirty I was dejected, disappointed, foolish and beaten. Even if he came now, my pride told me that he must not find me waiting for him, full of fear and resentment. That was not part of the deal. Except there wasn't a deal, it was all tacit, and between the lines, and me putting my feet carefully on the ground with each step, for fear of missing the mark.

I drove back, trying to chase the treacherous demon thoughts from my head, the ones that said everyone was right and I was wrong and this was what came of it and I had only myself to blame. I stopped the car, surprised to find I was outside Louey's door.

I didn't want to run for help, to find a shoulder to cry over. I didn't want anyone to say they had told me so. But then Louey hadn't told me anything, he had just let it ride, because that was the way he did things.

I rang the bell, tentative, ready to turn and go, ready for him to be out, or asleep. But the door opened at once, as if he had been waiting for me. He didn't say anything, just took me in and sat me on the sofa, turned off the television which was flickering with some old late-night black and white film, reminiscent of the days when boy met girl and everything was happy ever after.

'I'm sorry,' I said.

'It's all right,' said Louey. 'I was just watching the tube. Couldn't sleep.'

I didn't know he suffered insomnia. I always thought Louey could do anything. I thought perhaps I should stop making so many assumptions and start asking some more questions.

I started to cry. Louey held my hand and gave me a handkerchief. I sat there and cried into it and despised myself.

After a while, I stopped. Louey still didn't say anything. He just sat, close to me, comforting me by his presence. He knew that there was nothing he could do to make it all better, to make it all go away. How did he get to be so wise?

'I feel like a fool,' I said at last, my voice very small.

'You don't have to,' he said. 'Not with me.'

He got up to find some cigarettes. He gave me one.

'Do you want some tea?' he said.

I shook my head. I didn't want tea. I wanted everything to be different.

'I got stood up,' I said, trying to make a joke. 'Isn't it stupid?'

'Do you want to tell me?' he said.

'I don't know what I want,' I said. 'I don't know anything. I thought I was being so grown up.' I stopped. It sounded such a stupid expression, childish.

'I mean,' I said, trying to start again, trying to explain. I wanted him to know, because he would understand, but I didn't know how to say it. 'I thought it was all real, you know, life. That I had this affair, someone there, for me.

Everyone was saying, oh, he's no good, he's no good for you, but I thought they didn't know what I did, that they were jealous, something, I don't know. It was so lovely, at first. It has been lovely.'

I looked at Louey, wanting him to answer all my questions, wanting him to tell me that I was getting it all out of proportion, that it didn't mean anything.

I knew I couldn't make excuses for Jack, but I hoped he would. He didn't. He knew better than that. It was one of the things that he knew and I didn't. He just sat, watching me, listening. I rubbed my eyes. I felt tired and old.

'I went round, after seeing Lil,' I said. 'It was nice, we had a good time. I hadn't seen her for a while.'

I looked up at Louey. I hadn't seen him for a while either, except at work. We hadn't done any of the things we used to do. We hadn't had Friday nights, just us, or the weekends that we used to spend, just sitting. I had deserted everyone. I had put all my bloody eggs in one fragile basket. I had a sudden terrible sure feeling that the handle had broken, and they were all smashed. I waited for a moment, wondering if Louey was going to tell me what I had done, but he didn't.

'I was supposed to meet him at eleven,' I said. 'He's always late. He has this thing about time. He's no good with time. I waited in the flat, thinking it was just that, it was just that he was late, that he's always late, but he didn't come. He just didn't come. I had all these terrible thoughts, that he was with someone else, or he was dead, or something.'

The something was the really hard part, the part I could hardly admit even to myself, that maybe he had been arrested, that even now he was being read his rights, asked if he would like a solicitor present. I couldn't tell Louey that.

'I mean,' I said, trying to be reasonable, 'I know it's stupid of me. He never promised me a rose garden.'

He hadn't. I hadn't asked him. But I had hoped that there might be one, after all. That it would be a surprise, that it would just turn out to be perfect anyway. I thought I had been treading so carefully, but I had tripped up, and I didn't know what to do about it.

Louey put his arm around my shoulders.

'You're allowed to cry,' he said. 'It's normal. I would be hurt, too.'

'What do I do?' I said.

Willa would have told me to shoot him, but Louey knew better than that.

'I should tell him,' said Louey, eminent with reason. 'Tell him that you were hurt and you didn't like it, and ask him not to do it again.'

'I can't,' I said, frightened.

I knew I should, but I couldn't. I couldn't let him see that I was so far in, that I minded so much, that I wasn't the free spirit that I had pretended.

'All right,' said Louey. 'What do you want to do?'

I wanted to scream and shout and throw things. But I knew what I would do. I would pretend I didn't care. I would tell him that I had waited half an hour and then got bored and gone home. I would say, all light and careless, And what happened to *you*? as if I hadn't given it a minute's thought, as if I had more important things to think about. I would make him feel it was his loss, not mine.

'I'll let it go,' I said. 'It's not such a big deal.'

I looked up at Louey, apologetic, because I had acted like it was a very big deal, I had come to him in the middle of the night and asked for comfort. And now he had helped me put the pieces back together and I was saying it was nothing.

'It's too soon to start making waves,' I said. 'It's early days. I'm not sure how much boat I've got to rock.'

'Whatever,' said Louey, philosophical as always. 'You know him.'

I wished I did. This was the side I had heard about, that they had all warned me about. I hadn't seen it until now, it had come as a shock. But I could ride it out. I had done it before.

'I'm sorry,' I said. I got up. 'I'm sorry I disturbed your film.'

'It wasn't very good,' said Louey. He kissed me on the forehead. 'Sometimes,' he said, 'things can seem better in the morning.'

'Yes,' I said. 'They can.' They could, I knew they could. Everybody said so.

'Goodnight,' I said, turning to go.

'Sleep well,' Louey said.

I did feel better in the morning. I got up and told myself that it was just one night, that it didn't mean so much, that it was dangerous to read anything into it. I told myself that love wasn't just a walk in the park, that I should have to learn to take the rough with the smooth, that it wasn't Snow White. I told myself to grow up and be a big girl.

Jack called in the afternoon. I kept myself busy all morning. I had pride. I was going to keep away from the telephone if it killed me. I thought about other things and remembered how good I was at my job. I grew businesslike and got the new section ready and told Bob maybe I would talk to Louey about a rise after all.

'Nice to have you back,' said Bob. 'Your mind has been wandering lately. If I didn't know better, I'd say you were in love.'

He laughed, as if he couldn't imagine anything less likely.

'Really,' I said. 'What a thought.'

Violet, who seemed subdued today, her mind on something else, didn't ask me anything. Louey didn't say much either. He just asked me how I was, like he did every day, no extra emphasis, letting me know that I could tell him if I wanted and leave it if I didn't. I said I was fine. I gave a small rueful smile, as if the night before had been some kind of aberration, best forgotten.

So when the telephone went, I really was thinking about something else, and I was almost surprised to hear Jack's voice.

'What happened to you?' he said. 'I called last night.'

'I forgot to put the machine on,' I said, in a careless voice. I wanted to say, You *bastard*, how dare you turn it back on me. How *dare* you?

'I called twice,' he said, making it sound suspicious and mean and underhand, as if I had been out sleeping with mobsters.

'I went to see a friend,' I said, thinking it wasn't at all a bad thing if he did think that. Let him think. Let him wonder what friend meant. Let him wonder about me for once. Let him think about the secrets I might have.

'I came round to your place,' I said.

I wanted to say, I came round, like you said, like we planned, like we did every night. I wanted to say, You *fuck*, couldn't you have waited a while longer before making it not perfect any more. It wasn't that I loved him less, it was that I could see what he could do to me, with his carelessness, and I knew I had to be careful now where I had been carefree before.

'I couldn't be bothered,' I said, 'to wait.'

Couldn't be bothered. It was heroic. It was a lie. It was the first lie I had told him, and it made me sad, as if I had lost something and I wasn't sure if I would be able to find it again.

'I got held up,' he said, still in that suspicious tone of voice.

'Mm,' I said, not much interested, as if I had twenty-seven other things to worry about, as if where he had been, who had held him up, were way down the bottom of the list.

Bob came over, waving a sheaf of paper at me.

'Hold on,' I told Jack. I put my hand over the mouthpiece. 'What?' I said to Bob.

'Can you look at this?' he said. 'It needs cutting. Vi says it won't fit with the layout you wanted. I've marked the places.'

'I'll check it,' I said, businesslike and in control, mistress of my destiny and the August issue.

'Hello,' I said to Jack. 'What were you saying?'

'Nothing,' he said. There was a hard sullen note in his voice that I hadn't heard before.

'Don't want to interrupt your heavy schedule,' he said.

'It's that time of the week,' I said.

There was a pause.

'Do you want to do something later?' he said, unwilling.

'I can't tonight,' I said.

I pushed my nails into my palm. It hurt. It was the first time I'd told him no. I hated it. I wanted to say Yes yes yes, tonight and every night. But I didn't.

'I've got to work late,' I said. 'I've got a couple of openings to go to.' It was true. There were new places opening up and I had to go and check them out and write about them and tell people where they were, because that was my job.

'Maybe tomorrow,' I said, relenting a little. 'Things will have calmed down by then. I could come round about nine.'

I wanted to say, Will you be there. I wanted to ask if I would have to sit, all over again, in that strange darkened apartment, wondering horrible futile haunting thoughts about where he might be and what he might be doing.

'Yeah,' he said. 'All right.'

'See you then, then,' I said, and disconnected.

21

So the game started. Sometimes, when I was in it, I would look back on those early weeks and remember how simple everything had seemed and wonder how it all got so complicated. I had a vague idea, but there were so many reasons it was hard to separate them. I thought it was survival, that I was protecting myself, because if I gave everything away too easy I might just be left with nothing.

I thought it was wisdom too, because every agony aunt ever invented talked about keeping a little mystery, not handing yourself over on a plate, take me, I'm yours. I remembered what Willa had said, about holding yourself back, making it worth a fight. I thought she was right, after all. I thought I was really growing up, turning into a woman at last. I thought I was taking control of my life, putting myself in the driving seat. I thought I had more aces up my sleeve than I knew what to do with.

The part I couldn't admit, the part I'm not even sure I knew was there, was the real small scared part. All these games were just to cover up the great helpless love I had for him. I thought if I could play clever enough, if I could win gold medals for my sleight of hand, then I could make him love me as much as I loved him. I thought it was up to me. If I wanted it to be perfect, I would have to do it.

I thought if I gave enough, if I put in enough effort, the roses might just make an appearance after all.

From the outside, it wasn't such a great dramatic change. It was just that I went back to my life, the side I'd neglected, the part I'd deserted without a backward glance. At the start, it had just been Jack – every night, every weekend. There had been a kind of sweetness to it, even an innocence, as if I could forget everything else. I had forgotten everything else, as if I were eighteen again, when you could still do that kind of thing.

There were many reasons why I couldn't do that sort of thing now. It wasn't just that warning shot across my bows, that sudden shock when he hadn't come that night. It wasn't so much the fact that he hadn't come. I could have forgiven him that; I did forgive him that. It was all the fears that came crowding in, while I waited.

And apart from anything else, you can't just throw up your entire life for the sake of a man. No-one did that any more. We weren't living in a novel by Jane Austen. We were living in modern times.

I concentrated again on my work. I didn't leave my desk every night at six, whether I'd finished or not. Some nights I worked late. Some nights I went with Bob to the new exhibitions and clubs and restaurants, instead of letting him go by himself. Some nights I couldn't see Jack, because I needed my sleep and I had to get in to the office early. He didn't like that very much.

'What is this with your job?' he said.

'It's my work,' I said. 'It's important to me.'

He hated it when I talked like that. He seemed uncomfortable that I had a regular job and a regular salary and a regular boss. I thought it was because of what he did. So many times, I almost asked him. But I didn't. It was still too early for that. There were still things I didn't want to hear.

I went back to my people, too. I went back to 21 and the Corner, and Willa and Davey and Dexter and Jimmy and Ned, and Lil. I apologised for being a bitch, and said that everything was fine with Jack (it was always fine, just peachy, don't you know), but that I had missed them and I wasn't going to disappear again.

So when he called, often I had to say I was sorry, but I was busy, I had things to do. I did have things to do. Life was going on around me. Things were breaking out all over. Willa was opening in her play, for one thing. I went with Lil and Dexter and Davey, and Jimmy and Ned hired a minibus and brought along a whole load of punters. I didn't take Jack. Theatre was another thing he didn't do, along with reading.

It was a carnival, that night. It was hot, and England had just won another match in the World Cup, and the streets were filled with people celebrating. Complete strangers smiled at each other and rhapsodised about the scoreline, and all the cars were hooting in celebration as they drove past, passengers hanging out of the windows, shouting and cheering.

'Hot dog,' I said. 'It's a party.'

'Too right,' said Dex. 'It's a game of two halves. It's in the back of the net where it counts.'

We fought our way through the ecstatic crowd which filled the pub into a small back room. Pub theatre was a new thing to me. It seemed so strange to walk through the bar room philosophers, the fog of cigarette smoke, the noise of the fruit machines, to find one still dark room where the aspiring came out and did their Tennessee Williams and Arthur Miller. I liked it.

Dexter bought us pints of Guinness, because the Irish

had been doing well at the football as well, and he said he had to stay true to his heritage, and we settled in and waited.

It was a new play, by a young writer, and it was sad and funny and angry and raw around the edges. It was exactly right for its setting, and it was exactly right for Willa.

I was moved, as I watched her, not just because she was good, and she was good, real stand up knock down good, and not just because the piece was sad, but because I suddenly realised why it was worth it, all the failed auditions, all the disappointments, all the dashed hopes. And for all that, here she was, as good as she was, still in a humble room south of the river. I thought she should have her name in lights all the way along Shaftesbury Avenue.

At the end, we clapped very hard, and they had to take four curtain calls. Willa looked tired and surprised, as if she had forgotten about the audience and was startled to see all these people making such a noise. Davey held onto my hand very hard, tears pouring down his face. I did think the English were strange sometimes. Dave was so reserved, usually.

Afterwards, Jimmy and Ned kissed Willa eight times each and drove their busload off to a new one-night club that had just started in Vauxhall, so the rest of us took our heroine off to celebrate in a funny little Greek place that Dex knew where you could get kebabs and kleftikos until three in the morning.

It was midnight when we arrived, but it was still full. There was a tall beautiful man on the door who seemed to know Dex from way back. They slapped each other on the arm for a minute, and then we were taken to a table hidden in the back and they brought us champagne on the house and we drank toasts and told Willa how clever and talented she was and she laughed and looked pleased and shy, which was not something I'd ever seen her do before.

Davey kept his arm round her all night, like a proud father, and it was two o'clock before we finally left.

Dexter put me in a taxi, because I was going in the opposite direction from the rest of them.

'You haven't forgotten about lunch tomorrow?' he said.

'Of course not,' I said.

Dex had asked me to go home to his parents for lunch, a few days before. We were drinking coffee round the Corner and he said, out of the blue, 'You should come and meet my mum, Nancy.'

I was surprised. I knew Dex went to see his family often – Lil and Willa, who considered themselves above that kind of thing, teased him about being a home boy, but I hadn't thought about it much more than that.

'That would be nice,' I said.

'She's always asking about you,' said Dex.

'She is?' I said. I felt flattered, that Dex had told her, that there was something to ask about.

'Yeah,' he said. 'Come on Sunday. I'm going to our house for lunch.'

'That would be dandy,' I said. I leaned over and kissed his cheek. 'Does this mean I'm in?' I said. 'Getting the go-ahead from the folks?' But I was touched, all the same. I wanted to tell him, but I didn't want to sound like a sap, so we changed the subject.

It was so odd, going home with Dexter to see his folks. It was strange to me because it was such a normal thing to do. That's what normal people did, Sunday lunch with the family. Except I didn't know people like that. Jack was never going to take me home to meet his parents. I wasn't sure if he even knew where they were.

I was pleased to be going with Dex, for all that. It seemed the kind of thing you did when you lived in a city, belonged in it, knew your way around.

He picked me up at noon, and we drove across the river and down through the common at Clapham, where people were doing Sunday things like football and walking the dog. The sun was out, and everyone looked pleased because it was the weekend.

'My family,' said Dex. 'There are a lot of them. I thought I should tell you.'

'Will I be terrified?' I said. 'And there I was, thinking it was just you and your old mum.'

Dex laughed.

'You'll like my old mum,' he said.

'So who else will be there?' I said.

'My dad, of course,' said Dex. 'He doesn't talk much. And my sister Oona, with her two boys, and my little brother Joe, who's still at school and wants to be a footballer, and that's it.'

'That'll be doing,' I said. 'To be going on with.'

Of course the last laugh was right on me, good and proper. We crossed Balham High Street and drove down past all those neat red brick terraces that they have down there, and when we got to Dex's house, and I was admiring the window boxes, the door opened and there was Dexter's mother. I'd imagined she would be a dear little old thing, grey hair in a bun, flowered apron on, baking all day. When people talk about their old mum, I imagine a sweet rosy-cheeked Mrs Pepperpot, making cups of tea with plenty of sugar.

'This is my mum,' said Dex. 'Mum, this is Nancy.'

We shook hands and she said, 'Call me Aileen,' and I was taken in and introduced to the family, Oona the sister, and Joe the brother, and Bobby and Liam, the two little boys, and Gordon, Dex's dad, who was the spit image of his son, sandy hair and freckles and quiet eyes, and I smiled and said 'How do you do,' and tried not to let my mouth fall open in amazement.

Dexter's mother didn't look anything like a pepperpot. She was a good inch taller than me, and she was a beauty. She had hair as black as a raven's wing, and bright blue eyes, and bones that people would kill for. Once I got over the shock, I just wanted to laugh quite a lot.

But then, for all that, she was like a mum, too. Dex gave her a bunch of flowers, and she smiled and ruffled his hair, and said, 'Oh, Dexter,' and all the others chorused, 'You shouldn't have,' and laughed, as if it were an old joke.

'Have you been eating your greens?' said Oona.

'You haven't been going out without a vest now, have you?' said Joey.

Aileen tut-tutted at them.

'Would you just stop it?' she said. 'I wouldn't be his mother if I didn't worry.'

'Come on, Mum,' said Joey. 'He's such a big boy now.'

'But Joe,' said Oona. 'Mum can remember when he was just the littlest bittiest thing that she could sit on her knee.'

Dex looked at me and shrugged and rolled his eyes, as if to say, What can I do? and Aileen told everyone to stop teasing, in front of his friend, and what were they thinking of, embarrassing him like that.

'Don't mind me,' I said. I was enjoing myself. This was a whole other side of Dex, something I hadn't guessed at. I had never seen him blush before.

We ate. There was beef and Yorkshire pudding and roast potatoes and parsnips and brussels sprouts and green cabbage and horseradish sauce and sponge pudding and custard and fruit. Everyone ate and ate and talked and talked, all at the same time.

This, I thought, this is what families do. This was my dream idea of what families were like, eating together and teasing and bantering and knowing things about each other. They teased Joey about his football mania, and Oona about her husband having a flash new job and a smart new car and what a grand lady she was becoming, and Dex about being a rock star and how soon he would be driving around in stretched limousines and having a fan club.

'You won't go forgetting your old mum, now, will you?' said Oona.

'You wouldn't do such a thing as to forget your old mum, when you're all famous?' said Joey. 'Will you buy her a nice house and a washing machine when you make a million?'

'Now then,' said Aileen. 'Let him be. He would never forget his old mum.'

'He's such a good boy, isn't he?' said Oona. 'Even if he does still forget to brush his hair.'

Joey started to giggle helplessly.

'When he's up on stage at Wembley stadium, and all the girls screaming for him and throwing their knickers, and him in his leather trousers, and there will be mum, chasing him round the mike with a hairbrush, trying to get that hair tidy,' he said.

'Very funny,' said Dex. 'You should go into stand-up, with a routine like that.'

'No thanks,' said Joey. 'Another Georgie Best, that's me.'

After lunch, Dexter's dad sat himself down in a corner with the paper.

'Not much reading,' Dex said to me. 'He'll be asleep in five minutes.'

Aileen chivvied everyone to help clear, and Joey grumbled and griped and told Dex he was just sucking up by washing the dishes. I dried, and Aileen told me I was a good girl, and that the last girl Dex had brought home had just sat around painting her nails. I supposed this was Arianna, the model with the walnut brain.

'Mum,' said Dexter reproachfully. 'She's the beat of my heart.'

'It's all very well,' said Aileen, 'but she was a Lady Muck all the same, picking at her food the way she did, and looking as if she had a bad smell under her nose. Not like Nancy,' she said, smiling at me.

Dex went red again, to the tips of his ears.

'Don't start, Mum,' he said. 'Nancy's just my friend.'

Later, Dex and Joey and the little boys went out in the garden to play football, and I sat inside with Oona and Aileen, smoking and drinking coffee. Aileen's mind seemed to be running on Dexter's poor choice in lady friends and she spoke of it again.

'I don't know where he finds these girls,' she said. 'I expect I could get used to them looking like little sticks, and all that make-up and high heels, but they don't treat him well at all, from what he tells me.'

'They don't,' I said. 'We all tell him. We all think he could do better.'

'He'll grow out of it,' said Oona placidly. 'They'll come and go, like they are, and he'll get bored. Blinded by beauty, he is, just now. He'll open up his eyes.'

'I hope so,' said Aileen.

'Of course he will,' said Oona. 'Remember, Mum, when he was little, he always went through fads, always a craze on some new thing, and it never lasted.'

They asked me about myself, after that, and I told them some. I told them about my father being a writer, and how we had never stayed anywhere for long, and about coming to London and my new job and how I met Dexter.

I said, shyly, because I didn't want to sound sad and corny, that it was nice for me coming here, to see a family, and Aileen patted my hand and said everyone should have their family, and Oona said it was nice but they could drive you mad sometimes, and then we laughed and talked of other things.

Afterwards, Oona went out to round up her boys and get ready to go, and Aileen and I stood watching them outside in the garden.

'So, it's just friends, with you and Dexter,' she said.

I knew it was, but there was a part of me, all that day, that had been wondering why I didn't settle for all this, that it would be so perfect, to have Dexter, lovely as he was, and to be able to come home for lunch every Sunday.

But it was fanciful, it was what Dex had said that night on his roof, about the world never being as perfect as we wanted. In that house, small as it was, it seemed that there was something near as perfect as we dreamed, but then perhaps that was an illusion as well. I was just an outsider, after all, watching other people have what I didn't, and that's always alluring. And besides, out in the world, I had Jack. Out there, Jack was what I wanted.

'Just friends,' I said. 'He's a very good friend, Dexter.' I felt I should explain. I didn't want her to think that her lovely boy whom she had raised so well wasn't good enough for me.

'I have a boyfriend, you see,' I said.

I have a boyfriend, you see. I'm wild and crazy in love with someone else.

'That's nice,' said Aileen. 'To be in love. Is he a good man?'

I almost laughed. I didn't know if he was a good man. I didn't know what kind of man he was. I had hope, was all.

'I think so,' I said.

*　　*　　*

'So,' said Dex, as we drove back. 'Now you know.'

I wondered suddenly if it had been a test, to see whether after my cosmopolitan childhood with my famous father I might just have turned my nose up at Sunday roast with all the trimmings.

'Now I know,' I said. Then I laughed and let him off the hook.

'Dex,' I said. 'It was the best day I can remember. It was the best lunch I've had in my life. I think your family are the nicest people I've ever met.'

He smiled happily and shot a red light.

'I knew you'd like my old mum,' he said.

Dexter dropped me off on the corner of my street, and I kissed him goodbye and said I hoped he'd ask me again and why didn't he tell me that his mum looked like Ava Gardner. He liked that. He was proud of her, I could see. He tried to hide it, but he couldn't. I think he knew it was a bit of a cliché, loving your mother, when most people heaped their parents with contempt. I thought it was like a gale of fresh air. Besides, if I had a mother like that, I'd tell everyone.

'See you in the week,' he said. 'Jimmy and Ned's on Thursday.'

'I'll be there,' I said. 'Thanks for the feed.'

I walked down my road. It was looking pretty in the afternoon sun. There was so much green in London. It still gave me a shock, after the hard urban streets of New York. I liked it that almost everywhere you went there were great big trees growing out of the pavement, and so many of the houses had windowboxes and hanging baskets. I thought maybe I should get a windowbox of my very own and plant pink geraniums.

Jack was sitting on my stoop, which gave me a turn. He looked very white and thin in the sunshine.

'Hello,' I said.

'It seems so long ago,' he said, 'Nancy was alone, looking at the late late show through a semi-precious stone.'

'You've been listening to Kid again,' I said. 'I thought no-one took any notice of what he said.'

'Are you going to ask me in?' he said.

I asked him in. He had never been to my place before, I don't know why. I always went to him. It wasn't as if we discussed it, but then we never discussed anything.

'Nice,' he said.

I looked round my empty white room. It did look nice. The sun came in through the high windows. It looked wide and new and clean.

'Have you read all these books?' he said.

'Some,' I said.

Books were all I had added, since I first arrived. It was one of the things I had done, in the early weeks in London, when I didn't know anyone much. I liked going down to the market in Farringdon Road and the book fairs in the Great Russell Hotel, finding old copies of Yeats for 50p.

'Not your father's daughter for nothing,' said Jack.

'It's just books,' I said. I felt defensive, I didn't know why; as if I had been caught out in something, as if I had to explain myself.

'Just books,' he said.

His voice trailed off into the afternoon. He walked along the bookshelves, his steps sounding against the wooden floor, until he reached the window, and he stood, with his back to me, looking out into the street. I watched him. His hair was dirty, lying lank over his collar, and his shoulders drooped a little, his arms hanging long and loose at his side.

I felt that familiar tugging in my stomach, a sudden knocking rush of love. I wanted to walk over and put my arms round his neck and lean myself against him and feel him close to me. I didn't want to hold anything back any more. I wanted to tell him that he was my sun and my moon and that my day was a drabber sadder place without him. But I couldn't. I was too scared. I was scared because there were still so many parts of him I didn't know, that I could only guess at. I left all the moves to him, following only when he set the lead, knowing then that I could offer him some small part of myself.

I made some coffee, and we sat on the sofa and drank it. He didn't say much. I heard myself chattering and chattering, filling the silence, glossing over the cracks with talk. I wished I could just sit, sometimes, and be quiet, like he could. That was another of the things I didn't dare do. I was afraid that once the silence started it might just stretch and stretch into infinity, and then there would be nothing.

He let the talk wash over him, sitting in the curious mood he was wearing that day, withdrawn and quiet. I wondered what had brought him to my door, why he had come all this way just to sit in my room and not say anything.

'Where have you been?' he said, eventually.

'With Dex,' I said. 'I went down to Balham to have lunch with his mum.'

He didn't ask why. I told him about it, a little. I wanted him to be jealous, that Dex had taken me home to meet the family, but he wasn't. Or if he was, he wasn't telling.

I felt a kind of sadness, as we sat there, talking about nothing, everything lying unsaid between us. Perhaps it was because I had spent the day with people who laid everything out in the open, people who didn't have to search for hidden meanings or mysterious subtext. I knew I didn't really want all that, I didn't want to be settled just now, with everything clear and nothing left to guess at. But in that sunny Sunday afternoon, I looked at Jack, at his pale closed face, and I wanted to be able to say just what I wanted, without having to fear that I might be giving too much away.

I wanted to ask him why he looked so sad, and I wanted to ask if I could do something to take it away. I wanted to ask if he missed his mother, if he wished his father was someone he could talk to. I wanted to ask if he sometimes got lonely, if he ever wondered what it might be like to have brothers and sisters and a home he could go to, for lunch.

Later, he asked me one of the unexpected questions that he sometimes came out with. He did that. I would be talking about something, telling him something, and he would just turn to me and ask something altogether unrelated.

He did it now. I was talking about Dex and his model and how it would all end in tears, and he turned round and said, 'Do you ever wonder if you got the wrong life?'

I didn't know what he meant. So many times, I didn't know what he meant. So much of what went on behind those translucent eyes was just a mystery to me.

'It sounds like the kind of thing I say,' I said, suddenly realising that it was, that it didn't sound like him at all.

'So?' he said.

I shook my head. 'Go on then,' I said, wondering if he would. Sometimes he just stopped, left half a remark hanging in the air, as if he had got bored with it.

'When you're born, and they're handing out the lives,' he said, just as if this was some piece of accepted dogma, that someone gave you your life and then you had to do your best with it. I wasn't sure if he meant the Gods or the Fates, or even if he believed in anything or nothing, but I didn't want to show the great dark spaces of my ignorance, so I nodded back at him, as if I knew what he meant.

'Well,' he said. 'What if they mixed it up, and you got the wrong one? What if there is someone out there, living your life?'

I looked at him. I wanted to cry. So many of his questions were the kind that there is no answer to.

'I don't know,' I said.

22 $\int$

The summer carried on. England got knocked out of the World Cup, just like Louey said they would, and we were sad for two days after. Jimmy and Ned started a new club for Thursday nights, and everyone went, and said how hot and crowded it was, which meant it was a huge success.

Dexter got ditched by his girl, which didn't surprise anyone, least of all him, and he said that he was giving up women for the rest of the year, and we pretended to believe him.

The Summer of Love issue came out, with my Notting Hill section in. I hadn't used Jack for it, after all that. It seemed somehow indecent and incestuous to ask, now I was with him, and he didn't refer to it, so I just got on with my global village idea without him. I did a food page about all the different places to eat, where you could get food from five continents; and a club section, about how you could find music from all nations and all eras; and I put in two nice little contrasting pieces, one from a seventy-year-old woman who had lived in the area her whole life and could remember Rackman and the race riots, and the other from a West Indian percussionist Dex knew who had just moved to St Luke's Road after years south of the river. I got Willa to do a paragraph on local argot, which she said was a real joke, coming from her; and, to keep Louey happy, I found a sceptical old man of letters who wrote me a nicely cynical piece about gentrification and middle-class delusion, and, all in all, I thought the whole thing was a grand success.

Maurice read it and said that I lived in cloud cuckoo land, which I thought was charming, coming from him, the thwarted poet, but Jack laughed and told me not to pay him any mind.

As July passed and August arrived and it got hotter and hotter, I felt some growing sense of sureness, and I started to believe that the balance I was looking for so hard was coming to rest. I didn't allow myself to give in to it, at first, although I wanted to. I still told Jack there were nights I was busy, I had people to see, plans which did not include him, but one night towards the end of August he said something which made me think perhaps I was right, after all.

It was late one Saturday afternoon, and we were walking back through the market after lunch. Jack was in a good mood. I had spent two nights in a row with him, and we had gone out and had fun. There was a party mood in his manor because it was approaching the carnival, and people were out on the streets building floats and erecting sound systems and putting up bunting. I had never been to a carnival before.

'It's just up your street,' Jack said.

I wondered how it was that he seemed so sure of all the things he knew about me when I knew so little of him. I wanted to ask him what it was about me that told him I would like the carnival, but I didn't. He was right, anyway.

'Why don't you come for the weekend?' he said.

I looked at him. We never made plans in advance. If I saw him at the weekend, it was one day at a time.

'The weekend?' I said, carefully, but he was smiling and

easy that day, and he just took my hand and kissed me on the cheek, and said,

'We'll have a party.'

We'll have a party. We'll have a bloody party. It was the carnival, and we were going to spend it together and have a party.

'Well,' I said. 'I'd like that.'

'Whoah,' said Lil. 'Hot potatoes.'

She was feeling better. She had a new commission and she was working hard and she was giving men a rest for a while because she said that it was all too tiring and she didn't fancy anyone anyway and she was reading a lot of feminist literature and said it was high time she went through a radical stage because the backlash was on in earnest and someone had to fight it. I agreed with every single thing she said and tried not to feel like a traitor to the cause because there was Jack.

I had told her something of the grand plan, because I thought it was right and fitting and I wanted to be honest with her. I had told her about being unavailable and letting him see that he couldn't take me for granted and that I wasn't just going to drop into his hand like an old apple which can't cling to the tree any more.

She listened to it all with touching attention, as if hearing the theory of relativity for the first time, and nodded her head and said well done, quite right. I wasn't sure if she did think it was well done, but she seemed in earnest.

'Just watch yourself,' she said now. 'Just be careful. But then,' she said, still sorrowing for her own lack of foresight, 'who am I to tell you anything? I didn't exactly win first prize, did I, in the prudence department?'

'Learning experience,' I said. 'And look how much you've learnt. It was Fate, testing you. And he wasn't right for you anyway.'

I thought enough time had gone by for me to say this, and the more I thought of him, the more suave and greasy and duplicitous he seemed. Revolting old lecher, I thought, with his horrible diplomatic arrogance and out-dated libido. Hadn't he heard of New Man? Lil was worth more than that.

'Who wasn't right?' said Willa, walking in with Davey, as usual, attached to one hip. She sat down, drank some of my coffee, and blinked her eyes at us. 'Is it lunch?' she said. 'Who wasn't right?'

'The Italian,' I said.

Willa twisted up her face in disgust.

'Please,' she said. 'Sleazoid scumbag. Pass the smelling salts. Put a paper bag over my head. Does anyone know the Heimlich manoeuvre?'

'I do,' said Davey seriously.

'Oh, Dave,' said Willa, coming to. 'I don't know what I'd do without you.'

I wondered what would happen if Davey met a girl and fell in love and got married and had children and he and Willa couldn't be one person any more. Perhaps they would just wake up one day and realise that they were more than friends after all, like an old country and western song I'd heard once.

'We don't have to dwell on it,' said Lil. 'We all make mistakes. Can we just put it down to foolish youth?'

'I had a foolish youth once,' said Willa. 'But he didn't last.'

'She's being funny today,' said Davey. 'It's all this work she's been doing.'

'No need to get on your high horse,' said Willa. 'Just because you've sold your book in Rumania.'

Davey, who lived more hand to mouth than any of us, was always staving off his visit to the bread line by selling his first novel in unlikely places like Poland and Uruguay.

Willa, when she was in the mood, got angry that dross paid and talent didn't, but inconsistency being a life choice with her, spent other times trying to persuade him to sell out and write a mini-series with a part for her in it. Davey said he didn't know enough about sex or shopping. Willa said she could tell him everything he needed to know.

'Anyway,' said Lil. 'You don't have to worry, it won't happen again. I've decided to learn from my mistakes.'

'Isn't she sophisticated?' said Willa, in admiration. 'This is what you can do in the nineties. Are we eating? What's Nancy looking so pleased about?'

I tried to straighten my face. I was the rebirth of the cool, after all.

'Jack asked me to stay with him, for carnival,' I said, as if it were nothing, as if it happened every day, as if we were an old-established couple who did things like that.

Willa knew better. She knew all about the dodgy ones. She kept quiet about it now, she had told Lil that she was in no position to preach and if I chose to go out on this particular limb she would just hold my hand and hang about to pick up the pieces. That's what friends were for, she said. She said that she should never have introduced me to Jack in the first place, because he was far too dangerous to resist.

She also said, charitable as she was, that I might be able to succeed where she failed.

'Maybe Nancy's got something I haven't,' she said. 'Maybe it will be all right for her.'

She had a nice store of humility, learnt the hard way, from months of rejection and failed auditions. She understood something about not being able to be all things to all men. So now she followed my progress with interest, no detail too small to be neglected. She had been impressed by the game I had been playing, saying that she had never had that much self-control. She said it was always very well carrying on about hard to get, which she did, but she had never learnt how to do it herself.

'I'm such an old slapper,' she said, 'I always go to bed with them on the first date, however much I swear I won't. It's all bleeding talk with me, all mouth and trousers.'

'To stay?' she said now, her eyes wide open, just to show that she understood the gravity of the situation. 'For the whole weekend? He asked you five whole days in advance?'

'That's what he said,' I said.

Say what you liked about Willa, she gave you the goods every time. She never pretended that every one wasn't a coconut. She said once that she had tried to be cynical and world-weary, in her youth, when she thought it might come in useful, but it had never really washed.

'I tried to be So What,' she told me once, 'but really I'm just *What*? You can't fight science.'

'Is this good?' said Davey, who was still trying to understand about this kind of thing. He was very good on the big human themes, he wrote with what one reviewer had called an elegiac sweep, but he always said that he had much to learn when it came to the small things. He said that was why he liked spending time with Willa. Willa said he was a sexist fink, but Davey said she just didn't know how to take a compliment.

'It's good,' said Lil. Now she had admitted all her folly and broken out the Marilyn French she had taken on some unspoken position as elder stateswoman, new with hard-learned wisdom. 'She's been ignoring him, you see.'

Davey took his spectacles off and breathed on them, something he did when he needed a minute. I could see the mighty tumblers of his brain ticking over as he struggled to get to grips with sexual logic. We watched him. It was never any point rushing Davey. He went back to the days of steam travel.

'No,' he said. 'Can I have it again?'

'From the top?' said Willa, sitting up very straight in her chair, sensing that she might have to tell a story.

'No,' said Lil, who had work to do. She didn't have two hours. 'A synopsis, please.'

'You can, Nancy, if you want,' said Willa, generous.

'You do it better,' I said, which was true. Besides, I liked hearing what I was doing from other people. It made things clear in my mind, or as clear as they were going to get.

'Well,' said Willa, 'are you taking notes, Dave? Nancy has chosen one of those difficult ones, maybe it's her destiny, we don't know, but no family car and drip dry shirts. Complicated, see?'

Davey nodded, used by now to her fractured use of the English language. For himself, he had never split an infinitive in his life.

'So,' said Willa, 'being an innocent abroad, she read too much A.A. Milne in her early years, I don't know, she rushes in where any self-respecting angel would take it on the lam, only to find that the shining armour was rusting and the steed not so white as the books had told her.'

'Happens to the best of us,' said Lil, as if she knew, which she did.

'You can say,' said Willa. 'But, making it all up as she goes along, she switches tactics, sharp as a whisker, and suddenly isn't home. Busy, you see, other things. Nothing personal, but there are different life forms. Our hero wakes up and finds that his princess isn't running round every time he wants his back rubbing, opens his eyes, and thinks maybe she'll just skip off as easy as she came, which gives him a nasty shock, because he's kind of used to her by now, so he starts behaving like a human being.' She looked round the table, checking her audience. 'I think that's everything,' she said.

'Very good,' said Lil. 'A dramatic monologue in under five minutes, you're coming along.'

'Live and learn,' said Willa. 'We all got to start somewhere.'

'So,' said Davey, thinking it over. 'You got what you wanted.'

I smiled.

'Yes,' I said. 'I got what I wanted.'

'Carnival,' said Violet, with a nostalgic sigh. Her eyes went all misty and far away, as if she were remembering something, something she used to know.

There was something with Violet lately, she had lost that sharp edge that usually gleamed so bright on her. She came in, did her work, didn't say much about anything, and went home again. I hadn't given it much thought, having my mind so occupied by matters of national importance, like whether I was going to return Jack's calls or not, and there was something strange about Violet anyway, some kind of mystery which made me shy to ask questions. She was the one who asked questions, it was her job.

'I remember carnival,' she said.

I looked at her closely. This really wasn't her at all.

'Is everything all right?' I said, hesitant. I didn't want anything not to be all right, not with her. Violet was my touchstone, knowing everything. She was my icon. I didn't want her to have feet of clay.

'Everything is fine,' she said. She fixed a smile on her face, looking at me squarely. 'There are days,' she said carefully, 'when I get nostalgic for my past. You know how it is. The days when I was young and single and I did carnival. Dancing in the streets and staying up for the whole forty-eight hours.'

That was one of the times I wanted to ask her more about her marriage, but I didn't.

'You don't go any more?' I said.

She shook her head. 'Oh no,' she said. 'Not any more. Can you imagine Reg at carnival, in his plus fours?'

I couldn't, but then I couldn't imagine Reg at all. Any time Violet spoke of him, he sounded unreal, like some kind of strange out-dated cartoon character. Sometimes I wondered if he existed at all, if she just hadn't made him up for our amusement.

'That's nice,' said Louey. 'For you.'

We were eating at his place. He had cooked me spaghetti and clams with tomato salad, and tiramisu for afters. He liked to cook.

'I think so,' I said, trying to sound as if it were nothing. But then I remembered it was Louey I was talking to, and I smiled all over my face.

'It's bloody fantastic,' I said. 'We never made a plan before.'

'Moving on up,' said Louey. 'You'll be talking china patterns soon.'

'Not I,' I said, in reproof. 'We don't want to put the cart before the horse.'

'Do you ever think about it?' he said, seriously, taking me by surprise.

'The rest of my life?' I said.

'Yes,' he said, as if it were a perfectly regular thing to think about, quite permissible, nothing strange.

I shook my head. There was some small forbidden part of me which occasionally indulged in fantasy, which wondered what it would be like, in ten or twenty years time, with me and Jack. There were nights when I couldn't sleep, and I imagined us sitting together, at forty or fifty. I imagined how we would look back and laugh at these early days – that there would be a time when I could tell him all the things which I now kept hidden. I sometimes wondered what our children would look like. But I couldn't tell Louey that. I could hardly tell myself that, so how could I tell him?

'Give me a break,' I said, giving him my best ironic look. 'Please. We don't even talk about tomorrow.' And then I turned it back on him, because I didn't want to talk about it any more, in case I gave myself away. 'Do you?' I said.

He looked thoughtful, for a moment. 'Sometimes,' he said. I was surprised by that, too. I had always thought he really did take each day as it came.

'Really?' I said. 'Wife and children? The whole nine yards?'

'Sometimes,' he said, 'I wonder what it would be like.' He paused, and then he really took me back. 'I almost did it, once, when I was younger,' he said.

'Louey,' I said, staring at him. 'You did? All this time and you never told me. What happened?'

'Cold feet,' he said.

'Hers or yours?'

'Mine.' He took out a cigarette and lit it slowly. 'I was twenty-six and I suddenly thought about the rest of my life, and how long it was, and I couldn't promise her that. Not really promise, you know. So I said maybe we could wait a while, and she took it the wrong way, and that was that. Goodnight, sweetheart.'

'And what happened to her?' I said. I was curious. It seemed so strange, that things could have been so different.

'Oh,' he said. 'She's in America. She went to New York and married a management consultant. They send me a card at Christmas.'

I laughed and took his hand.

'Serves her right,' I said.

I wanted to ask him if he regretted it, if he thought of her, wondered if he'd made the wrong decision. I wanted to ask if that was why he was still by himself, if he still felt that the rest of his life was too long to promise to anyone. But I didn't. I thought I'd asked him enough for the time being, and that we would have so many more nights like this one, and he could tell me then. So instead, I asked him if he would make me some coffee, and we talked about other things, because there were plenty of other things we could talk about.

23 ∫

Looking back on that carnival weekend, I don't think I've ever been so happy in my life. It was everything I could have expected, and then some.

I didn't see Jack on Friday, because Jimmy and Ned were having a party, and I had promised them I would go. I persuaded Louey to break his rule about parties, and took him as my date, and everyone was there, Lil and Dex and Willa and Davey, and we drank and danced and Bob Marley sang and the party grew and shifted and spilled out onto the street and everyone was in a good mood and strangers walked arm in arm and it seemed to me that the world really was one great big melting pot, just like they used to sing about in the seventies.

Saturday morning, I arrived at Jack's place with my overnight bag, and tried not to look too pleased with myself as I put my toothbrush next to his in the bathroom and my shoes in his wardrobe.

We passed the day walking round watching everyone setting up, the excitement and anticipation building, the sun shining and everyone laughing, and in the evening we went to the pub with Kid and Maurice and Mariana, and even Maurice seemed infected with the goodwill in the air, and forgot to be difficult, and sang a little song

that had been a hit for Jack Buchanan in the thirties until
Mariana told him to shut up.

And then, at last, there was the carnival itself. I had heard
of it, and seen pictures, but nothing prepared me for it,
for the sheer scale of it, the great numbers of people on
the street. It seemed to me as if everyone in the whole
wide metropolis had come to Notting Hill for those two
days, every single city dweller had come out to hear the
music and watch the processions and eat the food and
see the people, that the usual invisible barrier that they
wore round themselves had been let down, the normal
set expression that served to separate them from the herd
and keep their privacy had been put away for the weekend,
because the sun was shining and it was a party.

On every street the crowds moved and swayed, on
every balcony people danced and waved – everywhere
you looked there was colour and movement and sound.
The insistent beat of dub and ragga and calypso and
reggae and house and soca and ska reached out over
the streets, lifting them from their daily staid pace into a
frantic open-air dance hall. The shrill note of the whistles
that were sold on every corner rushed through the heavy
drum beat of the sound systems, lending some sense of
urgency and excitement and hilarity to the rest, and the
air was thick with the smell of a hundred different kinds
of soul food from the stalls parked along the pavements.

The first time we went out, the pressing mass of people
almost overwhelmed me. Not used to it, I felt fearful,
afraid that I might be swept away by the crowd and
find myself lost and miles from home, but Jack held on
hard to my hand, guiding me through the maze with the
canny knowledge of many weekends like this one, seeing
a steady way through where I only saw people.

And as I adjusted myself to the milling crowd, and let it

take me without fear, I felt some deep kind of exhilaration, because it was a day when all the rules were suspended. It's hard to explain. I felt as if I could do anything. I felt as if the world was mine.

We walked around, and went to watch the floats, with all their shimmering gaudy, and ate hot dogs and rice and peas, and drank tins of Red Stripe and danced in the street, just like Martha and the Vandellas.

Everywhere we went, Jack met people he knew. All that day and the next, we climbed up strange steps and went through unknown doors to find parties going on – the doors and windows open to let the music in, free for all.

In one flat, I found Lil and Dex, and we fell on each other's necks like men who've been lost in the desert, astounded to find each other among a million other people, but by the next day I was an old hand already, and when I ran into Jimmy and Ned in an all-day party in Colville Terrace, I just smiled and said, 'Small old world, isn't it?' and they looked at each other and said, 'Isn't she a dilly?' and we all started laughing like it was the best joke anyone could think of.

On Sunday night as Jack and I fell into bed, too tired to do anything but lie still at last, with the sound of music still floating warm through the window, he looked at me and said, 'So, you liked it?' and I said, 'It's the best thing I've ever seen,' and it was. It was the best thing I'd ever seen in my life.

Monday night, I left early. It was before seven, and Jack had gathered all his own crowd into his flat, and suddenly I didn't want to have to sit with Mariana and Maurice and Kid and all those other curious people that were his. They were starting to drink hard, and I was exhausted from two days on the streets, and I didn't want this big wonderful thing to shrink to just another night in Jack's flat. I didn't want anything about it to degenerate. So I took him into the bedroom, and said I was tired and I had to go home.

'Thank you,' I said. 'It was my best weekend.'

I leaned my head against his shoulder, and he ran his hand over my hair, and we stood like that for a moment, quiet and still, a small oasis in the wash of noise and laughter and music that came in from outside, and I had some fleeting thought that perhaps I wouldn't have to be so careful any more, that I could let it all slip away and he would still be here, because we had had this weekend, that the carnival was some magic bond that would hold us together always.

It took a long time to drive home. Many of the roads were closed to traffic, and the ones that were open were still filled with people, and I crawled along with the windows open, dumb with tiredness, watching the party wind down. The crowd was dissipating slowly, as if unwilling to admit that it was all over, dragging steps taking them away from the fun for another year.

Children, over-tired and over-excited, were wailing at their mothers. The policemen, who had worn an air of resigned jollity through the weekend, were looking harassed and businesslike again as they tried to guide traffic out of the area and stop drunks from disturbing the peace. There was something sad in it, as everyone remembered that it was just the same old London after all, and their same old lives, and they would have to return to reality tomorrow, all the usual rules back in place.

I felt like that too. I hadn't played any game with Jack that whole weekend. I had let the carnival infect me as it infected everyone else, and it seemed as if he had too. We had just been kids out on the street, along with all the other kids, laughing and having a good time and not worrying about the consequences, because it had seemed, in that strange suspended time, that there might not be any consequences.

Stranger still, as I reached Chelsea, there was no sign that anything had happened. The wide white streets seemed stately and unruffled, quiet and regal, indifferent to the noise and fuss that had been going on only a scant three miles away. It was like coming back to another world.

I lay on my bed that night, my windows as wide as they would go, my body still humming with the hard beat of the carnival music, and I thought of Jack, and I felt some fluttering optimism, I was filled with some nameless faceless feeling of hope. It will be all right, I thought, before I fell into a dark and dreamless sleep.

At first, after that, there wasn't anything to tell me that this feeling was misplaced. There wasn't any sudden change or precipitate disaster. September came, and it was still warm. I felt calm and happy, at home in the city. I worked, and I went out, and I saw Jack. I started to accept some of the things that had bothered me before. Perhaps that was where the trouble started. I still don't know, and I look back, over and over again, to see if I can put my finger on what it was, on where it all went so wrong.

One of the things I started to accept was that there were many sides of Jack that I didn't understand, that perhaps I would never understand. He was still a mystery to me in many ways; he kept his secrets to himself as much as he had ever done. I still had to guess at what drove him and haunted him and gave him joy, at what he wanted and hoped and strove for. But for all that, there were things I could say he had never done.

He never chased after other women, for one. I never had to watch him, the other side of the room, making up to someone, flirting and teasing and making me feel invisible and jealous. And he never attacked me, or belittled me or patronised me. He never frightened me.

Until one time. It was early October, and we had planned to spend the weekend together. After that time at carnival, I thought that perhaps I could start to ask him for things.

He had called early in the week and said Come round, and I said No, I have work. It was a busy week, and I had promised to go to the theatre with Violet, and there was Jimmy and Ned's on Thursday, and I was tired. I had a lot to do in the office, and I wanted to have one quiet night with Louey, because I hadn't seen him for a while, and I needed at least two nights in, with early bed and my full eight hours sleep, so I said What about the weekend. It seemed simple at the time, not something I was angling for, manipulating. So it became a plan, that we would spend the weekend together.

Once I thought of it, I was excited. I made him promise it would be just us, that he would have to tell the crowd who always came and went that the flat was off limits from Friday night to Monday morning. I wanted it to be the two of us alone, together, quiet and still and intimate. I thought somehow that it might be a turning point.

It all started off so perfect, just the way I had dreamed it. Friday night, I got to his place, and he had tidied up and lit candles and laid the table and sent out for pizza. And we sat there, solemnly, upright in our chairs, eating the pizza in our fingers and listening to Van Morrison singing about Tupelo honey, and it was one of the sweetest nights I ever had. He was solicitous and watchful of me, and he talked, for once.

It was that night that he told me some of the stories about Johnny Thunders. I know it may not seem like the most romantic conversation you can ever imagine, but for me, it was a sign. For Jack to tell me those stories was in some strange way the most intimate thing he could ever do. He was offering me his hero, and that's not such an easy thing to do when your hero has more than one fatal flaw.

I listened, and I watched him as he spoke, and I thought that I would remember the way his face looked that night as long as I lived.

Later, when we went to bed, he undressed carefully and slowly, which was unusual. Normally, he just threw his clothes off his body as if they were some kind of encumbrance, and they lay where they fell, in small rumpled piles. But this night, he did it with care, taking off one piece at a time, folding them neatly and putting them on a chair, as if he was suddenly shy, putting off the moment when he would be naked. I sat on the bed and watched him. And when he was done, he turned to me, and he said, 'Let's just go to sleep.'

All that night, as we lay together on that hard bed, and I held him against me, his head heavy on my shoulder, I felt as if it was the closest we had ever been. I felt that if I held him there for long enough I could take all his care away. I watched him, lying against me. I watched his sunken white face, clear in sleep, and I felt as if I were guarding him from all the fearful things that he could ever imagine, as I could save him from the terrors of the night.

The next day I woke late. Jack went and got me breakfast, and we ate it in bed, and he put an old Bob Dylan album on very loud, and we listened to *Desolation Row* and *Tom Thumb's Blues* and got crumbs on the sheets.

After that we walked through the market, looking vaguely for Dolls records that he didn't already have, and afterwards we went and drank coffee with cream in one of those dark little places hidden away in the antique arcades, and then we went back to his place and had a bath, and later we went out and ate dinner, stringing it out with that anticipation you get when you know it's only a matter of time before you go to bed again.

It was a fine dinner. We had three full courses, and a bottle of red wine. Jack didn't really like wine very much. He was a beer and spirits man, that was his taste. But that night, he had, without asking and without being asked, ordered a bottle of good burgundy. And when it was finished we had small cups of black coffee, just like we were the most civilised couple you could imagine. And then there was a pause, and in it, without quite meaning to, I looked at him, and I said,

'I love you.'

There was a moment of terrible fear as I said it, the moment the words left my mouth I thought I would give any money in the world to take them back, and I looked hard at him to see what his reaction would be.

Something flickered in his eyes for a moment, and I thought he was going to say something, but he didn't. He just smiled and took my hand. I changed the subject, but his hand was still warm over mine, and I remember thinking, it's all right. It's all right. I said the hard thing, and he's still here.

When we went back that night, and he laid me down on his bed, it was the sweetest and most gentle he had ever been. Afterwards, as we lay, holding each other, I thought, I've won. I've done the scariest thing of all and he's still here. So I said it again. I thought he should know. I had wanted to say it for so long, and now I had. It was a relief, in a way. I wondered for a while if he would say it back, but he didn't. He just held me until morning, and I thought that was enough. I remember lying there and thinking, at last, I can tell them all I got what I wanted.

The next morning started off badly. It was raining for one

thing. I woke all smiling and languorous, but Jack woke with a start, and got out of bed and walked impatiently round the room.

I watched him, puzzled.

'I feel like shit,' he said.

Suddenly, I had doubt. I had been so sure, and now I had doubt. I wondered if I should say poor you, or so do I, or I feel fine. I didn't know. In the end, I didn't say anything. I just watched him.

'I feel like fucking shit,' he said. He didn't look at me. He just walked out of the room. I heard the bathroom door slam, and lock.

I sat there, staring after him. I felt as if he had slapped me. He never locked the bathroom door. It was so pointed; it said, stay out, stay away, don't touch me. I wanted to cry. I wanted to run away. I took four deep breaths and told myself to stop. It was just the mood he was in that morning. It didn't mean so very much.

Hoping to pacify him, I got up quickly and went into the kitchen to make breakfast. By the time he came out of the bath, I had coffee, toast, bacon, ready. I smiled at him.

'Breakfast,' I said, brightly, like a nice little wife from the fifties, all tupperware parties and the new look.

He stared at me for a moment, his eyes blank.

'Fuck breakfast,' he said. 'Let's go for a drink.'

Of course, I thought. Breakfast was far too normal and bourgeois. How could I be so stupid? It was almost twelve. The pubs would be opening. We could go and be bohemian and pretend we were in Soho with Francis Bacon.

I really wanted to have a bath and wash my hair and make my face look new and pretty, but I didn't like to say so. He had some kind of imperious thing with him that day. If he wanted to go out and drink, it had to be now.

'Fuck breakfast,' I said. I went into the bedroom, slashed

some scarlet onto my lips, and decided it would have to do.

He took me to a place we hadn't been before. It was a strange dark room hidden away behind Oxford Gardens. It wasn't a pub, or even a club. It was just a room with a bar at one end. Jack ordered Bloody Marys.

'Let's get drunk,' he said, as if it was a good game, as if it was a challenge. I took the challenge.

'Let's,' I said. He still wouldn't look at me.

We got drunk. I matched him drink for drink. He was in some reckless defiant frame of mind that day. I refused to be surprised by anything he did. He ordered glasses of champagne after the Bloody Mary, and then vodka again, but straight up this time, and then tall glasses of lager.

By the afternoon, my head was starting to spin, but it was a duel to the death, and I was damned if I was going to show it. I was being put to the test. He was talking again, strange stories and curious non-sequiturs, challenging me to slur my words. I knew, with a deep sense of terror, that soon I was going to have to call halt, that I could go on no longer, that he would have won. There was some buried conviction in me that if he won this time, that if it was me who said stop, then it would be the end of everything. He was pushing me verbally now, quizzing me.

'Name me five generals from Waterloo,' he said. I felt he was laughing at all that education I had told him I had.

'You're a historian,' he said, some sneering note in his voice. 'Tell me who was prime minister after Palmerston.'

All my learning deserted me, flying sure and south for winter. I stared at him, bullishly.

'Not my period, Mac,' I said, which was a lie, the second lie I'd ever told him.

He changed the subject abruptly, which was something he could do without effort or apology.

'If I was driving an aeroplane,' he said, 'would you jump out of it?'

I didn't know whether he meant for fun, for thrills, for kicks, or for self-preservation.

'I never,' I said, with dignity, 'would consider jumping out of any aeroplane. Whoever was driving.'

He leant back in his chair, and laughed some curious mirthless laugh, as if he had boxed me into a corner, tricked me into submission.

'The girl with no fear,' he said.

I didn't know why he sounded so triumphant. I had never told him I had no fear. I had never told him that.

'The fearless girl,' he said. 'And you wouldn't jump.'

I started to tell him that I had never pretended to be invulnerable, but he changed his mood again, for the twentieth time that day, and put his hand hard over mine, and said,

'Let's go to bed.'

As we walked back to his flat, I breathed in the quiet Sunday air, and felt a huge access of relief, as if I had negotiated the rapids, spun the white water. But when we got back to the bedroom and I started smiling, with the illusion that the danger was past, he pushed me down on the bed, and said,

'All right, let's fuck.'

If I had thought he meant it, I would have said no. I could have said no. I still don't think for one single minute that he would have done what he did if I had said anything.

But I didn't think he meant it. I thought it was just talk, that strange alien mood he was in that day. I thought what he really meant was, let's stop this vaunting talk, let's give in and be gentle and still and quiet and close.

But the really awful thing is that it was just fucking. He'd never ever done that to me before. He pushed me down onto the bed, and he didn't even bother to undress. And all the time, he was saying, 'You're never frightened, are you? You're never ever frightened.'

I was frightened, the most frightened I've ever been. But some sick pride stopped me crying out, stopped me telling him that it was enough, it was too much, I couldn't stand it.

It only took a few minutes. I didn't make a sound. And all the time I was lying there, letting him scare me, all the time I was feeling used and abused and I was doing nothing to stop it, there was this little voice in my head, this strange lucid rational voice, saying how curious it is that he thinks that nothing frightens me, when almost everything frightens me. That's the biggest irony of all.

There was a terrible quiet when he had finished. For once I didn't break it. I wanted to wound him and hurt him and scare him as he had scared me, but I didn't know how. The only weapon I had left was silence.

He sat back on the bed and lit a cigarette. He wouldn't look at me. I stood up slowly, my bones sore and aching, and straightened my clothes. I stared at him for a moment, but his face was turned away, to the wall. I would have given anything, just then, for him to turn to me and say he was sorry for what he had done, but he didn't. I went into the bathroom and looked at myself. My lipstick was smeared over my mouth, in some clownish caricature. I rubbed it off. There were red marks on my neck from his fingers, and my eyes were black and empty.

I picked up my things and left the flat, closing the door hard behind me.

All that night, as I lay awake on my bed, wishing at least

I could cry, I wondered what I had done wrong. I thought I had been so clever. I couldn't understand how I could have thought I was being so clever when all the time I had got it so wrong.

24

The week went by. I went to work, just like normal. People called, just like normal. I spoke to Lil and Dex and Willa, and I told them everything was fine. I felt as if I might just burst wide open, there was so much fear and bewilderment and hurt pushed down deep in me, but I couldn't tell them that. How could I tell them they had been right, all along?

I clung on to some sad lost hope that Jack would call and tell me that he didn't know what had got into him and he would make it all better. I held tight onto a desperate hope that I might get back one day and find him on my doorstep, pale and rueful, telling me it was all a terrible mistake.

I woke early that Friday, and the sun was streaming in through my window, and I smiled, because it was a beautiful day. Then I remembered, and it was as if the sun had gone behind a cloud, the light blacked out. I hoped for a moment, some distant helpless longing that he might just call, that he would sound quite normal. But I knew, in my heart, that he wouldn't.

I dragged myself through the day, did my work, didn't say anything much. I sat in the office and acted normal, because I didn't know how to say any of it.

• Tania Kindersley

He didn't call. I wasn't surprised. The dead sadness I felt grew in me, hour by hour, like a lead weight in my belly. I watched everyone finish up for the weekend, wave goodbye, leave the office, smiling and chatting with the festival mood that Fridays bring. See you Monday, I said, smiling and nodding like a puppet on a string. Have a good weekend, I said, have fun.

I went home and sat in my white room and looked out on the street where everyone had somewhere to go, their steps hurried, their faces happy with the end of the week and two free days to be together. I didn't know what to do. I had nowhere to turn, no-one I could ask. I couldn't admit now that I was lost, just when it had all seemed to be going so well.

I walked in circles around my room, holding on tight to the panic inside. I could hardly move I was so frightened it would come up and overwhelm me. I smoked a cigarette to try and stuff it down, to stop myself screaming out. I thought that I had to find out, somehow. I had to know what was going on. Anything was better than this terrifying limbo. So I put on some lipstick and brushed my hair and went round to Jack's place.

The lights were on when I got there, music turned up loud. I was so frightened I wondered if I would be able to speak. My heart was beating so hard I could hardly catch my breath.

Pushing myself, I walked up the stairs and knocked. Kid opened the door.

'Hey, Nance,' he said. 'I've got your number written on the back of my hand.'

I smiled, like it was all dandy.

'Hey, Kid,' I said. 'What's going down?'

'It's a party,' he said. 'It ain't me, babe.'

He was right. It wasn't him I was looking for. I kissed his

cheek with sudden fondness, because he couldn't know, and he had always been kind to me, in his own way.

He smiled, and held open the door.

I walked in, and found the room full, all those shifting faces whose names I didn't know. The air was thick with music and smoke. Eyes looked up at me without interest. Whatever they had been taking, they had been doing it for some time. Jack lay idly along the sofa, a cigarette drooping from one hand.

'Nancy,' he said without surprise, as if he had been expecting me, waiting for me to come, set the scene ready for my entrance. 'Come to party?'

He squinted at me, trying to focus. His pupils had shrunk to the size of pin heads. This is it, I thought, this is what they all warned me about. I didn't believe them, and now I'm paying the price.

'Have a drink,' said Jack, laughing foolishly.

His beautiful face had disintegrated, the sharp bones blurred and ill-defined. I wanted to hit it. I had a terrible pain inside, as if I were wrapped in steel bands, tightening around the space where my heart should be. I wanted to do something. I wanted to swear and shout. I wanted to shake him, to turn him back into the man I thought I knew instead of this horrible grinning stranger. But I couldn't. He just kept on looking at me, smiling that stupid mocking smile, because he had all his defences about him, and I had none. I couldn't make a scene. I couldn't do anything.

I looked back at him for a moment, trying to see something in his eyes, some clue, some remnant of the tenderness he had once shown me, but there was nothing there. It was as if someone had wiped across his face with a sponge, turning it into a strange thing that I didn't know.

There was nothing to say.

'I can't stay,' I said.

*   *   *

I can't remember how I got home. When I got back into the flat I sat down, on the hard wooden floor, because I couldn't walk any further. I clutched onto myself, trying to hold myself together, but I couldn't fight it any longer, it came suddenly in a rush, like a wave breaking over me, and all at once I was lost, screaming tears, tears running everywhere, down my face, through my fingers. I was rocking, shouting, hitting my fist on the floor. I didn't know what to do with it, every part of me was hurting, it was pain like I had never known, all over. I wasn't sure that my frail body could contain it.

It passed, after a while. I was left, hunched on the ground, empty and exhausted. I dragged myself to the bathroom and ran some water over my face. I stared at myself in the mirror, my distorted face helpless before me. This is what you've done to yourself, I told it, this is what you've achieved. I hope you're happy now. I hope you're proud of yourself.

Eventually, I slept. In the morning, I woke under a dead weight. I thought for a moment that I was paralysed, that all my limbs were useless and atrophied, that perhaps I was dreaming. But I wasn't, I was awake, and there was no escape.

I knew I had to see him, have some explanation. I had to know why. I needed some logic to cling to.

I dressed slowly, smeared thick make-up all over my face, like a mask. I had no pride now, I wanted him to see what he had done to me. I wasn't sure I could drive, so I took a cab. The sun was shining and everyone was doing their weekend things. I looked out of the window with dead eyes, unconnected with the world outside. It seemed hardly possible that everything should be going on just as usual.

*   *   *

Jack's flat was empty. I let myself in. There was a horrible sinister mess everywhere, cigarette butts and broken glass, empty bottles, spilt ash, burnt silver foil, a terrible dead metallic smell. This was the real Jack, laughing at me for my ignorance, the part I had taken so much care not to see.

I went down into the street again, not sure what to do next. I felt small and lost and helpless. Does it have a wild finish, I thought, this story? Does it end with a man on a station platform in the rain, a comical expression on his face because his insides have just been kicked out?

I walked pointlessly round the streets for a while. I didn't know what to do or where to go. I didn't know what I wanted any more. I passed a small café where Jack and I sometimes went for breakfast, and I looked in the window, and there he was, sitting at a table by himself. I walked in, and sat down opposite him without saying anything. He looked up slowly. He didn't seem surprised.

He looked shrunken and old and ill. I didn't know what to say. I took off my dark glasses and looked at him with my red swollen eyes. Fat tears rolled slowly down my cheeks.

I'm not sure what I thought he would say. My mind felt like some blank battered thing that has no shape or meaning left to it. When he finally did speak, he asked me one of those questions, one of those strange unexpected questions that he sometimes did, the ones that I never knew the answer to.

'What would you do,' he said, 'if you were pregnant?'

I was so surprised that I wondered for a moment if I had heard right. I wondered if he thought I was pregnant, if it would make a difference, or whether he hoped I was, or whether he thought it was the kind of thing I might go and do, to trap him. I felt some deep fury stirring in me.

'You bastard,' I said. 'You bloody bastard. You know I wouldn't do that. You know I wouldn't. I'm not fucking pregnant,' I said.

I tried to stop myself crying, but I couldn't. The tears ran down my hot stretched cheeks, onto the table. I was too tired to wipe them away. I was too tired to do anything.

'I'm not pregnant,' I said again.

'Go away,' he said. His voice was low and cracked and empty.

'What happened?' I said.

I meant about everything. What happened to us, to you, to what had gone before. He couldn't answer any of those questions. He didn't know the answers any more than I did.

'You made me do it,' he said. His voice faltered, tired and slight. It cut into me. I didn't understand any of it.

'I didn't,' he said, 'ask you for any of this.'

I sat silent for a moment. It seemed like years. I didn't know what happened next.

'I don't understand,' I said, at last. 'I don't know what you're saying.'

'No,' he said. 'You don't.'

He turned away from me, turned his face away. I tried one last time.

'Jack,' I said. 'Please. Please.'

'Go away,' he said again.

There was nothing else to do. There wasn't any point in saying goodbye. I didn't say it.

I took the week off work and sat at home. I couldn't face doing anything. People came round to see me, concerned. They all knew what it was like because it had happened to them, too; it had happened to Dex and Lil and Willa, and they came and sat with me and didn't say much because they knew that there wasn't really much to say.

'I don't understand,' I said, over and over again. 'We were happy. I thought we were happy. It was fine.'

'It wasn't perfect,' I said. 'But you never really get perfect, do you? It was close enough. It was fine.'

'I don't understand,' I said. 'I don't understand any of it. Out of the blue. Just like that. Why did he go and do it, just like that? Why did he?'

They didn't give me an answer. They didn't know any more than I did. Only Dex tried, late one evening.

'Maybe he was happy,' he said. 'Maybe that was what did it. People like Jack don't want to be happy, they're not used to it. They don't know what to do with it. They're afraid it might be taken away.'

Afterwards, looking back, I remembered that. Afterwards, I thought that he was right.

'Why?' I said again. 'I don't understand.'

I didn't understand, because I thought that everyone wanted to be happy. I thought that was the one basic desire which we all had in common. That was how naive I was.

I stayed in the flat for another week, mostly in bed. I called Louey and said I was sick. I couldn't think of a single thing I wanted to do, so I just lay there, staring at the ceiling, running and rerunning what had happened in my head. I thought about the nights we had spent together, and I went back over them all, like a beachcomber, trawling for clues.

I despised myself most of the time, for more reasons than I could count. For my gullibility, for my ignorance, for my blindness, for my weakness. I told myself, over and over, that it was just a man, that I was young and strong, that I would get over it.

Dex had to go up north, on tour with his band, but Violet and Lil took it in turns to come and sit with me, as if I were one of those patients who shouldn't be left alone, the kind that are a danger to themselves. They were concerned, sympathetic. I found it hard to bear. I wanted them to tell me that it was my fault, that I deserved everything I had got, that they had told me so. But they didn't. They were doing their best. They were doing everything they could. But everything wasn't enough. They couldn't put all the pieces back together again. It was all smashed and broken. My dream, of Jack, of myself, was sullied and spoiled. I had never felt so wrong in my life.

At the end of the second week, I had a brainstorm. I woke up one morning and it hit me so hard I couldn't think why I hadn't worked it out before. Drugs, that what it was. The strange thing, the thing that had baffled me most, was how he could change so much, from the person that I was starting to know to the complete stranger who had sat across from me in the café the last time I saw him, the stranger telling me to go away. That wasn't the same person who had held my hand through the carnival.

It wasn't Jack at all, all this. It was whatever it was he was taking. And you can stop taking things, people did it all the time. He didn't have to be Thunders, after all.

I got out of bed and got dressed and, full of hope and resolve, rang up Narcotics Anonymous. I spoke to a man who told me his name was Phil and that he was an addict and he'd been in recovery for three years. He was the nicest man I'd ever spoken to in my life. He was calm and sympathetic and rational. I told him I had a friend who I thought had a problem, and he said he was sorry and he would send me some leaflets.

They arrived the next day, and I read them, and the hope I felt grew. It was a disease, that was all. And there were twelve steps for it, and Jack could take them, and he could be like Phil, sane and clean, and it would all be all right.

I drove up to his flat and knocked. There was no answer, so I let myself in. It was quite tidy, for once. It seemed different, somehow. I looked around, and then I saw what it was. His records were gone. My new hope started to drain away. I went into the bedroom. The sheets were rumpled and cold, and his wardrobe door stood open, empty wire hangers where his clothes had been.

Steps sounded out on the stairwell, and I walked back into the sitting room, thinking it was Jack.

It wasn't Jack. It was Kid.

'Nancy,' he said, in relief. 'I thought it was squatters.'

'Where's Jack?' I said.

'He went away,' he said. 'I just check on the place, to make sure it doesn't get squatted.'

'Where's he gone?' I said urgently. 'When will he be back?'

'He didn't tell you?' said Kid. He looked affronted.

'No,' I said.

'I don't know,' he said. 'He didn't say. He just went.'

He couldn't just go. People didn't just go. They didn't just pack up their records and go.

'I've got to run,' I said abruptly. 'See you later.'

'Later,' said Kid, in his amiable way. As I clattered down the stairs, he leant over the bannisters and called after me.

'Hey, Nancy,' he said. 'It's not over till the fat lady sings.'

At first, it wasn't so bad. I was so convinced he would come back. I thought many things. I thought maybe he had gone away to sort things out in his mind, or perhaps he had run from shame, and would return when he felt brave enough to face me, to apologise. I thought he might have gone to a clinic, to cure this illness that he had in him.

At first, I didn't think he could have gone far. I drove to

his flat most nights, and sat outside in the car, watching for him. It's strange, when you lose someone, how many people look like them. The streets seemed to teem with tall dark men, men whose shoulders were narrow like his, whose boots scuffed along the pavement like his did. So many times, I started after someone, to find it was the wrong person. So many times, I ran up to a stranger, the cry of greeting dying on my lips as I saw it wasn't him.

I didn't tell anyone about the nights of waiting. I made a good show of it. I didn't want to become one of those sad victim women who carry their sorrow with them like some kind of totem. I went back to work. I told Louey I was all right now, I was a big girl, I was better. I told him Jack had gone away, that he would be back soon, and then everything would be sorted out. I don't know if he believed me. He just nodded and said, fine, and did I want to have dinner Friday night.

'Not Friday,' I said quickly. I laughed, to cover it up. 'I'm busy Friday,' I said, trying to look quizzical. He didn't push me. I was glad. I didn't want to tell him I couldn't come out Friday, or any other night, because I had to keep a vigil outside Jack's door. I couldn't be out the one night he came back.

I got good at making excuses, any time anyone called and wanted me to do something. I thought there was some kind of irony to it, that this was the way the secret life I had always aspired to had come about. Weekends I spent driving around Ladbroke Grove, past all the places we used to go together, in case he came out of a familiar doorway. Sometimes, I saw Maurice or Mariana or Kid, and I followed them. I didn't want to go up and talk to them and ask if they knew where Jack was. I couldn't have borne it if they did know, and I didn't.

One time, I thought I had found him. I saw a Mustang in the street, the same colour as his. It wasn't a car you saw too often in London, and my heart started beating, because I knew it was him. I followed it along the Bayswater road, down Park Lane and past Buckingham Palace. I almost lost it round Trafalgar Square, and then found it again on the Embankment, heading out east towards the docks. The Embankment was looking pretty in the autumn sun, the leaves turned red and gold, the tourist coaches parked in long ranks, the floating restaurants gleaming white against the river. I felt happy, following Jack to his destination. I wondered where he could be going, and what he would say when he stopped the car and got out and found me behind him.

We drove on, past the Tower of London and towards Canary wharf, through the Limehouse tunnel, up over the flyover that led towards the City Airport, past the Tate and Lyle factory. It was not an area I had ever been to before, and I thought how strange and unreal it all looked, the wastelands of derelict buildings contrasting starkly with the glittering empty new developments.

Just as the looming silver arcs of the Thames barrier came into sight, the Mustang pulled into a petrol station. I followed, and stopped the car, starting to smile. The driver got out, and turned round to the petrol pump, and I felt as if someone had punched me in the stomach. It wasn't Jack. It didn't even look like Jack. It was a small man in spectacles and a beard. He couldn't have looked less like Jack if he had tried.

I got lost on the way back, and ended up in Hackney, and I found myself in a dark littered street with peeling houses, worlds away from my nice little safe haven of Chelsea, and I sat in the car and looked at the broken windows and the fly posters and I cried as if my heart would break.

25 ∫

'What have you been doing?' said Lil.

'Nothing,' I said. 'Things,' I said.

She had come round one Saturday in late November. She had just called up and said she wasn't going to listen to one single excuse about how busy I was, and that she hadn't seen me for over a month, and it wasn't good enough. She could be bullish, Lil, when she put her mind to it. She could decide that no wasn't an answer she would entertain.

In the end, I gave in.

'Come on Saturday,' I said. 'Come round to my place.'

I thought at least I would be in, then, in case the telephone rang. I thought at least I would be somewhere he could find me.

Saturday came. It was one of those sharp bright winter days, and the sunshine came in through the window, filled with little motes of dust. I looked around listlessly and realised that I hadn't cleaned since I could remember. The flat didn't look wide and white and clean any more. It looked cluttered and dirty. I didn't want Lil to see that and draw conclusions. I didn't want her to know that I wasn't all right. I was all right, anyway, it was just I didn't have much time for cleaning.

I got my rubber gloves out and a bottle of Ajax and a tin of Mr Sheen, and I polished the whole place. I scrubbed the rings off the bath and poured bleach down the loo. I piled all the dirty cups and plates into the sink and washed the mould off them. I wiped the dust off the bookshelves and threw away the piles of old newspapers which I hadn't read.

When Lil arrived, she found me with my sleeves rolled up and my pink rubber gloves on, and she laughed.

'Nice Marigolds,' she said. 'You should wear them always.'

'Just cleaning,' I said.

'Housewife dementia,' she said obscurely. She kissed me and went into the kitchen and put a bag full of food down on the side.

'I'm going to make you lunch,' she said. 'I'm worried you're not eating.'

I didn't want her to be worried about me.

'I am eating,' I said. 'I am.'

She gave me a pointed look.

'You're the size of a stick,' she said. 'Anyway, people never eat when they're unhappy, it's in the constitution.'

'I'm not unhappy,' I said. 'I'm not. I'm fine.'

She looked like she knew better, but she let it go.

'I'm going to make you chicken soup,' she said. 'With dumplings. I'm going to be a Jewish mother.'

'But you're not Jewish,' I said.

'My granny is,' she said. 'I lived in Hampstead half my life. Come on.'

'So glad you're not falling victim to cultural stereotyping,' I said.

'It's a woman's prerogative,' said Lil, with dignity.

She cooked the soup and she watched me while I ate it, and then she said, 'You're obsessed, aren't you?'

'Obsessed?' I said. 'Obsessed? Of course not. I'm fine. What would make you think that?'

She looked at me sadly.

'Dex saw you,' she said. 'Sitting in your car, outside Jack's flat. He saw you a few times.'

I was furious. I was furious that they were spying on me.

'He never said anything to me,' I said, crossly.

'When do you see him?' said Lil.

'You know,' I said. 'He calls.'

He had called. He had asked me to go out with him, like they all did, as if I needed baby-sitting or something. He had asked me to go down and have lunch in Balham again, but I had refused. I couldn't tell him that was the thing I could bear least.

'Well,' said Lil. 'He saw you, anyway.'

'I was just in the area,' I said. 'Is there a law against that? Is there?'

'And,' said Lil, inexorable, 'who are all these people you suddenly have to see? It's not me or Dex or Willa or Dave. It's not Louey. Who are they, all these new people you suddenly have to see all the time, so you're always too busy to come out with us?'

'What is this?' I said. 'Mastermind?'

I really didn't want to get angry. I didn't. I didn't want to scream at her and tell her to get the hell out and leave me alone. I heard the rising anger in my voice, and I tried to make it into a joke, to show it was nothing.

'I wasn't expecting the Spanish Inquisition,' I said, in a comical voice, but it didn't work, and the words came out flat and wrong, and hung in the air between us, like an admission of guilt.

Lil watched me for a moment. I looked at her kind open strong face, and I noticed for the first time the fine lines that were starting to fan out from her eyes, and the frown marks that showed on her forehead. 'Don't frown, darling,'

I remembered my mother saying. 'Don't grimace. You'll get wrinkles.'

We weren't girls any more, I thought, irrationally. We weren't little girls with smooth unmarked faces unclouded by time and trouble.

'I did this,' said Lil, suddenly. 'I did all this. I know about this. After I left Paulo, I used to go to his office and follow him home, to see who he was with. I never told anyone.' She ran her hands over her face, and sighed, a tired old sigh, and she smiled at me, with a kind of rueful shame.

'Do you know what else I did?' she said. I shook my head. I didn't know.

'I went round to his house,' she said, 'when I knew he was away for two weeks. And I dialled one of those 0891 numbers on his telephone, the ones that cost 45p a minute, and I left it off the hook.'

I didn't know what to say. It was the kind of thing that I used to think was clever and funny. But it wasn't, hearing Lil say it now. It wasn't clever and funny at all. It was awful and sad and bitter.

'I'm not obsessed,' I said again.

'Nancy, please,' said Lil. She came and sat beside me, and put her arm round my shoulders. 'You can't go on like this,' she said, and all at once, I couldn't.

'Oh, God,' I said, my voice coming out all ragged and sore with unshed tears. 'He's got to come back. He must come back.'

'I know,' she said, her arm about me, rocking gently. 'I know.'

Grief is a strange thing. At least, I thought it was strange. Perhaps it was just that it had never happened to me before, not really, not like this. There were days when I really thought I was all right, that I had put it all behind me, that I had stopped thinking about him, stopped hoping he would come back. There were days when I woke with a start of surprise because that great black boot of despair wasn't stamping on my face, and I thought, oh, thank God, it's over. And then the next day, it would be back again, worse than ever, and I didn't know why, or what I could do about it.

There were times I went out, with Lil and the others, times when it seemed just like it had been before, and we went up to 21 and made all the same jokes we used to, and I found myself having a good time. But then there were days when I couldn't bear it, when I missed him so much I didn't know what to do with it, and I would sit in my flat and smoke a whole pack of cigarettes and cry and listen to Leonard Cohen records.

I listened to all those old songs, those long lonely nights I would sit up, thinking of all the times Jack and I had spent together, remembering all the sweet times, the times when he had looked at me as if it was love he felt.

I listened to the one about Suzanne, taking you down to the river, feeding you tea and oranges that come all the way from China, and just when you mean to tell her that you have no love to give her, then she gets you on her wavelength and you want to travel with her and you want to travel blind and you know you will trust her because she's touched your perfect body with her mind.

I listened to *Lady Midnight*, and *Bird on the Wire*, and *The Bunch of Lonesome and Quarrelsome Heroes*, and the one about waiting rooms and ticket lines and silver bullet suicides; and *Last Year's Man*, where the skylight is like skin for a drum I'll never mend, and all the rain falls down, on the works of last year's man.

There was one I listened to in December, over and over, the saddest of all, about a man who runs away, far away from his friends and family, to build a little house deep in the desert. It made me think of Jack so much. I wondered if he was building a little house deep in the desert. I could see him in the desert, miles from anywhere, New Mexico maybe, or Arizona, in some strange lost one-horse town.

The last time we saw you, it went, you looked so much older, your famous blue raincoat was torn at the shoulder; you'd been to the station to meet every train, but still you came home without Lili Marlene.

I thought it had been written for Jack. I wondered if he was going to the station to meet every train, if he was waiting for someone, if there was someone for him to meet. I listened to that dark grainy voice and the lone guitar behind it, and I thought that I would never feel anything but despair ever again. I see you there, the song went, I see you there with the rose in your teeth, one more thin gypsy thief. And I wondered if that was what Jack was, just one more thin gypsy thief, who had stolen away in the night, taking all my happiness with him.

The week running up to Christmas was pretty bad. I stayed at home because I couldn't face all the jollity and the seasonal cheer and the lights in Oxford Street and the families out shopping, and I sat in my room and watched television. I watched *Singin' in the Rain* and *An American in Paris* and *Smiles of a Summer Night*. I watched *Casablanca* and *Last Year in Marienbad* and *The Gay Divorcée*.

On Christmas Eve, Violet turned up on my doorstep with a bottle of champagne and a suitcase.

'My husband,' she said, getting right to the point, 'is fucking his secretary. I've left him.'

'Tidings of comfort and joy,' I said.

'Deck the bloody hall with boughs of sodding holly,' she said.

We sat and watched *North by North East* and drank the champagne and ate a tin of cold baked beans. Then we smoked some cigarettes and listened to Billie Holiday.

'Have you ever been obsessed?' I said.

Violet gave me a curious look.

'No,' she said. 'I did it the other way round.'

I didn't get it.

'I don't get it,' I said.

'All that sleeping around I did,' she said. 'In New York. All that sex. That was my defence. I just slept with people and I always left in the morning. They couldn't leave me, because I got there first.'

'I get it,' I said.

She laughed. Then she took a pull on her cigarette, and she laughed some more.

'Do you?' she said. 'I don't.'

'You get it,' I said. 'You got it.'

'And then there was Reg,' she said. 'I didn't love him or anything.' She gave me an accusing look, as if I had suggested that she had. 'I thought it would be safe. You know, after all that fucking.'

'I get it,' I said. 'What?' I said. 'Don't give me that look, I get it.'

'Men,' she said suddenly. 'Do you believe them? Do you believe what a cliché they are? I mean to say, of all the people he could have slept with, of all the women in all the gin joints in all the world, he had to choose his *secretary*?'

And then we really did laugh, because it was funny. It really was funny. We laughed and laughed until tears were running down our cheeks and we were holding our sides.

'Do you know what the really funny thing is?' I said. 'The really funny thing?'

Violet looked at me and shook her head.

'I don't know,' she said.

I pointed to the clock. 'It's Christmas,' I said. 'It's ten past one, and it's Christmas morning, and here we are, two jilted women, eating baked beans and drinking champagne, and it's the best bloody Christmas I've ever had.'

Violet lifted her glass.

'I'll drink,' she said, 'to that.'

The other strange thing was that life just carried on, all around me. Nothing in the rhythm of the city changed. I walked round the supermarket, blind and stupid, and all the mothers still told their children to put that Mars bar *back*, and all the single guys in pinstripes carried round their wire baskets with one aubergine and a six-pack of Stella, and the New Men still looked pleased with their savvy as they debated between five different brands of washing powder. On bad days, I wanted to scream at them, I wanted to ask them if they knew what had happened to me, I wanted to tell them that it seemed hardly possible that they should all be carrying on regardless, just as if everything was blithe and bonny, when I was bleeding to death inside.

You see couples everywhere, that's the other thing. Everyone says that, don't they, when they get left. I had heard people say that, and I hadn't thought so very much about it. But it was true. Everywhere I went were these beautiful pairs of people, gazing up at each other with sweet goony looks, holding hands, heads bent together as they laughed at their own private jokes.

'Bloody couples bloody everywhere,' I said, one day at lunch. It was the end of February and Willa, Lil, Violet and I were having Saturday lunch at my place.

'See,' said Lil, generally. 'She's getting better. She's talking about it.'

'I agree with Nancy,' said Willa.

She had got a part in a series for the BBC, and since her career was now going well and she had more time to think about her personal life, she had a new theme, which was how there wasn't a single member of the opposite sex out there that she even wanted to have a five-minute conversation with, let alone a meaningful relationship.

'Bastard bloody couples,' she said. 'If I see one more, I'm going to buy an Uzi and mow the lot of them down.'

'Don't say the Uzi word in front of Vi,' I said. 'It'll give her ideas about her husband.'

'See,' said Lil. 'See? She is getting better.'

I was getting better. I was. There were still nights when I sat up and missed Jack and listened to Leonard Cohen, but there were also nights when I had rational thoughts, thoughts like, he wouldn't really have done in the long term, he didn't really have what it took to make a woman happy, that perhaps I had been saved. There were times when I could think sanely of all the things that were wrong about him. There were times when I thought, when I really believed, that he would never come back, and that it was better that way.

But then the winter was over, and spring came, and the sun came out again, and the air grew warm and gentle, and people put away their heavy clothes and stepped out on the street with that free easy stride that warm weather brings, and the city stirred after months in the cold, and came back to life.

And just as I thought I was safe, just as I thought I had put all the pieces back together again, it started to fall apart. It was the anniversaries that did it. It was all the this time last year.

Violet had moved out, into a little rented room off Westbourne Grove, and I had no-one to watch over me any more, so I went back to hiding. Not that I thought I had anything to hide until I found myself walking past the house where the South American had given his party.

A year ago today, I thought, I first met Jack. I remembered how young and dauntless I had felt. I remembered seeing him across that garden, decked with its coloured lights; I remembered his pale mysterious face. I remembered asking him if he had a light, and him saying No, and me, so brave, so unknowing, just laughing, and saying, Well, that didn't work did it? And I walked slowly home, and it was as if it had just happened yesterday, and I couldn't bear it.

Oh, it's all so boring, isn't it? It's so bloody monotonous. I didn't want to bore people with it, so I didn't. I kept it to myself and hoped it would go away. Most of the time, I brushed through all right, but sometimes I didn't.

The worst giveaway was in May. It was the day that Jack and I had had our first date, and I was trying so hard not to remember that strange intimate dinner, not to remember him taking me back to his place and playing me his Thunders records and kissing me for the first time.

It was a Sunday, and I had gone up to 21 to meet Jimmy and Ned and Lil and Dexter for lunch. Lunch had been fine. The others were in a bright summer mood, drinking double expresso and smoking too much and making bad jokes. That was all right.

Then Jimmy suggested we went for a walk in the park, which made everyone laugh because we never did that. But the sun was shining and it seemed like a perfect idea, as if no-one had ever thought of it before. So we went down to the park, and it was all open and green and hot, and there were families out walking, and kids roller-skating, and tiny little babies feeding the ducks, and boys playing five-a-side football, and couples, of course.

'Don't look at them,' said Lil. But she was only joking, because the received wisdom was that I was all better now.

'We'll protect you,' said Jimmy. He and Ned came up either side of me, putting their arms through mine. 'We'll look after our dilly,' he said, laughing.

He was in a fine mood that day, laughter rising up to the surface even when no-one had said anything funny. Lil and Dex fell behind, and I held on to Jimmy and Ned, and I thought how lucky I was, that I had made friends like this, that they felt they should look after me, protect me, and I wondered what I had ever done to deserve it.

'Nancy,' Jimmy said suddenly. 'We've got something to tell you.'

He was serious for a moment, and I looked up at his face, and I could see that it was something big, whatever it was he had to say. I felt my heart lurch in me, thinking it was Jack, that Jack had come back.

'What?' I said. 'Tell me.'

Jimmy looked over my head, across at Ned, and Ned nodded slightly, serious too, and I knew then, I just knew they were going to tell me that he had come back.

'What?' I said again.

'Well, you see,' said Jimmy. 'You know me and Ned? Well, it really is me and Ned.'

I didn't get it for a minute, I was so shocked that it wasn't about Jack. And then I looked up at them, and I understood.

'You and Ned?' I said.

Jimmy nodded. If I didn't know him better, I would have said he was shy.

'Oh, boys,' I said. I squeezed their arms, trying not to betray the leaden disappointment in my belly. I tried to look pleased for them. I was pleased for them, really I was. I couldn't have been more pleased.

'Was it always?' I said, wondering that I hadn't worked it out before.

Ned nodded. 'Always,' he said. 'We just never could face telling people.'

'Oh,' I said. I looked at them, at their happy faces. 'That's lovely,' I said, 'really, really lovely,' and then I burst into tears.

They were very good. They made jokes and gave me their handkerchiefs and sat me down under a tree and held my hand until I was recovered.

'Is it Jack?' said Ned. I nodded.

'It's so stupid,' I said. 'Some days are better than others, you know.'

'We know,' said Jimmy.

I blew my nose and regained my composure. 'I don't want to talk about boring me,' I said. 'I want to talk about you. What made you decide to tell people, after all this time? Why didn't you do it sooner?'

Jimmy gave me a comical look.

'My dearest dilly,' he said. 'I come from a family where people march about draughty halls talking about bloody homos and damned poofters. It's not exactly considered desirable, down my way.'

'Oh, please,' I said. 'Could people just come out of the dark ages for a minute, or is that not allowed?'

'You don't know the English aristocracy,' said Jimmy. 'I'm supposed to carry on the family name and marry a nice suitable horsey girl and produce a son and heir. Ned has many hidden talents, but I don't think giving birth is one of them.'

Ned smiled, like he knew better.

'Oh, Jimmy,' I said. 'Sod them if they can't take a joke.'

'Sod 'em,' he said. 'Not much else I can do. They're not best pleased, I can tell you. My mother,' he said, 'asked if I was sure I hadn't made a mistake and it wasn't too late to change my mind. As if it was a choice, that one morning I'd woken up and said to myself, Oh, I think I'll be a bugger now. Just to get the folks going.'

I started to laugh. Seeing it, Jimmy and Ned laughed too, and when Lil and Dex caught up with us, they found us like that, rolling around on the ground, laughing fit to bust.

'See,' said Lil. 'I told you she would be pleased.'

'No,' said Jimmy. 'I told *you* she would be pleased.'

'Not,' said Dex. 'I was the one said she'd be pleased.'

I was pleased. Really I was. But seeing them so happy and together struck a terrible deep chord of longing and loneliness in me. I stayed long enough for form's sake, and then I made up an excuse and left. I drove home through the sunshine, and it made me think of that time I'd driven back after meeting Jack at lunch with Willa and the rest of them, and I felt terribly irreconcilably alone.

I was pleased for Jimmy and Ned, but watching them together reminded me too poignantly of those early days with Jack, and I wished, more than I've ever wished anything, that when I got home I would find him there, waiting for me, returned from wherever it was that he'd been, and everything could go back to how it had been, before it got so crazy.

26

It was Dex told me Mariana had gone into treatment. I thought what an odd expression it was. The Americans talked about rehab and detox, which sounded strange but somehow scientific. Treatment just made me think of something you got for piles or head lice.

Everyone was doing it just then, all those peripheral people I didn't know very well, the kind of people I saw around, knew enough to say hello, not staying for much conversation. They were there and then they weren't. People who usually went around in pairs were suddenly on their own, wandering about looking spare and forlorn and not sure what to do with themselves. Where's Billy, you said, where's Dawn gone? Treatment, that's where, that's where they'd gone. It was becoming such a commonplace that people didn't even need to specify. 'They've gone in,' they said, and everyone knew what they meant.

It puzzled me, because the ones that went didn't seem the way I expected. They were often the ones who were doing well, the ones who actually had jobs or publishing contracts or screenplay commissions, the ones who dressed nice and cracked jokes. They were the ones who were the life and soul of the party, the ones who seemed like they didn't have a care in the world.

It made me sad, as I wandered about Notting Hill. I had

lost the excitement of my early love affair with that part of London. Where I had once seen gloss and glamour and colour and spirit, I now saw the litter on the streets, and the winos with their matted beards and their dirty clothes and that bitter smell that hung about them, and the dealers lurking outside the pubs, and the hookers winking at the cars, and the crazies muttering to themselves about the end of the world. Where I had once seen individuality and non-conformity, I now saw people just counting the days until it all got too much and they would have to go into treatment, to get cured.

I went to see Mariana. I didn't tell anyone. I didn't want to have to explain. I knew I shouldn't go. I knew I didn't want to see her, I just wanted to find out about Jack. I wanted to know more, as if having some nice neat explanation would make things better. I didn't know if it would make things better, but I knew I had to go, all the same.

She was in a place not far from London. I drove out through the suburbs, thinking how strange they were, all those houses exactly the same, with their net curtains and their square windows. I wondered who lived in them. I wondered what they did. I wondered if they knew anything about people getting in so much trouble they had to go and get treated for it.

I got lost twice before I found the right address. It wasn't what I was expecting. I had some vague idea of a big white building, like a sanatorium, something clean and clinical, but it was nothing like that. It was an aged mock tudor house, ugly and rambling, and there were lawns and trees and a tennis court. It looked like the kind of place where a stockbroker might live, with 2.2 kids and a shiny Rover parked outside.

I stopped the car, feeling scared and out of place. I had no idea what Mariana would say. Nervous, I walked into the hall, which had low beams and thick carpets. There was a woman sitting behind a desk, with a bright friendly face, some kind of efficient sympathy coming off her.

'Hello,' I said, tentatively. 'I came to see Mariana.'

She smiled at me, as if I had a right to be there, and told me to wait. I heard her voice coming back from the next door room. 'Visitor for you, Mariana,' she said, as if it were all regular and above board.

Mariana came out after a moment. She stopped when she saw who it was, and she looked surprised, and then knowing, as if she could work it all out.

'Well,' she said. 'Nancy.'

'I'm sorry,' I said. 'I should have called. Do you mind?'

She shrugged. 'It's OK,' she said. She gave a small bitter laugh. 'I don't get many visitors. They're not breaking the door down.'

I didn't know what to say. She looked different. All the spiky make-up and the tight clothes were gone. She looked younger, and tired, and resigned somehow. But the memory of those times in Jack's flat was still too recent, and the fear I always had of her rose in my eyes.

'It's OK, really,' she said, seeing it. 'Let's go outside.'

We walked across the long lawn. People were wandering around in tight little groups. I couldn't tell which were the visitors and which were the inmates. Some of them said hello to Mariana as we passed by.

We reached the lake, and sat down on a wooden bench, watching a mother duck with her chicks glide across the water. Mariana lit a cigarette.

'So,' she said, with a little ironic gesture. 'Here I am. The end of the line.'

'What does it take?' I said slowly. 'Before you know?'

'It's not the obvious things, so much,' she said. 'Over-doses, or finding yourself flat broke. It's fear, you know, because it stops working.'

'Stops working?' I said, stupidly. 'What stops?'

'It,' said Mariana. 'Whatever it is you're taking.' She looked at me, some kind of ironic sorrow in her eyes.

'Hello, I'm Mariana and I'm an addict,' she said. 'And when you're like me you don't take anything for fun, so much, although you think you do at the start. You take it to stop all those unbearable feelings you have when you're straight. And you feel good, and it's such a relief, but then you want to feel better than good, you want to feel really good, you want to fly, so you take a bit more and a bit more, looking for that ultimate good feeling, like you could hit the stars, but you never quite get there, and you take more and you take more, but it's not working quite as well as it was, and not only are you not flying any more, but even the good feelings get a bit patchy, and you start to panic because the bad bits, the bits you thought you had got rid of, start showing through again.'

She stopped, and ground out her cigarette. I could see the pain in her face, stark and naked. I wanted to look away.

'You're running and running,' she said, 'and you're not getting anywhere. And one day you wake up and you know that all the things you thought were working aren't working any more, and it's the worst feeling in the world. Bottom, they call it. Rock bloody bottom. And then you come here.'

'It was Maurice, too,' she said, later. 'He lives on pharmaceutical heroin and methadone. He gets it on prescription. If he didn't take his dose every day he couldn't get out of bed. I didn't want to get that old and find that I was like that. Mind you,' she said, laughing, as if it were funny, 'the way I was going I probably wouldn't have got old.'

I felt strange, hearing her talk like this, so matter-of-fact, as if knowing that you were sliding slowly into the twilight zone wasn't such a strange affair. Knowing one day you might not wake up scared the sense out of me.

She looked at me suddenly, and then away. She took out another cigarette and lit it from the butt of the last. Then she laughed again.

'This is all that is left to us, in here,' she said. 'Everyone lives on caffeine and cigarettes. It's the only addictions we can still call our own. You didn't come here to talk about me, did you?' she said.

I wondered if I should pretend, but I thought it wouldn't sit well with her new candour. 'No,' I said. 'I didn't.'

'I didn't think so,' she said.

'I did, in a way,' I said, trying to make it sound better. 'I wanted to talk about what you're doing here, what you were doing before. I thought if I knew a bit about it I might be able to understand about Jack.'

She started to laugh again, but it cracked in the middle and she stopped.

'No-one has ever understood about Jack,' she said.

'Do you know where he went?' I said.

'No,' she said. 'He didn't send out change of address cards. It's not surprising. Doing a geographical, they call it here. The one thing you never believe when you're using is that wherever you go, you take your problems with you. Running away always seems like such a good solution.'

'And it isn't?' I said, some sudden hope rising in me. Mariana heard it and shook her head sharply.

'Don't think he'll realise that,' she said. 'He won't. He'll just go on taking the pills and finding another aeroplane to get on anytime he gets near to desperation, and then it will be all right for a while, and then he'll move on again. He's not going to come back with his tail between his legs and say it was all a big mistake and he's seen the light.'

'How do you know that?' I said, holding on hard to

the possibility that it might all work out rosy. 'How do you?'

'Oh, I know,' said Mariana wearily. 'You get to know. There are the ones who are reckless, take anything they can get their hands on. They're the ones that get treatment, mostly. And there's the kind like Jack and Maurice. They're careful. They protect their habits. It's all rigidly controlled, so it never gets out of hand, they never hit that bottom, like I did. Jack liked pills. He had six or seven doctors all over London, they'd give him things like Tuinol, those things you're not supposed to be able to get any more. Jack liked cocktails, see? He'd mix all these weird things together, and he always knew exactly what effect they would have and the right doses to take. He was very disciplined. Him and Maurice were snobs about their consumption. They looked down on all those people who shot up smack, looking for that quick fix. They said you got dead that way. They ration themselves, so they will always get to the edge but never go over. That's why they will go on forever, as long as they can get the money. And Jack will always have the money, because he deals, and he's good at getting those things that no-one else can. He's clever, like that.'

I didn't understand any of it. I didn't think it was clever. I wanted to scream, but I didn't.

'And you?' I said.

'Ah, me,' she said. I thought for a moment that she was going to sneer at me, like she always used to, but she didn't. She put on a light voice, and told me straight, as if I had a right to know.

'I was a poor little rich kid who had too much money and spent it all on cocaine. And one day I felt too sick and too scared and too tired. So I came here.'

'Is it awful?' I said. I was angry suddenly with Jack. Why couldn't he get the point? Mariana could get the point, why couldn't he?

'It's OK,' she said. She crushed out her cigarette fiercely. 'It's screaming hell, actually, most of the time. I want to get on the next train and score most days. I think about it all the time, just one little hit, and I'd feel better.'

'But you don't?' I said.

'I'm with the programme,' she said ironically. 'I'm scared shitless of staying, but I'm more scared of going. This is my shot. Sometimes you know you won't get a second chance.'

We walked along the side of the lake, past the other families, trying to make sense of what went so wrong with their darlings.

'I feel so blind,' I said. 'I had no idea.'

Mariana laughed, a bitter undertone breaking through.

'It's not your fault,' she said. 'We were good at putting on a front. Jack always said, Don't tell Nancy, don't do anything in front of Nancy.'

I looked at my hands, at the nails all bitten and ragged. I wanted to cry.

'What a fool he must have thought me,' I said. 'That I didn't see.'

'It wasn't that,' said Mariana. 'I was the one that thought that. I thought you were a fool. I liked fooling you.' She looked me very straight in the eye, bold with the catharsis of confession. It's strange how people can admit to dreadful acts, with a confidence in amnesty because at least they are being honest. As if that makes it all better.

'I'm sorry,' she said. 'It was a bitch thing to do. I encouraged him. I laughed and laughed when you came round and we had just taken half a gram of charlie each and you never noticed.'

That had been the animation, I supposed. All those times I thought they were in a good mood, and it was just half a gram each.

'Jack liked it,' she said, 'that you were different. I don't think he ever met anyone who looked so hard on the bright side. He liked it that you didn't do drugs. You were a kind of amulet to him, I think. You were his symbol of purity.'

'Great,' I said. I was bitter now. I loved him more than any human being I'd ever met, and all I was to him was a bloody symbol of purity. 'Thanks very much.'

Mariana twisted her face in some kind of apology.

'It wasn't fair,' she said. 'I know that. But that was Jack. I think he did love you, in his way, more than anyone else I ever saw him with. It's just his way wasn't much good to anyone.'

'I still don't understand,' I said. I felt as if this was my last chance, my last shot at making some sense of it all. 'Why he went like that, out of the blue.'

She looked at me with pity.

'You made him feel something,' she said. 'He couldn't afford that. That's why he ran away.'

She said it as if it was so obvious, so simple, something I should have worked out before, but I hadn't and I still couldn't, not really. Maybe I never would. Maybe that had been the trouble, all along.

'Did you see him before he went?' I said. 'Did he say anything about me?'

She looked at me for a while, considering. I think she was wondering whether she should lie or not, to save my poor singed feelings. In the end, she told the truth.

'No,' she said. 'He didn't.'

We turned and walked back to the house. At the door, she stopped, shuffling her feet.

'There's group, now,' she said. 'Family and friends. Do you want to come?'

I didn't. I wanted to drive away as far and as fast as I could. But I felt I owed her something.

'Of course,' I said, trying to look like I meant it. She seemed pleased.

'I don't have any friends or family,' she said. 'Except my husband and Maurice, and they wouldn't be seen dead down here.'

'No,' I said, 'I can see that.'

We went in and sat on hard schoolroom chairs, gathered in a circle. The sun shone pale and dusty through mullion windows. When the room was full, everyone avoiding each other's eye, the bright sympathetic woman came and sat down and said she was Jennifer and she was a counsellor and we would start now.

We went round the room. People said, 'Hello, I'm John and I'm an addict.' Some went one better than that, multiple dysfunctions rolling off their tongues.

'Hello,' said one girl, 'I'm Sandra and I'm an anorexic addict alcoholic co-dependent.' The inmates laughed, and the visitors looked shifty and nervous, trying not to stare at Sandra's tiny stick arms, livid with razor scars. When it got to me, I said, 'I'm Nancy and I'm a friend of Mariana's,' and I felt like a fraud.

I felt a cold sense of terror, as I sat there, listening. They told war stories, like Vietnam veterans talking of napalm in the jungle. They told stories of sitting in crack dens when the police bust in, of sleeping with people to get money, of robbing and thieving, of lying and cheating. They talked of misery and despair, of fear and loathing. I spent a thousand pounds a day, they said, some strange pride lurking in their voices; I lost everything.

'Louise, tell us what damage your husband did to you while he was using,' Jennifer asked one of the wives, a quiet dark woman, carefully made up and smartly dressed. Louise paused, looking round the room, at everyone except her husband.

'Well,' she said. 'He sold all my jewellery, he lost his job, he ran up thirty thousand pounds on my credit cards, and in the end he broke my collar bone.'

Jennifer nodded. 'And how did that make you feel?' she said. Everyone looked away. It was too much.

'I felt it was my fault,' said Louise in a quiet voice.

Some of them cried. One man got angry and started shouting. The families seemed lost and baffled, while their loved ones, new with learned wisdom, talked in the jargon of recovery, unfamiliar expressions – they spoke of inappropriate behaviour, and acting out, and unmanageability, of a day at a time, and handing over, and trusting in a power greater than themselves; of scoring and using and snowballs and parachuting, black bombers and reds and mandies – the strange exotic references to their previous life in the nether world of junk sitting oddly with the bright clean phrases of the programme.

Unexpectedly, the counsellor suddenly turned on me.

'How do you feel, Nancy,' she said kindly, 'seeing Mariana?'

I looked at her blankly. I didn't know what to tell her. Everyone was watching me, lassitude or interest or sympathy in their faces.

'I feel scared and stupid,' I said. Everyone nodded. 'I'm one of those ones who never knew what was happening. I feel like a fool.'

I stopped, hearing myself, worried that it was too negative. 'I'm glad she's getting better,' I said, lamely.

'What I don't understand,' said one of the old timers, someone's father, an outdated military type, 'is why you can't just train them out of it, like a dog.'

The junkies laughed, but the old man had tears of frustration in his eyes, and I knew what he meant, even if it was politically incorrect. I knew just what he meant.

*   *   *

Afterwards, everyone went into another room and huddled in small groups and smoked and talked and hugged each other. I felt awkward and depressed, and I told Mariana I should go.

She came out to see me off.

'Thanks,' she said. 'I suppose.'

'I'm sorry,' I said. 'Maybe I shouldn't have come.'

'It was nice,' said Mariana. She hesitated, and then she kissed me, with awkward restraint.

'I hope you got what you came for,' she said.

I looked at her helplessly. 'I don't know,' I said. 'I feel like that old man in there. I'm half a century out of date.'

I drove away, down the neat curving drive. Looking back, I saw Mariana, still standing outside the door, waving me goodbye.

I managed to make it back home and then I was sick. I sat all night, holding onto the hard white china of the lavatory bowl, huddled and hunched with tears and nausea, and I kept thinking about that poor old major general with his desperate rheumy eyes and everyone laughing.

In some perverse way, it made it worse, having seen Mariana. I kept thinking that if she could work it all out, Jack would too. I became more and more convinced that he would come back.

I started sitting outside his flat again. I didn't want to be seen, so I took a mini-cab, and I wore a scarf and dark glasses, and I paid a fortune to the driver to sit half the night in the street, waiting.

One night, I dreamt that Jack was flying in from South America. It was so vivid, and I woke in a happy mood, convinced it was a sign. I had always liked that line about there being more in heaven and earth than was dreamt of in our philosophy; I held a nebulous belief in omens and portents and other worlds and other lives. So it didn't seem at all strange to get in the car and drive out to the airport.

I reached Terminal Four and parked the car, and I felt all the excitement you get when you are going to meet someone back from a long trip. I went into the arrivals hall, and sure enough, there was a flight from Brazil, landing in half an hour. I went and had a cup of coffee, and I bought a couple of papers, because I thought he might like to see what had been going on since he'd been away. Then I remembered about him not reading, and I laughed, and I looked at them myself, and thought I could tell him well enough.

When it was time for the flight to come through, I went and stood with the crowd that had gathered to meet the arrivals, families and friends and suited men holding placards with names scribbled on them in black felt tip. I watched as the first stream of passengers came through; I watched as people rushed up to greet them and they were borne away. I watched and watched, until the crowd had dispersed and there was no more. I looked round the hall, wondering if I could have missed him, but he wasn't there. There were only a few people wandering about, changing money, clustering around tourist information.

I went over to the flight desk and asked if there was a Mr Jackson on the plane from Brazil, but a smiling girl told me that she couldn't give out passenger information. I argued with her until she stopped smiling, and in the end she called Security, and I was escorted from the building, and I found myself standing outside, on my own, as people streamed past me towards the taxi rank.

When I got back and turned the corner into my street, I could see someone sitting on my stoop, and I almost burst into song – he was here after all, I must have missed him in the crush. But it wasn't Jack, it was Louey.

He didn't have to ask me anything. He knew me better than that. He just had to look.

'Is it still that bad?' he said, when we got upstairs.

I was angry, suddenly.

'Still,' I said tightly. 'Still. It's still that fucking bad.'

He looked at me curiously, but he didn't say anything.

'After all this time,' I said. 'That's what you're all thinking, aren't you? Aren't you?'

I sat down heavily on the sofa and lit a cigarette. Louey just stood, leaning against the wall, waiting for me to finish. I got up again, and walked round the room.

'It's over eight months since he went,' I said. 'That's what you're all thinking. She should be over it by now. It wasn't nine years of marriage, after all. It was just one summer with someone who wasn't even very suitable in the first place. I know that's what you're saying,' I said, turning and staring hard at him. His face was still, his eyes unblinking. I wished he would deny it so I could throw it back in his face.

'Isn't it?' I said. 'She's better off without him, he's not worth any of her tears, it's a bloody blessing that he pushed off, she shouldn't spend two minutes of her time missing him and thinking about him and wondering if he'll come back. That's what you're all bloody thinking, isn't it?'

'No,' said Louey. 'We're not.'

I stubbed out my cigarette, and walked away from him, over to the window. Outside, the trees were green and full against the nice white houses.

'I am,' I said. I lifted my hand in a curious supplicating gesture. 'You don't have to think it. I can just think all those things all by myself.'

I stood there for a while, looking out. The silence filled

the room, and spilled over. I was getting good at silence, at least, I was getting better at that.

'Time,' I said, at last, 'is supposed to be such a sodding good healer. Well, it isn't bloody working.'

27

It was a week later that my father arrived in my flat, without warning. Of all the people I might have expected, he was the last. There was a knock on the door, and I went to open it, and there he was.

'Hello, Nancy,' he said.

I stared at him for a moment. He seemed smaller, older, than I remembered. He didn't look like a revered man of letters. He didn't look like a father either, but then he never had.

'Jonathon,' I said. 'Come in.'

I had never called my parents Mum and Dad, it had always seemed inappropriate and bogus, even when I was very young, too young to know why. Other people had mums and dads. Mine weren't like that. So, when I was seven or eight, I just started calling them by their names. They never remarked on it, but then they wouldn't.

My father kissed my cheek and walked in and looked around him and stood in the middle of my room, as if waiting for me to tell him what to do.

'Well,' he said. 'You've got yourself a place.'

I remembered now, that way he had of making bland anonymous remarks. I remembered as a child, thinking that he saved all his important words for the people who counted, his peers, the ones who deserved them. He could talk all night about morality and mortality and causality, about magical realism and existentialism and the romantic poets. But he never talked to me about those things. He saved the mundane for me.

'Sit down,' I said. 'Make yourself at home. Will you have some coffee?'

He said coffee would be good. Good. There he sat, a living lexicon, and he thought that coffee would be good.

I made the coffee, and we sat and drank it, and didn't say much. He said he would have called, but he thought he'd drop by instead, on the off-chance. He said he was in town to give a lecture. He said my mother was well. He said thanks for the postcards.

'How are you?' he said.

I looked at him closely, wondering if he really wanted to know, wondering if I should lie, or tell the truth. But he was my father after all, whatever that was worth, so I told him.

'I'm desperate,' I said. 'I was in love with someone, but he left.'

I wasn't sure what he would say. I wasn't sure what I wanted him to say. He didn't seem surprised. It was the most personal thing I'd ever told him, and he just nodded, and said,

'Yes. I see.'

'Do you?' I said.

And then he really did surprise me.

'It's always difficult for us, love,' he said.

'Us?' I said. 'You mean you and me?'

'Of course,' he said. 'You don't get it from your mother.'

I still didn't understand.

'Get what?' I said.

'This great romantic yearning you have,' he said. 'This way of projecting all your dreams and desires onto another person, hoping they will fulfill them, and then wondering why it doesn't work that way.'

'Is that what you do?' I said.

'Yes,' he said. 'That's what I did. Only once. It was a long time ago.'

'Oh, dear,' I said. My voice caught on the words, breaking. 'I don't know what to do.'

'No,' he said. 'I can't tell you that. I don't know, either.'

He took me for lunch in an Italian place near World's End. When we got there the owner, a broad smiling man with a tweed coat and spectacles, exclaimed in delight, shook my father's hand, clapped him several times on the back, and ushered us with some ceremony to a table in the garden. They spoke for ten minutes in rapid Italian while I sat and watched. My father had always been a good linguist, I remembered that. He spoke Spanish, French, Italian and Russian. I never understood about the Russian, it was one of the places we had never lived. I had always thought it was a literary affectation, so that he could say that he read Dostoevsky in the original.

'What was all that?' I said, when we were left alone.

'That's Alfredo,' said my father. 'It's his place. He started off in the King's Road, in the sixties. He used to let me eat for nothing when I had no money, before I could get published. I haven't seen him for thirty years.'

I thought it was curious. I hadn't known. I tried to imagine my father as a young man, a struggling artist, broke and hungry, while the sixties swung about him, but I couldn't. He suited success; it sat well on him, as if it were something he had always had. I suddenly realised how little I knew about him. He was not interested in his past, it was something he never spoke of. He didn't keep snapshots or postcards or mementoes. I didn't even know what he looked like as a young man.

'I didn't know,' I said.

I felt sad and awkward. I wondered what I was doing

here. What would happen? We would sit and make polite distant conversation and he would leave, and go home to New York, and nothing would have changed. There was a part of me which wanted him to do something paternal and reassuring, hold my hand and offer me sympathy. I wanted, with sudden urgency, to be small again, to be able to crawl onto his lap and be held and petted and soothed, as children are. I wanted to ask him why he never had held me and comforted me, even when I was young enough for it. But I didn't. There wasn't any point. You can't turn a complete stranger into a perfect father in one lunch, just because you're feeling lonely. It was too late for that.

Years before, I had met a clever nervy boy in Spain, who went everywhere with a copy of Solzhenitsyn under his arm and thought about things too much for his own good. He told me once, sitting up late in a deserted bar looking out over the sea, that the saddest two words in the English language were Too Late. I always remembered that. I thought of it now.

'Why did you come?' I said. 'What are you doing here?'

My father looked at me steadily for a moment, and then he surprised me again.

'I came to say I was sorry,' he said. 'For all the things I never did. I never was much good to you, was I?'

'No,' I said. 'You weren't.'

He nodded slowly.

'I didn't think so,' he said.

We sat looking at each other for a moment, unsure what happened next, and then a waiter came and asked us what we wanted to eat, so we looked at the menu and ordered some food, and then the waiter went away, and we were left where we started.

'Are you,' said my father, very carefully, 'angry with me?'

I shook my head.

'Not any more,' I said. 'I used to be, when I was younger. I used to resent it that other people had families and I didn't. And then I got used to it. You can't make a pig's ear into a silk purse, isn't that what they say? I even quite liked it, that I could do what I wanted, and you never asked any questions.'

My father nodded again. I lit a cigarette and watched him as he thought.

'You always were like that,' he said. 'Even when you were very young. You always did things for yourself. I remember that.'

'Yes,' I said. 'I remember too.'

'It's age, you see,' he said. 'There's a moment when you stop and look at yourself and ask some of those questions that you've avoided for so long. It's a very good job for avoiding things, writing. I was always dimly aware that I wasn't much good at actual living, people, you know. But it didn't seem to matter very much, because there was always the work. That was always the most important thing. There was always that idea that it was a worthy sacrifice, something noble almost. And you look at all the great precedents – Hemingway, Fitzgerald, O'Neill, Faulkner – at how they messed up their personal lives, but the work. The work.'

My father paused for a moment, as if in silent homage to his heroes. I wondered what it must be like, to be part of that illustrious company. His name was up with theirs. I wondered if it felt different, if he felt his talent, if he was aware of how apart it set him.

'But then I started to wonder,' he said. 'Just lately. About the business of living. There are some people who are good at that, just living. I never saw the point of it. Everything that ever happened was for me just so much material. Nothing seemed to count until I had used it, in a book. Then it was mine, I had shaped it, made it mean something. It seemed to me that there was no point to events, by themselves – that they only took on resonance and sense once they had been written.'

He stopped suddenly, and looked at me.

'I'm not sure why I'm telling you all this,' he said. It was the most human I'd ever seen him. I'd never seen him unsure of anything before. It made me feel comforted in some vague way, I don't know why.

'I'm not sure either,' I said. 'It's all right. I'm interested.'

I was interested. I had always liked listening to him talk, even if the talk had never been for me.

'You see,' he said, 'whatever you believe in – whether or not you believe in God or Fate or divine intervention – life is something that just happens to you. It has no form or structure – it just happens, a random series of events, over which you have little control. We all like to think that we can control things, but we can't, not really. There's always the inexplicable, the unknown. There's nothing ordered or tidy about it. So if you take it and write it, you can mould it, give it a structure, take control of it. Then it truly belongs to you, it's yours, you have made it your own. It's much less of a risk than actually doing it. The worst thing that can happen is a bad review.'

'Was that why we were always moving?' I said. 'So you could stay in your ivory tower?'

'I think so,' said my father. 'I didn't want to get drawn in. If you live in a place long enough, it's hard to stay apart. That's why New York suits me. It's a very anonymous town. And living so high up, too, that's no coincidence. There's something about the forty-second floor. You can look out on the city, at all those little figures on the street, going about their own personal dramas, but you're removed from it, literally. Above it, looking down.'

'Do you regret it?' I said.

'No,' he said. He shook his head slowly. 'It's more curiosity than regret. I wonder what it might have been like, if things were different. I wonder what it would be like to be so involved in your own life, to be right in it, instead of standing to one side, watching. I wonder what I might have written, if it had been like that, even if I would have written at all. That's what made me think of you, because you always dove right in. You were always out there, doing things, while I sat and wrote about them.'

'And look where it's got me,' I said.

'Is it very bad?' he said.

He put his head a little to one side, watching me, curious. I had a sudden irrational thought that perhaps he would use this too, that one day I would buy his new book and find this very scene in it, find myself, written to the life. But then, I thought it wouldn't matter so very much if he did.

'Yes,' I said. 'It's very bad.'

It was strange, how easy it was to tell him that.

'I don't know what to do,' I said. 'I feel small and hopeless and weak. I feel I should know what to do with it, but I don't. I loved him very much, as much as I've ever loved anyone, and he just went away. He didn't say anything. He just went. I feel as if part of me went with him, that there's a part that's missing, and I have no idea how to get it back.'

I looked away across the little garden, at all the nice neat tables with the nice well-dressed people eating the good Italian food and making nice lunchtime conversation.

My father sat still and quiet, waiting for me to continue. I wondered if he really wanted to hear it, or if this small moment was his way of offering me an apology for all the missing years. Whatever it was, I felt a sudden gratitude towards him. It's strange how misery can make you grateful for the smallest mercies.

'I feel like half a person,' I said. 'As if I'm just going through the motions. And I feel ashamed, that I should be better than that. That I should be able to dust myself off, and get on to the next trick.'

'It's curious,' said my father. 'I can only imagine.'

'That's what you're good at,' I said. There was a slight pause. 'Were you ever in love with my mother?' I said.

He shook his head. 'No,' he said. 'That wasn't the point. We suit each other very well, we always did, but that's all.'

'Yes,' I said. 'I can see that. I almost envy it.'

'Oh, no,' said my father, with conviction. 'You will now, while you're deep in the painful part. But later, when you feel stronger, you will see that it is I, in a sense, who should envy you.'

He didn't elaborate, and I didn't ask him. I felt tired suddenly, worn out, so we changed the subject, and finished our lunch, and ordered coffee. The proprietor came and sat down with us, and shook my hand, and told stories about my father when he was young, and what Chelsea was like in the sixties. He was such a nice man, a real old-time padrone, and for a while, as he talked and laughed and drank small cups of expresso with us, I forgot my sadness and joined in.

My father walked me back to my apartment. We stopped as we reached the door, and looked at each other for a moment. I think that we were both wondering what to do, whether this strange lunch, this long conversation, had put us on a different footing. So we stood for a moment, in that quiet London afternoon, wondering what happened next.

He smiled a strange little twisted smile at me, and gave me the formal kiss which I was used to.

'It's my heart, you see,' he said. 'That's really why I came. It's murmuring.'

He laughed, as if he really found it funny. I was shocked. I had always thought he could live forever. I stared mutely at him.

'It's ironic, isn't it?' he said. 'I never used it much, but it's wearing out.'

'What will you do?' I said.

'I have to have an operation,' he said. 'It will be all right. I'm not in mortal danger. But it made me think, all the same. So, I thought I should come and see you, say some of the things I never said, before it was too late.'

I looked at him for a moment, and then I put my arms round him and held on to him, the first time I ever had. I felt him put a hand on my shoulder, and we stood like that for a moment, a little awkward, doing the best we could.

'Oh, Dad,' I said.

He stepped back and smiled at me.

'Funny,' he said. 'You never called me that.'

'No,' I said. 'I didn't.'

He nodded.

'I hope things come right for you,' he said.

I knew he meant it, in his own strange way. It didn't make any of it any better, but then I wondered if all the things I wanted from him would have made it better either. If he had been another kind of father he might have shown fury or indignation over Jack's behaviour, he might have been protective and outraged. He might have tried to take me home with him, offered refuge and comfort.

But even if he had been that kind of father, which we both knew he never would be, it still wouldn't have made much difference. Jack still would have gone. There would still be the aching void in me. There would have a been a Band-Aid on it, was all, a small salve to my wounded heart. I knew that what he had done, little as it seemed, had been difficult for him, out of character, and I appreciated it for what it was. It didn't change anything, but it was worth something, all the same.

'Yes,' I said. 'I know. I'm glad you came.'

He nodded again, as if he understood.

'Goodbye, then,' he said.

'Goodbye,' I said. 'Have a safe trip.'

He turned, and walked away down that long straight tree-lined street, and I stood and watched him go until he turned the corner and was lost from sight.

28 ∫

August wore on. It got hotter. I felt terrible. I couldn't sleep, I just lay sweating and turning in bed all night wondering when Jack would come back and what I would say to him when he did.

It was coming up to Carnival. I walked the streets and watched everyone getting ready, the holiday mood already building, people laughing and talking, music turned up loud. I felt a growing panic, that if he didn't come back by carnival, that would be it. It would all be over, I could have no more hope. I wondered how it could be a year ago that we spent that magic weekend together, and how it could be that I still missed him so badly.

I took the week before the carnival off work.

'That's a good idea,' said Louey, when I asked him. 'You should take a holiday.'

I looked at him closely. It was the first time he had ever told me I should do anything.

'Is it that bad?' I said.

He knew just what I meant. I never had to explain myself to Louey. I never had to add or elaborate. I wondered, for about the six-hundredth time, why I hadn't just fallen in love with him, and then there never would have been any

Jack, any of this. I wondered why we couldn't make our lives turn out the way we wanted, but I knew we couldn't and he knew we couldn't, and we both knew there wasn't one single thing we could do about it.

He smiled slowly at me and took my hand in his.

'Nancy,' he said, very seriously, the most serious I'd ever seen him. 'You are a lovely shining woman, and you deserve a break.'

I tried to smile back, but it didn't work very well.

'Oh, Louey,' I said. 'I don't feel very lovely and shining.'

He didn't say anything. He just kept on holding my hand and looking at me with that generous sympathy that I felt I didn't deserve. I shrugged, putting the façade back into place.

'It's OK,' I said. 'I'll go away. I'll be fine.'

I pretended to myself that I really was going to take a holiday, fly off somewhere, sit on a beach and get a tan and feel better. I even went round to the travel agent and got brochures and asked about flights and prices. But all the time, I knew I wasn't going away. I didn't. I went back to Jack's flat.

It was strange, going back. I felt nervous as I walked up the stairs, the same fearful excitement in my stomach that I used to feel in the early days, when I was to meet him. There was a small hidden hope that I might just open the door and find him there, maybe with Maurice and Mariana, and Kid, watching his goldfish video and rolling his spliffs; that they would be drinking and telling stories and bitching, just like they always had; that nothing had really changed, that the last few months had been no more than a mirage, that he hadn't gone away at all.

He wasn't there. There wasn't anybody there, of course

there wasn't. It was like the Marie Celeste. Everything was in the same place it had been before, covered in a heavy layer of dust.

In the bedroom, the sheets were still rumpled, and the wardrobe door still stood open, empty except for the three shirts he had left behind. It made me think of one of those old black-and-white films, the ones with a deserted gothic house in, like Sunset Boulevard. I almost expected William Holden to come walking in, smoking on a Lucky Strike and saying he had always wanted a swimming pool.

I put my bag down, and went over to the bed. I picked up one of the pillows and pressed it to my face. I thought there was still the faintest scent of patchouli clinging to it, that heavy incense smell that always hung about Jack like smoke. He must come back, I thought. He must.

I had bought groceries with me, and cleaning stuff. I put on one of his shirts, and I rolled up my sleeves, and I cleaned the whole place until all the dust was gone. I cleaned the windows so the sun could come in, and it muddled over the beautiful furniture and dappled on the Persian rug. I thought how lovely it looked, and how pleased he would be when he came back and found it all gleaming and clean.

Then I cooked myself some supper and ate it, and after that I made some coffee and smoked a cigarette, and sat back and waited.

Someone did come, but it wasn't Jack. It was Kid, just like the last time.

'Nancy,' he said. 'It seems so long ago.'

I smiled. It did.

'Have a beer,' I said. 'I'm going to.'

'Beer would be fine,' he said.

He didn't seem at all surprised to find me here, and he didn't ask what I was doing. He wasn't curious like that; life for him wasn't the big mysterious thing it was to me.

We didn't say much, at first, just drank the beer, and listened to an old Bob Dylan album I'd bought with me, one of the ones I used to listen to with Jack. I felt some vague comfort having Kid there, because he was Jack's friend, and it was a little like the old times.

'You haven't heard anything?' I said, eventually.

'Nope,' he said.

He didn't ask what I meant. He didn't have to. He shrugged, philosophical. He knew Jack better than I did, after all.

I changed the record. I put on a New York Dolls album I had bought in the Record Exchange in Pembridge Road.

'Thunders died,' said Kid.

I didn't know. I was shocked for a moment, as if he had told me that Jack had died, the two were so connected in my mind.

'When?' I said. 'I didn't know.'

'Spring sometime,' said Kid. 'Overdosed in a motel room in New Orleans. Rock and roll suicide.'

'Poor Thunders,' I said, because I didn't know what else to say. Poor dead Thunders, never getting the point.

'They all go,' said Kid, some lingering sadness in his voice. 'All the good ones. Hendrix, Otis, Brian Jones, Keith Moon, Gram Parsons, Janis Joplin. They all go.'

I didn't know what to say to that either. They were just names to me, really. Names and voices, but to Kid they were more than that; they were his heroes, they lit up his days, and gave him their words.

'You know what Janis Joplin once said?' he asked.

I shook my head. I didn't. Just another thing I didn't know.

'She said, "Every night I go out on stage and make love to 20,000 people, but I always go home alone".'

After a while, he got up to go. He left me with one of those small pieces of wisdom that he had learnt so well from all the songs that he had listened to.

'You can't,' he said seriously, 'always get what you want, but if you try sometimes, you just might find you get what you need.'

After he had gone, I wondered if he meant something by it, or whether it was just that he was listening to the Stones that week.

So I sat the week out in Jack's apartment. I had found a book on Johnny Thunders in the market, the week before. It had a photograph of Thunders on the front, his face half covered by a mask, wary sleepy drugged eyes staring out from under his hair, a syringe in his hat. I thought about him checking out, alone, in some seedy motel room, only his junk for company.

I felt a deep sadness, and some unnamed fear too. I wondered if that was what had happened to Jack. I wondered if he had just stopped breathing in some empty room in some strange town, one of those sad lonely urban deaths when they don't find the body until weeks later, when the smell disturbs the neighbours or the milk bottles pile up outside the door or an unfed cat starts to yowl. I wondered if he was lying there, like Thunders, growing cold; unloved, unmissed.

I read the book. Right at the beginning, there was a quote from William Burroughs, the greatest junkie of them all.

'Dear Mom and Dad,' it said. 'I am going to join the Wild Boys. When you read this, I will be far away. Johnny.'

That made me think of Jack, too.

I didn't do anything, that week I spent in Jack's flat. I just sat and waited. Some of the time I wasn't even sure what I was waiting for. Some of the time, I thought he would just walk in, and everything would be fine. Some of the time, I knew that it might not be fine at all, that even if he did come back, nothing would have changed. But I thought that even if the worst came to the worst, at least the mystery would be solved, the mystery of where he had been and why he had gone. Even if he didn't want me back, at least I would know. That was why I was there, after all, because I needed to know.

I spent most of the time just thinking. I thought about the times we had spent there together. I thought about the reasons I had gone with him in the first place, and the reasons I forgave him for what he did.

I did forgive him, which was curious. I felt no bitterness or rancour towards him. I felt, as I always had with him, a deep unspecified yearning sadness, a hope for better things. I thought of what Mariana had said, that he liked me because he had never met anyone who looked so hard on the bright side. I had hoped that if I held on to my conviction that he could change, that he would. Just like that, just as simple as that. And sitting there, in his strange abandoned apartment, I remembered also what Dex had said, about some people not wanting to be happy, and I thought that maybe it wasn't so simple after all.

That was on the fourth day. It was that day that I started to think that perhaps he wouldn't come back, that my certainty that he would, must, return, was misplaced.

One of the things that made me saddest was the end of the Thunders book. It said that by 1986 Thunders was living quietly in Sweden with his girl. It said, things should be fine, he's earned that much. And here we were five years on, and Thunders was just another rock and roll casualty, his famed refusal to give a damn no more than a sad memory. I thought of Ziggy Stardust, and how he took it all too far, but boy could he play guitar, and I thought it wasn't enough. That was on the fifth day, the Friday.

I remember it so clearly, that morning. I woke up in Jack's bed, and I lay there, reading that sad stupid book, and I thought, he wasn't so very great after all, Thunders, he was just some kid from Queens who got a taste of the big time and didn't look beyond it and who got too fucked up for his own good.

Outside, someone was playing an old song by Toots and the Maytals, testing the sound system for the carnival to come, and I lay back in those musty sheets, and I felt angry, and I wondered for the first time, really wondered, what I was doing there.

I remembered something I'd read somewhere, that there were some people who didn't want to live. Mortido, I think it was called, a fine romantic Spanish name for the death wish. Except it wasn't really fine and romantic, it was sad and lonely and pointless and wasteful. I thought perhaps that was what Thunders had, that perhaps it was for that that Jack had idolised him, recognising the disdain for living that they shared.

It took me until Sunday to really get the point. I was sitting in the flat, and all the noise of the carnival was around me, and I was alone, waiting for someone who would never come.

Even if he did come back, I knew at once that the mysteries that surrounded him would never be solved. I thought Mariana was right, that he was one of the ones who was never going to change. I thought that if I could see that so clearly about my father, then I could learn to accept it about Jack. I thought that the only choice I had was my own.

I knew, finally, certainly, that this cause was utterly lost. I had always seen something alluring and exotic about lost causes, but I suddenly saw myself, sitting here alone, while about me in the streets people were living, and I thought it wasn't so much fun any more. I thought there was more for me than this.

I don't know what it was that brought me to this. I didn't know then, and I still don't know now, not really. I thought of those people who say there is a reason for everything, a catalyst, something concrete that comes to change things. But I don't think there was, with me, then. It wasn't anything specific. I think it was just that I had truly come to the end of the road. It had taken me a while, longer than I might have wished, but I had reached the end.

It was the strangest thing, as if the blindness had been lifted from my eyes and I could suddenly see what I was doing, and how futile it was.

That was what I felt, on that sunny Sunday. I was at the end of the road. The dark twisting ribbon of highway had led me to a dead end, after all that. I saw that, believed it for the first time, and I wondered why, why now, why this way.

I thought of all the words of advice and wisdom that I had been given, and how they hadn't done it, although I thought of them all in that dark silent time I spent sitting alone in that strange still apartment.

Whatever it was, I knew that I couldn't go on any more, caught in this lonely suspended vigil. And as I thought this, there was a great sense of relief in it, as if someone had lifted the weight of the world from my shoulders. There was an aching sadness too, because I saw for the first time that we all have to do these things, have our realisations and revelations, alone.

It made me sad, because I knew that Jack would have

to do it alone too, because that was the way the world worked, and I didn't think he ever would. I knew then, in that moment, as surely as if he were standing there before me, telling me, that he did not have it in him to make another person happy, because he didn't know how to do it for himself; and I knew why it made me sad, because for all his failings and all his blindness, there was something in him, the part that I had truly loved, some buried promise which he would never fulfil, which would stay lost and forgotten, whatever anyone tried to do about it.

And when I had come to the end of all this thinking, I opened the window, and I looked out, really looked, and I saw the crowds, laughing and dancing in the street. I leaned out, and down to the left there was a sound stage, and a great big West Indian woman was singing, her voice carrying out bluesy and grained and sad and joyful all at the same time. That's it, I thought. There's the fat lady. She's singing. It's over.

I packed up my bag and went down those familiar stairs for the last time. Out in the street, I looked at the crowd around me, took in the sound and smell and movement, and I gave myself to it. For once in my life, I didn't feel frightened. For once, it didn't matter that there was no-one there to guide me, no-one to hold my hand.

I wondered if I might run into Dexter, or Jimmy and Ned, or Lil or Willa or Davey, or someone I knew. I thought it wouldn't matter if I didn't. I thought it would be all right on my own. For the first time since I could remember, I really thought it would be all right on my own.

I walked away from the flat. I stopped for a moment, and looked at that window, remembering the times when just looking up at it had made my spirits lift and my heart beat faster. I felt, for just a moment, that familiar tugging sadness that Jack had so often inspired in me, one last shot of regret that the fairy-tale hadn't come true like I had wanted.

Then I turned away, and walked out into the crowd, out into the carnival streets, and I didn't look back.